LAND OF THE CRYSTAL STARS:

LAST RISE OF THE GUARDIANS'

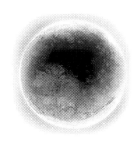

RIA MATHEWS

authorHOUSE®

AuthorHouse™
1663 Liberty Drive
Bloomington, IN 47403
www.authorhouse.com
Phone: 1 (800) 839-8640

Published by AuthorHouse 02/10/2020

ISBN: 978-1-7283-4605-2 (sc)
ISBN: 978-1-7283-4604-5 (e)

Library of Congress Control Number: 2020902455

To those who have always been there for me; to help me get back up and keep pushing me to succeed in everything I do and did. Too my loving husband, and my loving children. To the best parents a girl could ask for, and sisters and brothers that were always there for me no matter what happened or have happened. To my best friends Sonia and Kayla who are like sisters to me. This is what I call family.

The series includes

Land of the Crystal Stars:
Rise of the Guardians' Book 1

Land of the Crystal Stars: Second
Rise of the Guardians' Book 2

Prologue

As Andrew and Faizah had went into the portal of light to the Crystal Star of Water and Ice. As they stepped through the portal door they had covered their eyes because the sun was really bright on this Crystal Star but it was very beautiful. As they walked through the portal they were under attack again by the Dark Kingdom Zodiac. So they ran behind a tree hoping that it would keep them from being hit by the dark powers.

As they looked up they notice several people was running toward them being guarded by a water shield. As they looked they notice they might be the other guardians that Sue and Joey had informed them about. They felt the wind pick up and that it was going near the enemy. Faizah had a huge smile on her face; because they had friends that would always be there no matter the distance between them. She is aware that she had not met them yet but had a very wonderful, warm feeling that just made things seem to be better. As they are fighting their way to them the other guardians notice that two people were behind a tree trying to keep from being hit by the enemy. So they ran to them to send them away but notice that they were also fighting and using powers. This met that Sue and Joey had found two more guardians that were left out of twelve. So they would be facing a strong enemy this time around. So they needed to get their barriers straight before introducing themselves to the guardians.

Alena knew it was up to her since she was the one they counted as being the leader of the team, but could not understand why because Joey was found before her and the rest. She knew that no matter what happens in the near future that her friends old and new would be there for her no matter what.

The Crystal Star of the Water and Ice Realm

Chapter 1

Andrew walked through the portal to the court yard at the high school; Faizah was hiding behind a tree, and Andrew did not know why. When he looked in the direction that Faizah was looking; he saw why. His eyes got wide and he ran for the same tree that Faizah was hiding behind.

There are two swarms of some type of insect, and before he knew it a dark power ball flew by him hitting the tree, and turning it to dust. Then he heard people yelling at them, then he turned in their direction; and he saw them running toward Faizah and himself. As the six people were running Andrew notice Leroy, and he knew that they were the guardians. That they were supposed to meet up with. When the other guardians and the protectors reached them they are surrounded by a shield of water which was starting to fade because of the dark powers and acid hit the shield.

"I would say welcome to my realm, but as you can see the welcoming party has already arrive." Alena said.

"That is not funny Alena." Jenny said.

"Sorry, but it is the truth they didn't show up until the two new guardians had gotten here. Look we can introduce ourselves, but now is not the time for that." Alena said.

"Alena you are such a kidder and all. You are right we need to get rid of those swarms, and their trainer if not; we all will be dust soon." Lola said.

"Well we need to get on the move if not; we could be turned into dust just like Lola had said." Rich replied.

"Well in that case where is the trainer who is controlling these swarms. Are they black hornets and killer bees?" Andrew asked.

"Now that you mention it does look like that." Leroy said.

"Yeah, and it looks as if we are in a bind." Andrew said.

"So what are we going to do about these damn insects?" Alena asked.

"We are going to use our powers to get rid of them." Rich said.

"Okay then let us get started." Alena said.

"Ice comes to me." Alena called.

"Wind comes to me." Rich called.

"Water comes to me." Leroy called.

"Lightning comes to me." Faizah called.

"Earth comes to me." Andrew called.

"Fire comes to me." Lola called.

As the six guardians called their powers to them. That is when the tamer showed up.

"Well if it isn't the guardians of the Majestic Star Kingdom." Morgana said.

"So you have returned with more powers than you left with the first time. I came across you a few months ago." Alena yelled.

"Well guardian of the Crystal Star of Water and Ice it is good to see you are still a live, and it will do me the honor of destroying you myself." Morgana said.

"In your damned dreams, you witch." Alena said.

"Let us combine our powers together to get rid of her." Leroy said.

"Listen you little weasel there is no way to get rid of me without getting rid of the Dark Kingdom Zodiac because I'm its Queen." Morgana said.

"We don't care if you are the Dark Queen or not we still will stop you here." Alena said.

"Then let me introduce you to the tamer of these beautiful insects. Here is my general Sasha Beedrill. She is the master of these insects and their dark acid, and dark plasma." Morgana said.

"Whatever you say, but don't get all dramatic on us when we wipe the floor with your general. Also let us show you that we are stronger together. Now that there are at least six of us guardians together now!" Alena said.

"Rich! Why don't we combine our powers and show these losers who is boss; and that we can take whatever they throw at us." Alena said.

"You got it." Rich said.

"Oh, please like your powers have any chance against my general." Morgana said.

"Ice Storm." Alena and Rich said together.

As the attack hit the swarms all it did was make the swarms stronger. As well as added more to the swam when the attack hit them; they multiplied by another hundred. The swarms started to attack again and as they did the general finally shows herself to the guardians. Morgana is smiling from ear to ear; when the general shows herself; laughing at the attack by Rich and Alena.

"Well guardians' I heard that you were strong, but I expected a little bit more power than what you showed today. I am Sasha Black the general of these insects which are my babies and they are under my control. I will take this Crystal Star from you and make it my home." General Sasha said.

"So you choose now to show your ugly face to us." Lola said.

"Who you calling ugly. I am the most beautiful general in the Dark Kingdom Zodiac's army. We will take you all out and take over all the realms, and there will be no one to stop us." General Sasha said.

"In your dream's you monster." Faizah yelled.

"We will see." General Joselina said.

"Come on Andrew let us show them who is boss and can stand up against this Dark Army of the Dark Kingdom Zodiac." Faizah said.

"Let us go, we can stop them. This is for all our realms, and for the future that is at risk with them still here." Andrew said.

"Stone Net." Lola and Andrew said together.

As the attack hit the swarms it caught them in the net of fire, and earth so that they can't move, and doing so it made the swarms turn to stone, and are trying to get away. It only was able to take only half of the swarms' out which are hornets and killer bees. Now it was up to Leroy and Faizah to take care of the rest.

"Come on Faizah let us show them how it is done. I use my water and you can use that as a conductor for the lightning and wipe out the rest of these swarms." Leroy said.

"You got it." Faizah said.

"Water attack." Leroy said.

"Lightning attack." Faizah said.

As the attacks hit the rest of the swarms they are started to disappear into dust. The general took her leave and vowed to be back soon to wipe the ground with the guardians, and show them who is more powerful than the others.

The guardians came out from the tree in the court yard to the school and started to introduce themselves to each other.

"Hi, my name is Faizah Carter." Faizah said.

"Welcome to my realm, I am Alena Patches the guardian of the Crystal Star of Water and Ice Realm." Alena said.

"I am Leroy Addams guardian and Prince of the Crystal Star of the Elemental Realm." Leroy said.

"My name is Lola Brown; I am the guardian of the Crystal Star of the Fire Realm." Lola said.

"My name is Richard Springer; I am the guardian of the Crystal Star of the Wind Realm. You can call me Rich." Rich said.

"It is nice to meet all of you. I hope that I can be a great assist to you all in this fight for our freedom and the Star Princess." Faizah said.

"Well everyone I have seen you once before, when the Dark Kingdom Zodiac had attacked you at the dance. I was forced to return to my realm to regain my powers over the earth. My name is Andrew and I am the guardian of the Crystal Star of the Earth Realm." Andrew said.

"Hi Andrew and welcome to my realm." Alena said.

As all the guardians get know each other and the protectors in the court yard of the high school. They need to make a plan for another attack by the Dark Kingdom Zodiac. As they all set talking to one another and make a plan to counter another attack on the guardians by this general and the Dark kingdom.

The Crystal Star Realm of Water and Ice is blue, has blue flowers all over and their national flower is a Carnation that is Blue and White. There are a lot of buildings around the Crystal Star Realm of Water and Ice. There are many homes that people have. Some have white fences, big yards, and nice size homes for large families; there are beaches that go on for miles. There are ice skating rings all over the place. There are malls, factories, and all kinds of stores; ice skating is the main sport that most people like to watch and be a part of. The next best thing that people love to do in this realm is football. This is the other sport that gathers people from all over.

The flowers look like ice in the sun light, but have the deepest blue of the ocean. The most things the people care about besides their families is the waters in this realm which is good for fishing, swimming, and just hanging out. As the guardians talk into the night they make agreements of who will stay where. Faizah and Lola are staying with Alena. The boys Rich and Andrew will be staying with Leroy at his home. They all agree to meet up at the beach and have a little fun and let each guardian enjoy themselves.

"Oh by the way; Sue and Joey said to tell you all that they are doing great and they are still working on their mission to find the last of the guardians. Lola, Joey said to tell you he is thinking of you each and every day and night. That you are in his dreams always." Andrew said.

After Andrew told them this Lola blushed really red and started to giggle because she knows that the words are true because she is always thinking of him to.

"Well; let us meet up at the Rose beach tomorrow everyone. Let us hope that we can find some peace there and maybe have tons of fun." Alena said.

"Why do you call it Rose Beach?" Lola asked.

"You will see. If you need to use a swimsuit, both of you are more than welcome to borrow one of mine." Alena said.

"Sounds like a plan to me." Leroy said.

"Cool. Then have a safe trip home and a good night' sleep everyone." Alena said.

As everyone went their own ways each group knew that there is going to be a really big storm coming and that the Dark Kingdom Zodiac will be at the eye of the storm. The kingdom will be the most damaging one is when the Star Princess is found. They all have a bad feeling about this. They also know deep down inside that the Dark Kingdom Zodiac is up to something.

As the girls are walking back to Alena's place they stop at a restaurant and went in to eat. The chef came out and started to talk to Alena and the girls. As they take a seat near the back of the restaurant to keep from praying eyes of the other customers in the restaurant. The restaurant was elegant it was something out of a movie where the rich and famous would go. The restaurant has glass tables with red table clothes and lace, with pink and white roses in vases on the tables for center peace's', the dishes are white plates with a gold trim, the glasses are flat with a design of flowers on them, the wine glasses are of different shapes and sizes, the silverware is nice with some type of design on the handle, and the floors are wooded with a throw carpet at the door with a podium for guest.

"Alena this is a very nice restaurant fit for a king." Faizah said.

"Thanks Faizah, it is my mother's restaurant." Alena said.

"Oh, is it just you and your mother?" Faizah asked.

"Yes, my father died when I was very young serving our country." Alena said with a sad face.

"Oh, I'm so sorry to hear that." Lola and Faizah said together.

"It is okay, I never got to know him, but my mother never remarried and there are many pictures of him in our home, even one with him holding me as a baby. This restaurant was both their dreams together so my mother got a loan to start it up, and now it is one of the greatest places to eat at. She gets' a lot of business and I work here during the week if she needs me." Alena said.

"That is cool of you to do." Faizah said.

"Thanks. It is hard sometimes with school, friends, and other things going on." Alena said.

"I know how that is." Faizah said.

"Yeah me too." Lola said.

"Well we should order something to eat. It is on the house; my mother said that we don't have to pay and that we can have whatever we want." Alena said.

"Well in that case, let's look at the menu." Lola said with a giggle.

"Yeah let's look." Alena said with a very big smile.

As the girls are looking over the menu a woman walks over to their table and clears her throat to get the girls' attention. The girls look up and they see the most beautiful woman ever. She had short hair the color of a black panther, she was tall, and was wearing a white coat type that chefs only wear. She had a smile that was so friendly; the girls could not help but smile back. She looked to be in her low to mid forties, but could have been younger. Alena got up and gave the woman the biggest hug and smile on her face that could go for miles.

"Lola and Faizah, I would like to introduce my mother to you. This is Aubrey Patches." Alena said.

"It is nice to meet you ma'am." Lola and Faizah said together.

"Mom this is Lola Brown, and Faizah Carter. They just moved here and will be starting school with me this fall." Alena said.

"How nice it is to meet you two girls. How did you all meet?" Aubrey asked.

"Well Alena and I meet at the Greenbay Beach." Lola said.

"Yeah, Alena goes to the beach a lot during the summer. That is why she is always dark." Aubrey said with a little laugh.

"Alena and me, meet at the school today when my parents came in to sign me up for the next school year." Faizah said.

"Well that is nice, and you became instant friends?" Aubrey asked.

"Yes we did, Alena showed my parents and me the way to the office. We ran into each other when she was leaving and we were coming." Faizah said.

"Well that is good. She doesn't have many friends. Sue, Joey, and Leroy are the only friends she has right now, and now you two. This is great for her she needs friends her age." Aubrey said.

"Thanks mom." Alena said getting flushed.

"You are welcome dear. Well I will let you girls get back to the menu, you can order anything you want except for the alcohol beverages. I am guessing you are not old enough to drink." Aubrey said.

"No ma'am we are not, but thank you for the food and soda we will be having." Faizah said.

"You are most welcome." Aubrey said.

As Aubrey walked away from the table back into the kitchen the girls start to breathe normally and started to laugh at the fact that it was a close call. The girls' start to look over the menu when a waitress with brown hair and a small face came over to take their order.

"Are you girls ready to order? What can I start you three with to drink?" Waitress Amber asked.

"What kind of soda do you have here?" Faizah asked.

"We have Pepsi products." Amber said.

"I would like a Serra Mist." Faizah said.

"You?" Amber asked Lola.

"I would like a Mt. Drew. Please." Lola said.

"Okay and Alena I assume you would like a Dr. Pepper." Amber asked.

"Yes that would be just fine." Alena said.

"Okay, I will get your drinks and be back for your orders." Amber said.

As the waitress walked away the girl started to look over the menu and was looking for some really good food to eat. There was a lot of good looking food which makes it hard to order food in a restaurant; which is one of the most famous. As they kept looking it started to get dark in the restaurant and the girls' sense something evil in the air. They put down their menu and looked up to see if the Dark Kingdom Zodiac had enter the restaurant. Alena remember not too long ago that the Dark Kingdom Zodiac had came into her mother's restaurant and everyone had fallen under the spell of darkness and that is when she first found out that she was a guardian to protect the Star Princess and Prince of the Majestic Star Kingdom.

Alena left her ravine and looked up, and that feeling went away just as fast as it came. All the girls looked up and there is Amber the waitress standing waiting to take the girls' order.

"Excuse me are you all ready to order?" Amber asked.

"Yes." Lola said still looking at how white Alena had become just moments ago.

"What will you have missed?" Amber asked.

"I would like Meatloaf, for my sides I would like steamed asparagus, and mashed potatoes." Lola said.

"Okay and for you?" Amber asked Faizah.

"I would like Roasted Lemon Chicken, mixed vegetables, and a baked potato." Faizah said.

"For you Alena?" Amber asked.

"Oh; sorry. I would like a T-Bone Steak medium well, sweet corn, and a salad that will be all." Alena said.

"Okay I will put this right in, please enjoy these rolls." Amber said.

The girls did not notice that she had put the rolls on the table. It must have been the feeling they got just before she arrived back at their table. As Alena and the other two girls were sitting there; Alena seemed to have gone as white as ghost. As if she might have seen a ghost or at least something evil. Both Faizah and Lola seemed to have been much censured to notice that Alena did not look like herself. As the girls pick up the rolls to eat something did seem off to all of them. Faizah looked back Alena and started to say something.

Chapter 2

"Alena what was that all about you just went as white as a ghost?" Faizah asked.

"Faizah it was a feeling that I got whenever the Dark Kingdom is near or getting ready to attack us. I know you both felt it as well as I did. It just gave me a flashback to when I first found out I was a guardian and they attacked my mother and the people who was working and eating here last time. It just happened a few months ago and it seems that now we are facing a stronger enemy than before." Alena said.

"Well we need to eat, head back to your house, and make a plan on how to deal with this enemy that has appeared here." Lola said.

"I agree with you and we should keep our guard up too just in case they do attack us here." Faizah said.

"I agree with you both." Alena said.

The girls sat looking around for the enemy to attack; and the feeling went away but it still kept them on edge for an attack that might just come at any moment. As they are sitting waiting on their food the restaurant started to fill with fog and everyone started to pass out. The girls jumped up and covered their mouths so that they could not smell the fog. Then it started to get dark, and the girls ran for the kitchen, and everyone in the kitchen had passed out as well; so Alena ran into the kitchen, and turned off the grill to keep the restaurant from going up in flames. As the girls started to look around to who was controlling the fog and why they choose to attack them now they did not know. Then they heard a male's voice in the fog and Alena had frozen at the sound of the voice. Her face went even whiter than it did when she felt that unfriendly sense early.

"Who is there?" Faizah yelled.

"Well I can see there are more guardians now than there was when I first came for you guardian of the Crystal Star of Water and Ice." Prince Jordan said laughing.

"Show yourself?" Lola yelled back.

"Well guardian of the Crystal Star of the Fire Realm. I see you made it back here in time to see me take the guardian back to my Dark Kingdom." Dark Prince Jordan said.

"WHO ARE YOU? Faizah yelled getting flustered.

"He is the Dark Prince Jordan from the Dark Kingdom Zodiac." Alena said finding her voice again.

"She is right he appeared in my realm when Joey and Sue showed up there; and ran with his tail between his legs leaving his general to fight the battle he started. Just like the crowed he is." Lola said with angry.

"Don't be so rude guardian of Fire Realm; I had another engagement that needed my attention far more important than fighting some weak guardians'." Dark Prince Jordan said with a snarl.

"I don't give a damn; who you are here for, and what engagement you had. YOU ARE STILL A CROWED!" Lola yelled.

"I think we should wipe the floor with him now and get it over with." Faizah said.

"Guardian of the Crystal Star of the Lightning Realm you are no match for me and I did not come here for you. I WANT THE GUARDAIN OF THE CRYSTAL STAR OF WATER AND ICE!" Dark Prince Jordan said getting angry.

"Again I don't care who you are here for and I am glad you are not here for me because you are not my type. I will not let you take her or any of my friends." Faizah said.

"LIKE YOU HAVE THE POWER TO STOP ME!" Dark Prince Jordan said.

"We will see." Faizah said.

"She is the next best thing to having the Star Princess and by taking her away again to my realm she will become my wife and we will rule these realms together." Dark Prince Jordan said.

As Alena is standing stun by his appearance and the memory of being back at his castle in the Dark Kingdom Zodiac. She started to shack and cry with the way she had been treated as much as them trying to turn her evil. She knew that she was the most powerful guardian out of all the guardians. Which made her a target since the Star Princess is still missing; and there are still four guardians that still need to be found. Then her tears started to fall like a waterfall she did not want this she loved someone else. She still could not move, but something happened she started to get angry with the display going on in front of her and she found her voice again. Not hearing what the others were saying.

"What do you mean again?" Faizah asked.

"He means when he took me the first time from the park that Joey, Leroy, Sue, and me where at just before school was let out working on our school project. That is also when I found out that Leroy was a guardian too." Alena said with angry.

"So you remember guardian. It was fun with you in that most beautiful dress I gave you. I still think that the Light Blue would look great on you. I also know that the dress would fit you as well." Dark Prince Jordan said to Alena.

"You can take that dress and put it up your nose. I will not be wearing it ever for you. It did fit when I tried it on the first time I was in your Dark Kingdom, but I was not going to give you that satisfaction of wearing it around you." Alena said laughing.

"So you lied to the maids and me about it not fitting." Dark Prince Jordan said with angry.

"That is right. I am done with you." Alena said.

"You are only done with me when I feel you are done with me." Dark Prince Jordan said.

"Like you have the power to make her yours." Faizah said.

"I agree she will never go with you again as long as we are here with her." Lola said.

"Thanks girls. Let us finish this NOW!" Alena said.

"Water come to me please." Alena called.

"Lightning come to me." Faizah called with a smile.

"Fire come to me." Lola called.

As the girls called their powers to them the Dark Prince Jordan smiled at them with their roughness. He started to laugh at them and could not hold back his amusement at them. The girls was not going to take this from the likes of him anymore.

"Let us combined all our powers together to stop him." Faizah suggested.

"You got it." Lola and Alena said together.

As the attack hit the Dark Prince it had turn pure white and it was like heavenly music in the air. This is the true power of the guardians and it is their strongest power as a team. After the powers hit the Dark Prince the guardians passed out and the Prince ran again with his tail between his legs. Alena saw him go and then she finally passed out could.

"Excuse me miss." Amber said.

Alena started to stir and she was looking up at the waitress standing over her along with Faizah and Lola. They had been crying and started to smile at her as if they were scared that she would not wake up again.

"Why is everyone staring at me?" Alena asked turning bright red.

"You passed out after the battle and didn't wake up when the fog cleared up." Lola said.

"Are you okay? You used up a lot of your power." Faizah asked.

"Yeah, I think I'm okay. Just feel drained. Has our food finally got here?" Alena said with a smile, and laugh.

"You and your jokes. Yes it has. Let us eat and get the hell out of here." Lola said with a smile.

The girls were glad to see she was going to be okay. The waitress had walked away after she woke up to get Alena's mother. As she approached the girls Aubrey was staring at her daughter and was glad to see she had come too.

"You scared me to death young lady. DON'T YOU EVER DO THAT TO ME AGAIN?" Aubrey said.

"I won't mother." Alena said with a weak smile on her face.

"I think you girls need to eat and go back to my house and get some sleep. You all are looking pinkish." Aubrey said.

"You got it ma'am." Lola and Faizah said together.

"Okay mom we will." Alena said.

"Good. Now eat up and get going." Aubrey said.

As the girls finished up their meals and head out the door; it had gotten even darker than it was when they went into the restaurant. As they are leaving the restaurant Alena looks up at the clock and it had been almost four hours since they got there. The battle must have taken longer than she thought. As they walk out there is a cool breeze that hits the girls' faces and made them turn their heads to keep from losing their breath. As the guest of wind stopped they looked around to make sure that there were no more enemies coming at them. There was no one there at all.

"It is okay, we supposed to have fall like weather and a lot of rain." Alena said to the girls.

"It has been really crazy since we got here." Lola said.

"Yeah, it is like my realm wants us to fight back and doing so it has changed the way the weather has been." Alena said.

"Is your weather always like this?" Faizah asked.

"No; not normally, just in the last few years the weather has been crazy. I'm not sure want it is, but I think that my realm is feeling that the Dark Kingdom Zodiac is here to take it over." Alena said.

"Well it would seem that all the realms are feeling the Dark Kingdom Zodiac is here." Faizah said.

"What do you mean?" Lola asked.

"I mean; that even on my own realm; the weather had started to go crazy and now I think I know why. What about you Lola?" Faizah asked.

"Yeah, my realm's weather has been off lately too." Lola said.

As the girls kept walking, and talking about the weather, and how it is being affected by the Dark Kingdom Zodiac. Lola looks up and she sees all kinds of stars in the night sky. As she stops and keeps looking the two girls look back to see what is wrong and see her looking up. So the two girls looked up and felt that the world had been lifted off their shoulders.

"Alena your realm is so beautiful; you can see stars for miles." Faizah said.

"Thank you." Alena replied.

"She is right since I got here I have looked at the stars every night from her bedroom window wondering if there will someday be peace for us." Lola said.

"Well I'm glad you think that, but it is getting late and we do have an early start tomorrow. So we need to get moving." Alena said.

"Okay." Faizah and Lola said together.

So the girls started to walk again to Alena's house. So as they kept walking down the street to Alena's house they kept looking up at the stars and moon. The moon was full and bright as a shining white stone. This gave them even more peace and Faizah knew that she would be able to sleep tonight as well as to help find the Star Princess and save this realm and all the realms.

As the girls' reached Alena's house they stopped and looked. Her house was a nice size with pink paint, white fence, and a porch that people could set on and rest. It was a very nice and net house. They knew that it was going to be a very nice looking house on the inside too. As the girls walked in they see a sun room, a parlor, and living room with very nice furniture, a plasma screen that is about 70", and a surround sound. It was a nice and welcoming room. As they move though the house to the stairs to go upstairs to Alena's bedroom to sleep. The girls had not felt as drained as they did this night and that it would make them want to sleep better. As they reached Alena's room there are sleeping bags on the floor for the girls to be able to sleep. As they reached the sleeping bags Alena took her bed as Faizah took the purple sleeping bag, and Lola took the red sleeping bag for herself since it is the sleeping bag she has been using for the last few weeks since she got here. As the girls fall into a deep sleep and start to dream of the Majestic Star Kingdom and the beauty of the kingdom.

Faizah dreamed of being in a field of flowers that was so beautiful that they could be seen for miles. She looked around and someone was coming near her and for an instant she felt that she should run in the other direction, but her feet would not move. She stood there just wondering who was coming near her, then her dream shifted to a ballroom where people was dancing and Faizah was wearing a purple glittered formal dress with gems all though it with a lace back flowing all the way down to the floor with buttons. She looked around and everyone was dancing and watching someone in the middle of the dance floor. As she stepped forward there is a guy and girl dancing both into their own little bubble. The girl was very beautiful and the guy was very handsome. Then Faizah's mouth dropped it was Leroy dancing with the Star Princess. She looks a lot like Alena; Faizah was thinking. She just kept watching them dance and they seemed to be very much in love with each other. As she just watched them dance she could not help but smile and feel the warmth of peace from them. She could not help but keep smiling and watching them dance like from a music box.

Lola had fallen asleep almost instantly and was thrown into a dream of a castle that was made up of crystal of all colors. She was looking onto the castle and felt right at home and so much peace was radiating from it. As she looked she had turned around and there was Joey sitting right next to her holding her hand. She could feel his love and knew that she was safe. As she turned to him to start talking her dream shifted on her and she was wearing a red formal dress with share lace on it with gems in the middle of the flowers that flowed from her dress it was a halter top style and very elegant. She felt the material and found it to feel like slick and velvet. Joey was standing next to her and was watching someone dancing in the middle of the dance floor and as she looked she knew that it was their Star Princess and their Prince. As looked on her mouth fell open and it was Leroy dancing with the Star Princess who looked a lot like Alena. She was very beautiful and they danced as if they were the only ones in the room. Then Joey and I joined in with the dancing watching the Star Princess and Leroy dance. It was like swimming in a pool of peace. It felt so good to feel this warmth that it was a great thing to have. As they danced the night away Lola knew that there can be this same type of peace when all the guardians, Star Princess, Prince Leroy join together to bring this peace to all the realms.

As Lola was dreaming she woke with a startled by hearing the alarm going off around 9:30 am and she could not see why they were getting up so early. As she started to wake the others was waking up and the first to wake all the way was Alena she was shaking both Faizah and Lola to wake up.

"Girls get up if you want to go to the beach today. It is like a two hour drive from here and the boys will be waiting for us at the restaurant so we can go. Leroy is driving his new car he just got from his father for passing school and getting his Drivers Licenses." Alena said.

"I'm up." Faizah said half a wake and half asleep.

"Okay I'm getting up. Do you have a hot pink and black two peace swim suit I can borrow?" Lola asked Alena.

"I might have one." Alena said.

"Do you happen to have a purple Kimono monokini?" Faizah asked.

"Yes they are in the dresser ladies." Alena said.

As the girls run to the bathroom one at a time to get changed into their shots, tank tops, flip flops, and swimsuits. They all took their showers and got dressed, then headed out the door to head to the restaurant to meet the boys. As they walked down the street they looked around to see all kinds of buildings that have blue, white, and clear windows of glass as well as how the streets have all kinds of cars on them. Ranging from a Ford Mustang to a KIA Forte each of different colors.

"Alena when do you turn 16 years old?" Lola asked

"I turn 16 years old in 8 months." Alena said.

"What month does your birthday fall in?" Faizah asked

"Okay; if you two really want to know. It falls in March on the 15th." Alena said.

"Thank you." Lola and Faizah said together.

As they walked on they saw many stores, some with clothes, some with just shoes, and other types of stores that carry many things that a girl could want. Before they knew it they were at the restaurant and the boys where there waiting.

"What took you all so long?" Rich asked.

"We are young ladies and there are things we must do to get ready." Alena said.

Leroy starts to laugh and then looked away. They were sitting in the car with the top down on the mustang which was the color of Candy Apple Red with a white drop top. So all the guardians got into the car and headed to the Rose Beach. As the friends pile into the car they seemed to be all happy just waiting to get to the beach and they started to leave.

Chapter 3

As the group of friends is heading down the highway to the beach; they can see mountains as far as the eyes could see. There where all kinds of colors like gold's, browns, reds, yellows, and greens all by crystal clear water that was surround by the most remote mountain range in the area. It was breathe taking, so Leroy pulled over and they all got out of the car to have a better look. As they look on to view the clouds starting to turn black, and then snow and ice started fall as if someone had turn on the air-conditioning in the mountain range. The temperature started to fall rapidly and the guardians started to shake. They knew it was the Dark Kingdom Zodiac that came to rain on their fun. As the clouds got closer they could see someone in them that started to walk on air near them.

"What is this?" Faizah asked.

"I see you have not started to freeze guardians. So, what I have heard you are very strong." Dark Knight said.

"So you choose to freeze the realm for the Dark Kingdom scum." Lola said.

"How you are all so unwelcoming. I heard that you had some kind of manners. I guess they were wrong on how friendly you all are." Dark Knight said.

"We are only nice to those who are welcomed here. YOU ARE NOT WELCOME!" Alena said.

"So guardian of the Chrystal Star of Water and Ice Realm." Dark Knight said.

"So who are you really?" Rich asked.

"I am called Dark Freeze head knight of the Dark Kingdom Zodiac.

"We can careless what you are called or what misery rank you are in their loser army." Andrew said.

"Oh, Prince Andrew you hurt my feelings." Dark Freeze said.

"Who cares if we hurt your feelings? What do you want and why are you here." Leroy said with anger.

"In that case let's get this over with." Dark Freeze said.

"Fire come to me." Leroy called.

"DARK SNOW STARS." Dark Freeze said. As he calls the snow stars to him he throws them at the guardians making them all scatter to keep from getting hit. Making Leroy to lose his hold on the fire attacked he had called to himself.

As the snow stars hit the mountain behind them; it had turned into decay. Leroy landed by the car, Lola was near the edge of the road with the railing that keep cars from going over the mountain, Alena landed a few feet from the hard mountain face, Faizah was about a couple of feet from Alena, as Rich and Andrew landed a few feet behind the car. As Leroy started to get up he had notice that Dark freeze was laughing.

"What is so funny?" Leroy asked.

"You guardians are, because I have been told you are strong, and I can see now that my other colleague where very wrong." Dark Freeze said.

Leroy was standing with shaking legs from getting out of the attack that he could barely stand. As he did you was not going to let this monster win.

"Fire come to me." Leroy called.

"So you wanna play." Dark Freeze said.

"Dark Ice." Dark Freeze called. As Leroy had let the fire attack go Dark Freeze's dark ice attack had hit him square in the chest throwing him against the hard mountain face making him slide down to his knees then he became unconscious. Alena ran to him crying and praying he was not dead. As she reached him, she picked up his head and could not believe that one of her friends was hurt maybe even dead. It could have been the man of her dreams, someone she cared much about and now she was facing the fact that she might lose him. As she holds him in her arms her sorrow, anger, and confusion was taking hold and turning into adrenaline. She stood up and started to walk to Dark Freeze.

"You will pay for what you have done here today." Alena said with anger.

"So guardian of Water and Ice. Show me what you got." Dark Freeze said. As Alena started to pull all the moisture to her as Dark Freeze did two Ice Swards formed in her hands. To her everything seemed to be moving in slow motion. Dark Freeze seen what was happening through more Snow Stars at her only being blocked by Andrew's attack an Earth Wall. As Rich and Faizah run over to Lola and Andrew were only a few feet from Alena now. He went to Leroy to check on him and started to scream at Alena that he was okay, but she seemed not to hear him. As the wall came down Alena threw one sward at Dark Freeze making him to move and turn away from as the second sward hit him dead in the chest. Rich looked at his friends and knew what they needed to do.

"Come on team lets show him what we can do." Rich said.

"I'm with you." Lola and Faizah said together.

"Lightning come to me." Faizah called. As the lighting hit Dark Freeze it just made him weaker and the sward acted like a lightning rod.

"Wind come to me." Rich called.

"Fire come to me." Lola called.

"Come Lola let us combine our powers to get rid of this fool for good." Rich said.

"Let's do it." Lola said.

"Fire Storm." Rich and Lola called together. As the fire storm hit Dark Freeze he disappeared into darkness hopefully gone for good. As Andrew walked over to Alena who had passed out from her attack and the power she has gained from her friends being near. Andrew picked her up with a much unsteadied Leroy on his feet breathing heavy.

"He isn't gone just got rid of him for now." Andrew said.

"Andrew you can drive my car I will take the backseat with Alena." Leroy said.

"What do you mean he is only gone for now?" Rich asked.

"He will be back. It will take time. Andrew just take this road the rest of the way to the beach and the first intersection you come to take the left road, and follow that road to the end of the street and on your right hand side you will see a cabin with my family name on it Addams." Leroy said.

"Okay got it." Andrew said.

So all the guardians got into the car, and Andrew set Alena gently down in the backseat with Leroy next to her; and Lola behind Andrew. With Rich, Faizah, and Andrew in the front seat. As they start to drive down the whining road down the mountain and to the first intersection and Andrew turned left as they kept driving all they saw was green trees, and very blue skies. Alena started to stir and as she did Leroy lend up and help her to sit up straighter. As she is looking around she notice that they are in the car again and they are driving.

"What happened?" Alena asked.

"You passed out after using up a lot of your powers and energy." Leroy told her.

"What happened to Dark Freeze?" Alena asked.

"He has ran off for now, but you did do some damage." Andrew said with a smile.

"Yeah, girl well done!" Faizah said with a little giggle.

"So where are we going now?" Alena asked.

"We are heading to my cabin, and then we are going to relax on the beach for a little while." Leroy said.

"Oh." Alena said.

As Andrew came up to the first intersection he took the left turn and headed down the street and as he is driving they all seemed to have relaxed a little bit after the battle they just had. As he came up on Leroy's cabin and pulled into a drive that was very long, they come pulling up to a cabin that looked like it was out of a book or something. The cabin was very nice and big enough for them all, but it was all one story.

As the guardians pull up to the cabin they notice that the leaves started to change from green to gold. It was so majestic that they could not look away.

"Leroy it is very beautiful here. You must really enjoy coming every year?" Alena said.

"It is home away from home. I love it here even more during the winter when all the mountains are covered in snow." Leroy said.

"Dude you are like one of the richest people I know." Rich said with a laugh and then all the guardians started laughing together as if it would be their last at any moment.

"Yeah man, it is really nice here." Faizah said with a smile.

"How long has your family had this?" Lola asked.

"It has been in my family for as long as I know." Leroy said.

As they all start to get out of the car and head into the cabin before getting their stuff out of the trunk of the car. They walk into a living area that had a fireplace, nice furniture, a plasma screen T.V. voice active, some recliners, and a love seat. It felt like home and very comfortable to everyone. The T.V. was also a touch screen and they all are egger to touch it and start to watch something.

"Before we start to play with all the fun stuff we need to get our stuff out of the car and put into our rooms." Leroy said.

So everyone got up and headed back outside to get their things and something seemed off as if they had walked into a room with decaying flowers. As they look on they notice that there is a smell of something burning in the woods behind the cabin. As the guardians run around to the back they notice that someone was touching the plants and turning them to decay. It looked as if they were burning the leaves of the trees, and the petals of the flowers. It would smoke then turn to decay.

"Who are you and what do you think you are doing?" Alena yelled.

"Guardian of Water and Ice. You are as beautiful as the dark prince says. Your raven hair, golden brown eyes, and skin tone is tan. I can see why the Dark Prince likes you. I also can sense that you are very powerful compared to your other guardians." General Light-Feather said.

"We are all powerful in our own way. It doesn't matter who is more, we are equal." Alena said.

"You are also modest just as the Dark Prince said. You don't understand how he can compare you to those around you. Keep in mind guardians that I'm your enemy and that I am here to destroy all that is beautiful and precious to your realms." General Light-Feather said. As she said this she disappeared into the darkness of the Dark Kingdom Zodiac. The Guardians knew that she could come back at any time to do more damage to the trees, flowers, animals, and the people of the realms. They also know that if they don't meet this enemy head on that things could go from bad to worst. It was facing all of this that made the guardians question if they are strong enough to bet the Dark Kingdom Zodiac and still think that they may not be able to.

"What was that about?" Lola asked.

"I don't know." Alena said.

"Either way we will have to expect an attack at any time." Andrew said.

"I wish Joey and Sue were here to help." Alena said.

"Yeah, me to." Faizah said.

"They can't be, not that they don't want to be, they just can't." Rich said.

"Yeah, but what they are doing, is just as important as what we are doing. As soon as they fine the last guardians we will be able to stop this Dark Kingdom's advance on all the realms. Hoping we can find the Star Princess in time." Lola said.

"Well let us work just as hard as they are to keep the realms intact." Alena said.

"AGREED!" Rich, Lola, Andrew, Leroy, Faizah, and Lola said together. As the guardians walk back inside after gathering their things from the car. They all went to different rooms and met in the living room to prepare for the beach and an attack that can come at any moment. As the guardians enter the living room everyone was spread out on different seats talking in whispers as Alena enter the room. Then they all became really quite.

"What is everyone talking about?" Alena asked.

"Do you want the truth or us to lie to you?" Faizah asked.

"The truth is always best, please." Alena said.

"We think that it is not safe for you to be by yourself anywhere just in case the Dark Kingdom Zodiac attacks you." Faizah said with a sad face.

"You do know that I can take care of myself. Whether you think I can be trusted or not does not matter, but I will not go so willing to them if that is what everyone is thinking." Alena said getting mad.

"We know you can take care of yourself, it is not that we don't trust you. It is that we don't trust them. The Dark Prince has got it bad for you and he will stop at nothing to get you back there. We know how it was when we first saved you from the Dark Kingdom Zodiac. Our powers where drained badly and if they take you again we think that this time they might just successes where they left off at, when we got you out." Leroy said.

"What does it matter to you? All you ever did was given me problems from the beginning. Why don't you mind your own business?" Alena said.

"For your information, I care about you a lot whether you can see it or not. No matter what happens I will always be there for you no matter what." Leroy said blushing a lot.

"The thing is, you may care, but you and I can never be together because you belong to someone else. That someone else is not me." Alena said as she started to cry for the first time in months and finding out that she was the Guardians of the Crystal Star of Water and Ice. She could not help but feel that her friends were starting to get worried about her. That she did not want them to worry at all. As they all finished the conversation about how they were going to protect Alena whether she agreed or didn't agree she had no say. All she could think about was what Leroy said to her about caring what happens to her. Is it possible that maybe they can still be together even if they find the Star Princess, and he was destined to marry her, and be with her forever?

So after a long talk about protecting and getting ready to go to the beach, so that maybe they can relax for a while; and just be normal teenagers for once instead of protectors of the realms. They all get back in the car and head to the Rose Beach where they found a perfect spot to set up their towels, blankets, and coolers.

"I heard on the news this morning that it is going to be a least a 105 degrees today." Faizah said.

"Yeah, we do get heat waves like this sometimes in the summer time to fall. In this case it is not so normal this time of the year. Do you like the heat?" Alena asked Faizah.

"I have never been able to enjoy something like this my whole life. Yes, it is very nice." Faizah said with a smile.

"Come on girls lets' play some volleyball." Leroy said.

"Okay we will play, but it is girls against boys." Lola said getting up and holding a hand out to Alena to get up. Faizah was on her feet ready to go. As the girls and the guys set up to play volleyball they saw that there was something in the water and wasn't sure what it was.

"SHARK!" Male Life guard said. As everyone ran out of the water they were screaming and shouting that it was not a shark, but something not from this world. It looked like an alien that came from deep in the sea. As the guardians ran toward the water to get a better look, some type of tentacle came out at them grabbing Faizah who started to scream, and then she felt her powers start to drain. She tried to use her power against the mutant shark/squid type monster.

"Who the hell sent this thing here?" Alena said.

"Well consider a present from the Dark Kingdom Zodiac. Guardian of Water and Ice." Lieutenant Fishman said.

"You could have kept that present. Who sent you?" Alena said.

"My bosses, General Dark Freeze and General Light-Feather who have their own army working for the Greatest Kingdom of darkness, the Dark Kingdom Zodiac." Lieutenant Fishman said.

"You think they are the greatest kingdom, but it will never amount up to the Majestic Star Kingdom." Lola said.

"Enough of this talk. If we keep this up Faizah will drown in the lake Sapphire." Alena said. So instead of dealing with this moron from the Dark Kingdom Zodiac they ran for Faizah who was now unconscious and being dragged under water. Andrew ran to her grabbing her hands to keep the shark/squid from taking her underwater only taking him with her.

"We will not let you go." Andrew yelled.

"Hold on you two we are coming." Alena yelled.

"Lola can you use your fire power to keep them from going under." Leroy yelled at Lola.

"Fire come to me. FIRE STAR!" Lola said as the star sliced though the tentacle holding Faizah making Andrew to fall backwards into the water. As he gather himself and got to his feet carrying Faizah from the water Leroy summoned his powers.

"Fire come to me. Fire Ball Strike!" Leroy called. The attack hit the mutant shark/squid sending it back into the water disappearing into dust. As the guardians fall to their knees while Alena and Rich help Andrew with Faizah to get her to come to. The water seemed to be clear of any other type of mutant dark creature from the abyss. As the friends carry Faizah to their spot to let her rest after the attack. It still seemed to get darker as if someone was still there and before they knew another attack came from somewhere behind them. Sending the guardians flying back into the lake.

Chapter 4

As the guardians get to their feet looking around to see where the attack came from. Rich was running to Faizah who started to come to, and then they heard giggling.

"So how did you like my pet guardians?" General Light-Feather said.

"So you choose to attack now." Alena said.

"Well I just wanted to test your abilities. I can see why the Dark Prince and the Dark Kingdom Zodiac wants you." General Light-Feather said.

"They can want all they want, but it will never happen. I have told the Dark Prince that my heart belongs to another and he will never have it." Alena said.

"It isn't your heart he wants, just the power you have." General Light-Feather said with a smile.

"It does not matter either way he still has no chance." Alena said.

"We will see." General Light-Feather said while disappearing into the darkness. The guardians look on to see if anyone was hurt, but it looked as if the beach was clear of all the people. So they packed up their things and headed back to the cabin to regain their strength and to get some rest. As they pull up to the cabin they all seemed to be very tired and felt as if they were ran over by a bulldozer or some heavy equipment construction workers use. As they all file into the cabin and hit their rooms to get some rest Alena was having trouble sleeping with her mind wondering and all she could do was look up at the ceiling. She was so tired, but her mind would not let her sleep. "Why is he after me, and what does he want? Was all Alena was thinking about. "My friends are the world to me and if this keeps up they could get hurt badly." Alena was thinking out loud. Then before she knew she had drifted off to an uneasy sleep. Dreaming of monsters, Dark kingdom Zodiac, her friends, and many other aspects she could not tell or even knew. As she slept through the night into the mid-morning waking to a cool summer air going into fall she knew it was around 10 in the morning when there was a knock on her door.

It was Leroy checking on her and letting her know that breakfast was done to come eat before it was gone. She started to get up, but did not feel like it. It felt like she had not slept at all during the night.

"Alena are you awake, breakfast is done and starting to get cold." Leroy said.

"I'm coming, give me a minute, okay." Alena said through a yawn.

"Okay, just wanted to let you know and that there is food here for you if you are hungry." Leroy said through the door. Alena got up throw on some sweats, a t-shirt, and slippers to keep her feet warm, and head down the hall to the dining room where everyone was sitting talking and eating only stopping long enough to look up; and see her; and started to eat again.

"Girl you look like you have not slept at all." Faizah said looking at Alena.

"It feels like I stayed up all night." Alena said back.

"Well sit here and get some food before you fall over and die." Lola said laughing making everyone around her to start; including Alena which made her feel a little better about the night before.

As Alena sat down to eat she notice that she did not have much of an appetite and was looking at what was left on the table and she just grabbed a little bit of eggs, fruit, some coffee because she needed it, and a couple of pieces of toast. As she was looking around at everyone she felt that this was all her fault they got dragged into this fight with the Dark Kingdom Zodiac.

"Stop thinking like that." Lola said. Alena looked at her as if she had read her mind.

"Did you just read my mind, Lola?" Alena asked. Lola started to laugh and she smiled at Alena.

"No it is all over your face. This was not your fought and we are destined to be guardians whether you were found first or not we still would have been found if not by Jenny and Glen, but by the Dark Kingdom Zodiac. So it was better to be found by them than the Dark Kingdom. Okay." Lola said.

"You are right if it wasn't for all of you I might not be here today and would be working on the side of darkness. Thank You." Alena said.

"No need to say you are sorry, we are happy we met you, and we all became friends." Lola said. Alena smiled feeling a little better and notice that she was a little bit hungry after all. As she grabs a bagel and puts cream cheese on it she notices that everyone was still looking at her. She smiled and could not help but feel the love they have as friends. She knew that she would give her own life for them and all the realms just to keep them safe from harm.

As Leroy gets up from his spot at the table and goes into the kitchen to get more coffee he takes a look out the window and notice that soon the leaves will change color and then winter will be here. He wanted to enjoy these last days of summer with his friends more than anything so he was thinking about them all taking a hike in the mountains. He walks back into the dining room and everyone was just finished up eating and looks up at him.

"Hey guys why don't we take a walk into the mountains for some fresh air. As well as looking at the leaves, plants, and see if we can see anyone else." Leroy suggested.

"I'm game, and we might meet some new people." Rich said.

"You can count me in." Faizah said.

"I'm down." Andrew said.

"I'm up for some good nature looking." Alena said.

"Let us enjoy this time of peace we have. I'm going to." Lola said.

"Good then let us get dressed and meet at the back door in the kitchen. Okay." Leroy said. So all the friends get up from the table and go to their rooms to get dress or changed and they all met back at the kitchen back door. They headed out and started up the trail to have a nice view of everything and the guys brought back packs with drinks and food for a picnic after they have climbed a while. They all wanted to enjoy the peace while they still have it before a war breaks out with the Dark Kingdom Zodiac. They all walked for a good couple of hours and stopped to take a break and rest for a minute and have a drink. They were all smiling and laughing at those who have never been in nature before to enjoy it.

"You know Sue and Joey would have loved this." Alena said.

"I think that when they come back from their mission we should all do this as a team." Andrew said.

"Yeah, but Sue would not be up for it she is not much of a nature girl." Alena said laughing.

"I think it would change now that there is more going on them she knew, and then we all knew." Andrew said with a smile.

"Maybe you are right. I hope so she can be loads of fun. She brings the light with her where she goes." Alena said.

"That she does." Andrew said with a dream like look in his eyes and on his face.

"Don't get all dreamy Andy we might all melt from that love that is showing on your face for her." Faizah said.

"Tease all you want Faizah when it happens to you then we can tease you. Fair?" Andrew said.

"Okay you win. Now should we keep going then?" Faizah asked everyone.

"YEAH!" Everyone said together. So they started their hike up the Red Hawk Mountain trail where they saw, hawks of all colors, birds fling free, deer in the woods, and other people walking. Then it all started to freeze over, and the guardians started to look around.

"Who is here?" Leroy asked.

"Well guardians' I wanted to pay you a visit to see how you are doing, but seeing you all have fun and laughing I thought I would put an end to that." General Dark Freeze said.

"So you came back for more hurt. Hun?" Alena said.

"Well guardian of the Crystal Star of Water and Ice, I just came to pay my respects to you. But it won't be me you fight today. Met my son; Dark Freeze, Jr." General Dark Freeze said.

"So instead of doing your own dirty work; you let someone else do it for you." Andrew said.

"Aww, guardian of the Crystal Star of Earth, don't sound so hurt. He will give you hell, this I assure you." General Dark Freeze said.

"So bring it on then." Faizah said.

"Don't be so hasty guardian of the Crystal Star of Lightning realm. When he attacks you it won't be a walk in the park." General Dark Freeze said.

"Who cares, Fire come to me." Lola called as the fire went to Dark Freeze he just moved out of the way and put up his figure and waved it back and forth shaking his head no.

"Now guardian of the Crystal Star of the Fire realm that was a little careless on your part. If you would have hit me then all these animals and people would be gone. Now my sons come out, and play with your new friends, but don't be too nice to them." General Dark Freeze said.

The guardian heard laughing and was looking around to where it was coming from. As they look up there was an opening and someone or something was coming out of it.

"You call them strong father. Please they look like weak flies caught in a spider web. I hope you guardians give me some enjoyment to kill you." Dark Freeze, Jr said.

"You are sure of yourself." Alena said. As Dark Freeze, Jr. comes out the rest of the way he looks at her and then starts to smile. He could see why the Dark Prince wants her, he wants her. As he looks at Alena he was thinking that maybe he would keep her for himself.

"Well guardian of the Crystal Star of Water and Ice I can see why my Dark prince wants you so badly. You are very delicious and very beautiful. I might just have to keep you a live for my own enjoyment." Freeze Jr said.

"You will keep your dirty hands off her." Leroy said.

"Well Prince of the Elemental Realm, you have some taste, but doesn't your hand and heart belong to the Star Princess. If she could see how you drew over her; she might have to do something about it. So why care so much for a guardian girl you can never be with. You are supposed to marry the Star Princess; if you can ever find her." Freeze Jr said.

"Who I choose to love is my choice and not fate or destiny can change that. I will keep the promise made by my parents and I will up hold my vow. I will not stop loving those around me or my friends." Leroy said with anger.

"Now look who is getting mad. It would seem I hit a very tender spot you don't want to talk about." Freeze, Jr said.

"I don't care what you have to say." Leroy said.

"Well in that case I will take what I want and be done with you guardians." Freeze, Jr said.

"Wind come to me!" Rich said. As the wind picked up and was being aimed at Freeze, Jr, the attack didn't help it just made it even colder. So as the guardians' look on trying to figure out how to stop the freeze that was spreading down the Red Hawk Mountain and freezing everything it touches. Alena was looking around and felt helpless. She felt this was her fault because they came for her again.

"Don't you dare think like that?" Lola said. Alena looked at her and knocked her head to let Lola know she knew what she met.

"We need to find a way to stop that freeze and stop Freeze, Jr." Alena said.

"I know, but we can't if you don't stop feeling sorry for yourself, and blaming yourself for what happens." Lola said to her. As they look up at Freeze, Jr he seemed to be stronger than his evil father, but something was bugging them. If he can freeze everything then while are they not frozen? Then it hit Alena, like a light bulb coming on for the first time.

"I know why we are not frozen everyone. It is because our guardian powers are protecting us. So let us combine our powers to stop this freeze." Alena said.

"You got it, after that we can take care of Freeze, Jr." Faizah said. As the guardians' combine their powers to stop the freeze from spreading any more down the Red Hawk Mountain. Freeze, Jr smiled as he looks on to see how powerful they are. Then before the guardians know it they were starting to freeze as well. How can the guardians' get out of this?

Chapter 5

As Lola throws her element of fire at Freeze, Jr. it hits him, but it does not cause much damage, but enough to keep the guardians' from being frozen to death. As the guardians' start to unfreeze, Dark Freeze, Jr looks on and smiles even bigger.

"You are not as weak as I thought before guardians'." Freeze, Jr. said.

"You have no idea how strong we can be or we are." Lola said.

"Then show me how strong you really are guardians'." Freeze, Jr said.

"You got it." Rich said.

"Dark Birds attack." Freeze, Jr said. Before the guardians' knew what happened, the birds that was frozen came back to life, but was evil and being control by the power of the dark freeze. As they try and battle them off they knew that there would be a problem without knowing how to deal with; Dark Freeze, his son, and General Light-Feather.

"Guardians you look as if the world is about to end." Dark Freeze, Jr. said.

"You think that we are just going to give up and not finish this fight you have another thing coming Dark Freeze, Jr." Alena yelled. As she looks up at the evil in front of her friends and her. She was not going to let them win this battle or any at that; she will find a way to stop the Dark Kingdom Zodiac.

"Alena is right; I owe the Dark Kingdom Zodiac for killing my family." Andrew said.

"Guardian of the Earth Realm you are no match for me and my men." Dark Freeze, Jr. said.

"It does not matter what you say we will stop you all." Lola said.

"Then bring it on." Dark Freeze, Jr. said.

As the guardians start to get worry; how to bet their enemy, and to stop the Dark Kingdom Zodiac. They look on as to how to save the people on the mountain and themselves. Alena was sacred as is everyone, but they were not going to just give up and let them win.

"There has to be a way to stop this fool, and to beat the Dark Kingdom Zodiac?" Faizah spoke out loud.

"By working together and staying strong for each other; whether we are all together or distance apart." Lola said.

"I agree with you. We have to stop these three first and hoping that our friends can find the other guardians." Leroy said.

"Then let us put a stop to this battle." Alena said.

"You got it; let us finish this fast so we can finish our mini vacation before school starts up next week." Rich said.

"You got it." Faizah said. As the guardians look on they knew what they had to do to end the battle, they were in and enjoy summer; what they had of it. So as they look at each they choose to go for it and looked up to see that Dark Freeze, Jr. was still looking at them laughing as if they were a big joke.

"Let us show him who he is truly missing with everyone." Alena said.

"You got it." Everyone said together. As everyone stood up and started to call their powers to them they felt a really cold breeze and looked up Dark Freeze, Jr. was aiming a bow and ice arrow at them and let it go. As they all jumped out of the way to keep from getting hit by the arrow. It started to snow where the arrow had hit making it hard to see and do anything.

"We need to find a way to get him to stop long enough for us to use our power." Lola said.

"Leave it to me." Alena said as she ran around the arrow and away from her friends. As she did Dark Freeze, Jr. turned his head long enough to keep her in sight.

"So you plain to give yourself to me so that I can return you to the Dark Kingdom Zodiac?" Dark Freeze, Jr. said.

"Not on your life. NOW!" Alena said. As Dark Freeze, Jr. turn the other guardians had gathers their powers and putting them together to force Dark Freeze, Jr. out of this realm. Alena had enough time to do as well and when she finally got her power together, she added it to the others and they let it rep and before they know it the power had turn a bright white light and it hit Dark Freeze, Jr., his father, and Light-Feather back to the Dark Kingdom Zodiac. So the friends to each other and was happy that the fight was finally over. They knew also that this was only the beginning for them all. It started to warm up and everyone that was on the mountain was turning back to normal with no memory of what had happened to them. So the friends enjoyed what was left of the summer together before school started. As they went back to the beach Alena sat on the beach and watched her friends have loads of fun. Lola and Faizah came over to her and sat down next to her.

"What up girl?" Faizah said.

"What is on your mind?" Lola asked.

"I was just thinking about Sue and Joey, hoping that everything is going well, and that they are okay." Alena said.

"Alena don't be worried they were heading to the Crystal Star of Healing and Spirit Realm." Andrew said.

"Do you really think so Andy?" Alena asked wiping away tears of joy and sadness.

"Yes we all do." Andrew said.

"Believe in our friends. They are very strong." Rich said.

"I will believe in them." Alena said hoping up with a smile, and she began to splash in the ocean water. She felt at home there, as well as believing in her friends knowing that they are getting close to finding all the guardians. As Sue and Joey head to the Crystal Star of the Healing and Spirit Realm to find the next guardian, while the other guardians' keep the Dark Kingdom Zodiac at bay.

Crystal Star of
the Healing and
Spirit Realm

Chapter 6

As Sue and Joey had walked through another portal after Andrew had went through the portal to the Crystal Star of the Water and Ice Realm. Sue was still stunned by the sudden kiss she had gotten from Andy before he left her to do his mission and Joey and her can finish their mission which was given to them of finding the last of the guardians. As they do it would get them closer to finding the Star Princess. So Joey and Sue go through the portal to the next realm. As they step out of the portal they find themselves in a whole new place. Sue looked around the new realm, and notice they had appeared in a field of flowers that was as bright as the sun. Each flower was some color of white, and she could smell a light an aroma. It smelled so good; but relaxing as if all the worries in the entire galaxy was gone, and taken away.

"It is so beautiful here and relaxing." Sue said with a smile. Joey was looking around and his ground was up just to be safe. He could not agree more with Sue; it did seem to be very peaceful here, but he knew all too well that it could not last. As they looked around they notice all kinds of flowers, trees, even temples off in the distance. As they looked around they notice that there was a river a head of them that sparkled in the sun as if welcoming them here.

"So, Joey what do think of this realm?" Sue asked

"It is nice, but you and I both know that the minute we start to notice a nice thing; that is when things take a turn for the worse." Joey said with a laugh.

"You are right, well let's start to look around, maybe we can find someone to help us out." Sue said.

"You are right." Joey said. So they started to walk toward the river they seen sparkling in the sun a little ways back. As they a pouch the river they notice a person getting water. As they look the woman was wearing what looked like an old fashion kimono from history. As they look around they notice that there where many women getting water. So Sue walked up to the women and started to ask about the realm and what was going on.

"Excuse me miss." Sue said.

"Yes my dear?" Temple Lady said.

"Hi, my name is Sue and that guy over there is my partner, he is my cousin and we are looking for a special person with a lot of power. Also we would like to know if this is the Crystal Star of the Healing and Sprit Realm. What also happened here?" Sue asked.

"My name is Lady Julia, Yes; this is the Crystal Star of the Healing and Spirit Realm. You would be looking for a priestess of great power." Lady Julia said.

"What happen here?" Sue asked.

"We was attack by some dark force and it try to take over this realm, but my sister put up a barrier that kept demons away from the people around here and purified them." Lady Julia said.

"I'm sorry to hear that, but where can we find your sister? She might be the true guardian of this realm we are looking for." Sue said.

"That she might be, we have a temple here that she goes to for help from the accent ones and elders of this realm. That has passed down their own; pure powers of healing. If you head west for a few days and then go south from the village called Heaven's Light. Then you will go south from there to a city called Light's Hope. Does this help? There in the temple of Heaven's Gate you will find my sister praying. Her name is Lady Autumn." Lady Julia said.

"Thank you so much this does help us out. We will find your sister Lady Autumn and see if she is the guardian we seek." Joey said.

"I do believe that she would be; because she is very strong. Also she is as pure as can be." Lady Julia said.

"So, Joey shall we head west then south to the temple. What is the name of the temple that we seek?" Sue asked.

"The temple is called The Temple of the Elders and Gods." Lady Julia said.

"Thank you very much." Sue said. As they start to leave Lady Julia yelled at them to stop for a moment.

"You two please wait a moment." Lady Julia yelled.

"Yes?" Joey said.

"Take this; it will help with poison and here are some herbs that can help you two out; if you get hurt or need healing of some kind, until you find my sister." Lady Julia said.

"Thank you very much; we will use these herbs if the need arises." Joey said. They headed toward the setting sun in the west. As they looked at the site and the colors it was so breath taking that both of them stop to look. It was peaceful and very beautiful. The colors were violet, orange, red, pink, white, blue, and other colors of the rainbow. The scene was also breath taking as they took the time to look, it was like a paradise they always wanted to go to. The landscape looked as if it was painted there, flowers as far as the eyes can see of all colors, rivers and creeks in the background that shined like jewels, the view was so much peaceful that the thought of it being taken away is not believe. The guardians will not let this happen.

"Let us make camp here; we have a few days before we can reach the temple. So let us rest, since the fight we have not had a chance to rest since then so let us rest now. So that we can be at our fullest power. Okay?" Joey said.

"I agree with you, we do need rest and I'm hungry as well. So let us rest." Sue said. So they set up camp on a warm peaceful night, hoping they can have at least one night of good sleep. As each one choose to see who will take first watch for enemies it had been decided that Joey will take the first watch and Sue will take the last watch before morning. As Joey is sitting in the door of the tent he is looking up at the sky and can see many stars in this realm, he started to think of Lola and the others wondering if they are all okay. As he is watching he feels an uneasy disturbance in the air. It is as if someone was trying to avoid being found, so he stands up to take a better look and finds nothing. He can't shake the uneasy feeling that someone or something is out there in the field of flowers they set up camp at. As the time goes by Sue takes her turn for the watch when day break comes she wakes Joey and she felt the uneasiness as well.

"Joey did you happen to feel some fowl in the air while on watch. I felt a very uneasiness in the air." Sue asked.

"Yeah, I felt it too looked around while you were asleep and could not find anything." Joey said.

"Then let us get moving before that uneasy feeling shows itself." Sue suggested.

"Yeah; great idea, because I don't want to fight if we can avoid it then let us avoid for the time being." Joey said. So the two guardians started their trip to the temple which lies west from the village. As they head to the temple they started to get worry that the uneasy feeling they felt that late night early morning was coming back and they knew that it was a matter of time before the force behind the uneasy feeling will show up. They also knew that with that uneasy feeling that the Dark Kingdom Zodiac was not far behind. The only thing that they would happen is that they at least lay their hand before they get too far and it involved innocent people.

"Joey do you think that the Dark Kingdom Zodiac is toying with us." Sue asked.

"Yeah, I think they are, but I also think that they are waiting to hit us when we least expect it as well. When our guard is down. Here is to hoping it will be soon, unless they are waiting for to find the next guardian first. So that they can hit us all at once and test the new guardian's powers." Joey said.

"Yeah, I think that is what it is. They are buying their time to see were we going." Sue said. So they kept walking with their guards up and watching for any type of movement that might come at any time. As they walk toward the temple in the west they notice that there seemed to be no sound at all. Not even a bird was singing which is never a good sign.

"We know you are out there, show yourself." Joey yelled into the wind. There was no movement, or sound just water moving in the distance. So the two guardians continue on their way west to get to the temple. They had at least a full two days walked. They knew that it is only a matter of time before whatever enemy they are supposed to fight against shows themselves. Since they had a long walk a head of them they knew they could at least enjoy some of the scenery and make a good memory of it. As the guardians walk the scene there are flowers in the colors of red, pink, white, blue, black, purple, and yellow. They were mini roses, daisies, tulips, cat-lilies, and pennies. The sky look so brilliant that the colors blind together so well that you could not see where one started and the others ended. There are small villages in this realm that it looks to be from history of some kind. So they made sure to make great memories for themselves and share their experience with their friends back home. As they walked on till day was almost over they set up camp for the night. They looked up at the stars wondering how everyone was doing and hoping that Faizah and Andrew made it back without any problems. Sue was worried about Andrew and touching her lips remembering the passion in the kiss he gave her before leaving her to her mission with Joey. Joey was thinking about Lola and how it felt so normal to be with her. He missed his other friends, but not as much as his soul mate that he finally found in

Lola. Sue felt the same way about Andrew and the how it felt so normal to be with him. They knew that they had to find all the guardians' that was left to be able to return to their home and to those they care about and miss very much. They were starting to get home sick with all the traveling they have to still do and have already done.

"Sue will you take the first watch tonight and I will take the last watch?" Joey asked.

"Yes, I think it is a good idea. I have been enjoying this time with you and everything that has happened in the last few months. I still worry about our friends and how things are going there." Sue said.

"I do too. It seems like it has been an eternal since we have seen them all. I miss them all too. I hope that we can find this guardian in this realm soon so we can keep going to the next." Joey said.

"Yeah, me as well. You go ahead and get some sleep and I will wake you in a few hours to take the next watch." Sue said with a smile on her face.

"Okay, keep a good watch and try not to use to mush power." Joey said smiling at her. So Joey went into the tent and lay on the cot but could not go to sleep. He felt so uneasy it was not funny. It felt as if they were being watched by someone or something. He wish if the Dark Kingdom Zodiac would attack instead of holding off until they found the next guardian. "I wondering what the guardian is like in this realm." Joey was thinking. So Joey fell into a very uneasy sleep having a nightmare of something horrible that he could not see or get away from. It was the size of a huge bear with hair as red as a blood moon in the night sky. Then Joey woke suddenly up with cold sweats and breathing hard, as if he was running for his life. So he got up and went outside the tent to see Sue was still keeping watch. He sat down next to her and looked out into the darkness.

"Are you okay?" Sue asked.

"No, just a really bad dream I could not get away from." Joey said.

"What was the dream about? You only have been a sleep for maybe three hours." Sue said.

"It was about a huge bear with hair the color of red as a blood moon." Joey said shaking.

"Please, try to claim down and try to get a few more hours a sleep." Sue suggested.

"No, I'm okay. I will take the watch over from here. You go get some rest, we leave at first light. Okay." Joey said.

"I think I will stay up just for a little while, and then I will try to get some sleep." Sue said. So both Joey and she stayed up for a few more hours after that. Then Sue went to sleep thinking about the kiss she received from Andrew and feel into a deep sleep. Dreaming of a castle that was made up of all kinds of crystals with so much color and life that all you wanted to do was set there in the meadow and just look. Someone was sitting with her. As she looked at the person she realized that it was Andrew holding her hand. She smiled and then before she knew her dream took a dark turn for the worst of the castle being destroyed and people screaming for their lives. She stood up and knew just what to do. Before she could she woke with a start and was holding her chest and she felt tears falling from her eyes as if her life was being taken from her. She got up and went outside just before first light looked down at Joey and tears was still falling.

"What is wrong Sue?" Joey asked jumping up and grabbing her to hold her as she cried.

"I had the worst nightmare ever. It was as if I was there and the castle was being destroyed right in front of me. I went to help and I woke up crying. It is like I was reliving the last few days of the Majestic Star Kingdom." Sue said still crying.

"It was only a nightmare. I'm here we will not let that happen this time. We will find the guardians and the Star Princess of the Majestic Star Kingdom." Joey said. All Sue could do was nod her head while crying into Joey's shoulders and arms thanking, that her cousin was there with her.

"Let us get moving. I want to get to that temple as soon as we can. No more stopping let us keep pushing forward." Sue said.

"Okay, let us get a move on. Maybe I can summon a dragon to help us get to that village and temple sooner." Joey said.

"No, let us go by foot for a little while, but when we want to stop and make camp let us use the dragon then okay?" Sue asked.

"That is a better idea than mine was. Okay you got." Joey said. So the two guardians packed up the camp and started walking again until they came to the village they were supposed to reach in three days but cut it down by leaving sooner than later. As they reach the outskirts of Heaven's Light this is the village they were supposed to go to. They notice that something seemed to be off.

"Sue, let us move there might be trouble there?" Joey suggested.

"Yeah, let us move as fast as light." Sue said. So they ran the rest of the way to the village to see that a woman was defending the village with a barrier of pure light. As they enter the village they felt as if they had been healed by the barrier. They ran over to the priestess, she was wearing the colors of white and red. They ran over to her to help. Sue put up a light barrier that was as bright as the sun.

"Can you use some help?" Sue asked.

"Yes, and I thank you an advance if we don't make." Priestess said.

"Can you tell us what those are?" Joey asked.

"They are called demons of darkness. I do not know where they come from, but they are giving more trouble than normal." Priestess said.

"We see it would seem that they might be from the Dark Kingdom Zodiac." Joey and Sue said together.

"May I ask what that is?" Priestess said.

"It is a kingdom that is so dark that they only like to destroy things and most of realms with guardians of power on them." Sue told her.

"I see so this Dark Kingdom Zodiac is the reason we are seeing so more demons than normal. My name is Lady Autumn Williams." Lady Autumn said.

"It is nice to meet you Lady Autumn. My name is Sue Stang, and this guy over here is Joseph. He goes by Joey." Sue said.

"Is there any way to push them back of some kind?" Joey asked.

"Yes, if you two can hold the barrier I can use my powers to send them away." Lady Autumn said.

"Okay, we will hold the barrier the best we can. So please do it fast." Joey said.

"Okay, this might make me tired and weak." Lady Autumn said.

"Then we will make sure that you will get rest from someone in this town." Joey said.

"Okay, here goes nothing. I call HEAVEN'S ARROW COME TO ME. DESTORY THOSE DEMONS, AND PUSH THEM AWAY." Lady Autumn yelled. As she did there was a very bright and pure light and as it cleared all the demons were gone. The two guardians looked at her and could not believe she was so strong. She looked at them and smiled the next thing they knew she had passed out. Joey had caught her before she hit the ground. He picked her up and all the villagers came running over to say thank you. The head of the village offered them a place to stay for the night.

"I want to know who sent those damn demons and why?" Joey said.

"There is only one person that could do this and only one place could." Sue said.

"Yeah, that would be the Dark Prince and the Dark Kingdom. So who is their new general that they sent here to keep us and the next guardian from coming together." Joey asked.

"We will know soon enough." Sue said.

"Could she be the guardian of this Realm?" Joey wonder.

"She did say her name was Lady Autumn. She is most likely Lady Julia's older sister. So she has a hell of a pouch of power in her." Sue said.

"Yeah, there is no doubt she is the guardian of this realm we sink." Joey said.

"Let her rest for now she did use a lot of power back there to destroy and push demons back." Sue said.

"Yeah you are right. We need to rest as well. With using your powers and hers' we all can use some rest. Good thing we are all sharing a room for the night. We can always ask all the questions in the morning." Joey said.

"Yeah, good night Joey. Just keep your guard up and I will do the same." Sue said falling to sleep. She fell back into the same dream she had the other day only to wake to it never ending. As she looked up she notice that the head of the village's house was very different than she was used to. It looked like a mansion that had sliding doors made up of thin wood. Paintings on the wall of Cherry blooms, a mountain side with snow on top, and it had paneling made up of wood. They laid on rolled out matts with a pillow in the same of a circle. It was very nice and comfortable, she felt safe for now. She looked up and someone was standing outside the door. There was light coming in, which met it was morning. She got up and went outside and she seen the Priestess standing on the long pouch looking at the sky. She looked back at Sue and gave her a gentle smile. So Sue went over next her and stood there.

"I want to thank you for the help yesterday. You two are not from here, but I can sense some strong power coming from you both." Lady Autumn said.

"Yeah, we are the guardians of the Crystal Star of Light and Travel, and the Crystal Star of Summoning Realms. We are guardians sworn to protect the of the Majestic Star Kingdom." Sue said.

"Aww, I see, so you have come to seek me out to help. I'm the guardian of this realm. I am sworn to protect the Majestic Star Kingdom with my powers of heaven and spirit. But, before I come and help the guardians out. I need help to push out this enemy out of this realm so they people here can be safe. I'm a priestess and I also have royal blood in me. My family is the most powerful of priestess in this realm." Lady Autumn said.

"I see so you and your family are very spiritual. That is okay with us." Sue said.

"Yeah, we will help you out. We would not be happy or feel we did our job right if we let the Dark Kingdom Zodiac keep getting their way." Joey said.

"So how long have you been there?" Lady Autumn said.

"Not long, only to hear the last part of the conversation you two were having." Joey said.

"That is good. At least you don't ease drop much." Lady Autumn said with a little laugh.

"So do you have any idea what this enemy is or what they are after?" Sue asked.

"I have no idea who, what, or what they want. All I know is that they came here from a far off place that is not in the Majestic Star Kingdom realm, or any of the other realms that serve the Great Kingdom." Lady Autumn said.

"I see so even if they came from a far place they have not chosen to show who they are or what general who is pulling the strings." Joey said.

"Yes, I have no idea. They are very powerful, and that power is very dark. There is pure hatred there. They can for no one or nothing." Lady Autumn said with anger.

"The only thing we can do now is head to the temple of Heaven's Gate and get what answers we can." Sue suggested.

"I was heading there myself, when those damn demons attacked this village." Lady Autumn said.

"Then it is settled we are all heading to that temple in the south. We will find out what is going on. Who is behind all of this?" Joey said.

"We need to get a few things before we leave. Like food, water, stuff for healing, and other important things. Also as you can see I am just now getting into my powers and my most powerful attack would make me weak. I need to get myself a bow and arrows. I also can use twin katana which helps me with most of my powers. So let us stop at a weapons shop, a potions shop to get what we need, as well as an items shop for all other things." Lady Autumn said.

"Great idea. We could use some things as well. We need to restock on those things as well." Joey and Sue said together. So all three guardians headed to the items shop first to get things that can't be brought at the other shops. They went in the shop and saw many different things that caught their eyes. So they looked around the shop which looked like a pub, but did not have any chairs just a counter for which you paid for your things. They got rags, bandages, sprints, and other things you would find in an item shop. They next shop they went to was the potions shop which they got stuff for healing, poisons, trickery of the mind, not being able to more, and potions that gave them energy when they need it. The last shop they went to was the weapons shop where Lady Autumn found twin katana, and a new wooded bow and arrows which Lady Autumn put her spiritual and heaven powers into so they would be more affected. Then they headed for the boarders of the village so they can start their journey to the Temple of Heavens' Gate. As they leave the village and get a few miles away demons come back to attack them this time it was them they were after. As each guardian pulled out their weapons they knew that this fight was not gonna be easy at all.

"We need to use our powers as guardians to fight these demons and push them away." Lady Autumn said.

"So how do we do that?" Sue asked.

"By calling our powers to us." Lady Autumn said.

"I'm with you. But first let us find out who is behind this attack." Joey suggested.

"Great idea cuz." Sue said.

"WHO ARE YOU AND WHAT DO YOU WANT WITH US?" Lady Autumn yelled.

"Well if it isn't the guardian of this realm." Mystery guy said.

"I maybe the guardian in this realm, but you don't belong here. SO WHO ARE YOU?" Lady Autumn yelled again.

"As it would be guardian of the Crystal Star of the Healing and Spirit Realm, I am the general of Cruelty. My name is Amos." Amos said.

"So the Dark Kingdom Zodiac sends out another creep to do their bending and try to get rid of all of us guardians'." Sue said.

"I see that the guardian of Light and Travel and the guardian of Summoning is here as well. I see that my co-workers did not stop you two in the other realms. I WILL STOP YOU THREE HERE!!!!" General Amos said.

"You can try, but you don't have the power to stop us here." Lady Autumn said.

"I will leave you to my demons who only want to cause pain and suffering to these people in this realm. So fight my demons until your heart is grand." General Amos said.

"We will stop them, and then come after you. You just wait and see." Lady Autumn said.

"You can try guardian, but my demons will tear you apart here. If you can beat them I will see you at the temple of Heaven's Gate." General Amos said with a laugh disappearing into the darkness.

"COME BACK HERE YOU CAWORD!!" Lady Autumn said.

"Get ready, here they come." Sue said.

"We don't have time to worry about him right now. We need to do something about those damn demons that are in our way." Joey said.

Chapter 7

"In that case, let me show you how I do it." Lady Autumn said. As she was pulling out the twin katana.

"Okay, just try not to overdo it." Sue said.

"HEAVEN'S WAVE! As she put both twin katana together to use her powers." Lady Autumn called.

"I summon you Fire Dragon. Come to me." Joey called.

"Sun Burst!" Sue called. So as all three guardians used their powers against the demons that turned to ashes just from the hit.

"That was great you two. I did not think there were people who have such power. I'm glad you came here to help." Lady Autumn said smiling.

"It was nothing, but let us save the celebration when we have finished all these demons. Okay" Joey said.

"Yeah you are right. There are more demons coming our way. Sue you take the right this time, Joey take the front, and stay behind as I take the back because the power is going to just get stronger. That is the same for you two as well." Lady Autumn said.

"Yeah, I can feel it. That was the first time I even used that type of attack." Sue said.

"So let us finish this and make it to the temple before Amos does." Joey said.

"You got it." Sue and Lady Autumn agreed.

"Heaven's Crescent Moon Dance." Lady Autumn called.

"Fire Ball." Joey called

"Sun Burst." Sue called.

As each attack hit the demons turning them to ashes they still had a lot to deal with. So as it looked if they would not make even a dent in the demons attack. They knew they had to put their all into this fight to be able to make it to the temple before Amos does.

"This is getting us know where." Sue complained.

"Don't give up. I know we are low on magic but we can when. We are not just doing this for us or the people of this realm but for all realms, and the peace that will come with it." Lady Autumn said taking long hard breaths.

"I agree with you both, but we can't give up our friends are counting on us." Joey said.

"Then let us put an end to this. Both of you get behind me. This next attack will take them all out." Lady Autumn said.

"Okay." Both Joey and Sue said together.

"I call fourth DOORS OF HEAVEN! Please wipe out all these demons that attack us." Lady Autumn called. As she did there where many doors that looked really old with oak wood and gold on the doors. As Sue and Joey looked on they also notice that the doors had Angel Wings on them. Before they could see any more there was a very bright light and before their eyes the demons were gone. Joey's mouth fell open looking at Lady Autumn with high respect, and amazement. Sue could not believe that she had this much power. It would seem that she is as strong as Alena is if not stronger.

"WOW!" They both said together.

"Thank you, but it is an attack that can't be used often because it drains you of so much power that the caster has to be aware of their levels. I do believe that all the guardians hold this much power as I do. I can't wait to meet them all." Lady Autumn said falling to her knees. As Joey ran over to her and caught her before hitting the ground.

"Let us take a little break and rest. If not we all will be out of power soon." Joey suggested.

"We agree." Lady Autumn and Sue said together. As the three guardians take a break after the fight which drained them of almost all their powers.

Amos is on his way to the temple of Heaven's Gate to turn this realm evil and to take what it has; in souls, energy, and people to make into puppets for the Dark Kingdom Zodiac. As the guardians rest to gain some strength back they; know that the fight is just starting and that it will take a lot more effort on their parts to make it through; all this to find the last of the true guardians of the Majestic Star Kingdom. Amos is aiming to destroy this realm and to find the Star Princess to keep the Majestic Star Kingdom from rising again. So he plans to release all the demons he can on this realm and to also keep the three guardians from ever reaching the temple to stop him. He knows that they are strong but his anger is stronger. He will keep attack until the guardians can't stand any more. There will be no body to stand against the Dark Kingdom Zodiac if the guardians fall in this realm.

So the guardians must push forward to keep the realms from falling into chaos. The end of days will come, but they will always be there to keep it at bay, until the Star Princess is found again and is safe. It will take a lot more power for each guardian to stop the Dark Kingdom Zodiac from every reaching their goal of totally power. Amos can't wait for this to happen because he will become one of the strongest generals they Dark Kingdom has ever had. First he must wipe out those annoying guardians before they can gain all their true powers starting with the three that are on this realm.

As the guardians rest is over, they start to head south to the temple of Heaven's Gate to stop Amos from ever taking over this realm or any other realm for that matter. To keep all the realms from being destroyed by the Dark Kingdom Zodiac. When they find the rest of the guardians and the Star Princess peace will come at last. But, will it last? This is the question that is always on the minds of all the guardians as of late. The guardians know they have a major fight a head of them and that this fight might even be the worst and longest fight they ever had to do so that peace can come to this realm. It also means that they must fight to protect everyone. As they are heading south toward the temple they choose to rest new a Pub that is the next village they came to.

"What is the name of this village?" Sue asked.

"It is the Village of Holy Grace." Lady Autumn said.

"Oh, it sounds so formal. It also sounds like a village that worships gods of some kind." Sue said.

"It is a holy place that priest and priestess come from all over the realm to get the blessings of the elders and gods. The village people know that it is a holy place that surrounds the temple. It keeps some type of barrier around to keep demons away from the temple." Lady Autumn said.

"Oh, I see it is a magical place that uses barriers to protect scarred grounds safe." Joey said.

"Yes, you can put it that way." Lady Autumn said. So the guardians walked into the village, but things seemed to be off. It was like the air around was very dense and that it felt heavy in your lungs. The people seemed to be looking at them like they are way out of place. As the three guardians make their way to the inn for rooms to stay in for the night. They notice that the village had small houses made up of wood and hey, as well as some made up with stone and wood roofs. As they make their way through the village to the inn at the far end of the village. There are many different things from outside of the village to the inside of the village. Like the flowers seem to be of different and more depressing colors, of black, dark purple, or dyeing. The people didn't seem like a lot of people who have respect from the scarred grounds.

"Does it seem that something seem to be wrong?" Joey said.

"Yeah it does, it seems to be very strange and the people seem to be very hostile." Sue said.

"Something is wrong here. I can feel that the peace is being drained along with the energy. The air seems to be heavy as well." Lady Autumn said.

"Now that you mention it. You are right it does seem the air is very off." Joey said.

"I think we need to get rest and then get some information from the villagers. Also find out what is going on here." Joey suggested.

"DO you think that Amos made it here before us?" Sue asked.

"That is a really great question. It is also a very big chance he has come here." Lady Autumn said.

"Well, let us get a room then rest, eat, and then we will find out what is going on here." Joey said.

"You are right." Lady Autumn said. So the guardians went into the inn to get a room. As they enter it seemed to be very dark, and that the air in here is just as bad. So they walk over to the counter and ring the bell. As the desk person came out with a very bad look on his face. As if something dirty came through the door. As they look at him they knew that something is most differently off here.

"Excuse me sir, but we are looking for a room for the night. Do you have on available?" Lady Autumn asked.

"Yes, would you like a room with three beds?" Desk Front Man asked.

"Yes, that will be fine." Lady Autumn said.

"That will be 60 dollars for the night." Desk Front Man asked. So Lady Autumn paid the man and his bell bop showed them to their room which did not look all that great. At least there were three beds to rest on, instead of the ground in a tent somewhere else. So each one took a bed and set their things on it. Joey took the bed near the window, Lady Autumn to the one across from Sue, who took the bed near the door to the room. This way they all can defend themselves if it came down to it.

So the guardians went to get some food and made certain to keep their weapons on them just in case something happens while they are eating. As they make their way through the village again to the café which was not far from the inn. This made it easy to find their way back. They choose to start asking the villagers questions in the morning. So after each of them ate and headed back to the inn to get rest. Far as they knew they would not get the rest they needed. After they all fell asleep they woke up in a dark place wondering what happened, as they look around they notice that they were in a dungeon somewhere.

"Does anyone know where the hell we are at?" Joey asked.

"It smells like a dungeon in the village we came to yesterday." Lady Autumn said.

"Well this can't be good." Sue said. Looking around they could here others in the cells next to them.

"Is anyone there?" Sue yelled.

"Yes, there are a few people here who tried to stop the darkness from coming." Guy in cell next to them.

"What do you mean sir about darkness?" How did they break the barrier?" Lady Autumn asked.

"My dear priestess, it was a man from a Dark Kingdom we have never heard of. Trying to take the light from the temple. He was able to bring down the barrier with some type of power. I'm not sure what kind of magic it was, but everyone in the village joined this man, just so that they could keep their family safe and themselves safe." Guy in cell.

"Sir thanks you. What is your name?" Lady Autumn asked.

"It is Emery my lady. I'm a father and husband that wanted to do the right thing, and this is the result. Jail!" Emery said.

"My good sir Emery, you have done well, your wife and children will be very proud of you. Thank you very much for the information." Lady Autumn said.

"My lady if you could be so kind, what is your name?" Emery asked.

"My good sir, my name is Lady Autumn." Lady Autumn said.

"I see now, it is clear why you and your friends are here. You are of very bright light, love, and friendship." Emery said.

Chapter 8

"We need to get out of here; also we need to save all these people that are here." Lady Autumn said.

"Damn right, at least we have a great idea who did this and why we are here." Joey said.

"The only thing is that how did they get us without us waking up?" Sue asked.

"It had to been the food we ate, and the drinks we had at that café." Lady Autumn said.

"We should have known he would try something like this to keep us away from the temple." Joey said.

"Yeah, you are right." Lady Autumn said.

"Then let us get the hell out of here." Sue said with anger. As the guardians look out the dungeon down the hall both left and right. They could not see if there are any guards on duty. So to try and use their powers seem to drain them just as much as standing up. They did need to find a way to get out, but how? So they looked around their cell to see if they could find anything that might help them to escape from the cell without notice. The only thing that came to mind was that one of them yells for a guard that one of them had to pretend to be sick and clasp to get out of the cell.

"GUARD, GUARD, GUARD." Sue yelled down the hall as a couple of guards came running to see what the problem was.

"What do you want you traitor?" Guard one said.

"My friend is very sick, he clasped with a fever. Please help him. If your general was to find out that we are hurt in any way then it would be on you." Sue said.

"Stand back from the door." Guard one demand. So Sue did as she was told and backed up into the cell and Lady Autumn was hiding in the corner as the guards walked end making Joey to jump up and knock the first guard out and Lady Autumn using a pan of some kind to knock the other guard out letting them to escape the cell. As they run out of the cell they lock the guards in taking their armor for cover up. So they also let out all the people who trapped in the cells for believing in what is right by Amos.

"Hurry everyone we have to make a run for it before they notice we are missing from the cells." Joey yelled. So everyone ran out of the cells making their way through a labyrinth of tunnels and dungeons. As the three guardians work on finding a way out of the labyrinth of tunnels something seemed to be off. This was too easy for even them. Something was up; they just didn't know it yet. As the group with the three guardians makes their way down each tunnel and turn they finally make it to the middle of the labyrinth just to be stopped by a huge demon with horns, red skin, fire for eyes, and tenacious for arms and legs. People started to scream, run in all directions, as the demon reached out to grab them they moved to keep from being grabbed. People from the village that was in the cells were so scared that when the demon would grab them, it would swallow them and it became bigger.

"What the hell is that thing?" Village one yelled.

"It looks to be a demon of some kind." Joey yelled back.

"Well, my guardians welcome to my labyrinth. I hope my pet gave you a good welcoming party?" General Amos said with a smile.

"So you planed on us escaping and set up this trap for us." Lady Autumn said.

"Aww, don't sound so hurt. You don't like my little gift?" General Amos said.

"Why the hell would we enjoy something like this when it is eating all the villages you had in the cells." Joey said with anger.

"Oh, guardian of the Crystal Star of the Summoning Realm. Don't be mad at me. I wanted to give you a most welcoming gift. It will keep you from leaving this labyrinth and heading to the temple for which I have made my home." General Amos said whiling laughing.

"Only until we get out of here." Lady Autumn said with pure hatred in her eyes along with pure anger.

"Guardian of the Crystal Star of the Healing and Spirit Realm, you are more than beautiful, you are also very powerful for which we can not a loud you to join up with the other guardians." General Amos said.

"I will defeat Dark Kingdom Zodiac and you if it means that it will cost me my life. So let these people go. It is us you want, not them." Lady Autumn said.

"Now why would I do that? My pet is taking the energy from those ants and making him stronger." General Amos said with a smiling and started to laugh.

"It would seem that we would have to beat the crap out of that damn demon to save the people and the hell out of this damn maze." Joey said.

"Then let us show him how strong a true guardian is of this realm, and save all the people." Sue suggested.

"Then let us give him something he will never forget." Lady Autumn said with a smirk.

"You guardians can try, but my pet is not that easily beaten." General Amos said.

"We will see to that, it is." Lady Autumn said.

"Then give it a try, when you bet my pet come see me at the temple of Heaven's Gate. We will finish this guardians." General Amos said just before he disappeared. As the guardians look onto the demon it had double in size. As they started to move the demon moved and hit the ground making it to split in two with flames shooting up from the floor. So the guardians jump out of the way. Telling the villagers that were not eaten to stand back. As the demon hit the floor again this time were Joey was standing making him to jump back even closer to the wall of the labyrinth. As the two girls are over on the other side. The demon hits the floor this time next to Sue causing her to fall and grab onto a ledge were the floor had spilt shoot up lava this time along with flames. Lady Autumn runs over to Sue and grabs her by the hand trying to pull her up. With some help from Emery they were able to pull Sue up. Just as they did the demon grabs Emery and eats him, causing the floor to shift and buckle under them all. As the guardians look up the demon began to change as it did, it burled for a second and when they looked on it had spilt into two. Both demons just as big as it was the first time. This demon looked yellow skin, with fangs of black, scarlet arms and hands, with legs of an ape, and the eyes looked hallow. This one seemed to be putting off even more power than the first one did. It would seem if the demon eats a lot of energy and people that it can change adding more demons to the mix.

"What are we going to do?" Sue said to Lady Autumn.

"I'm not sure, but if it keeps eating people and their energy; then we will be here for a while. We have to defeat the demons before any more can come to the aid." Lady Autumn said feeling very unsure of her own words.

"We just can't give up. We can win this; we just have to try a lot harder than before." Joey yelled at the girls.

"You got it, but how are we going to stop this thing? If it keeps hitting the floor, in time the floor will give way. Some of it has already fallen and almost took Sue with it." Lady Autumn yelled back.

"Then we need to take to the air. How are you on flying?" Joey yelled at Lady Autumn.

"I'm okay with it as long as it isn't too high." Lady Autumn yelled back.

"Okay, I will summon one of my dragons to help us." Joey yelled at her.

"Okay, we will get the demons attention while you call your dragon to you." Lady Autumn said. As she did she picked up a broken break from the labyrinth floor and throws it at the demon's head. Sue followed suite and hit the other demon with a broken break from the floor as well. Making both demons to take their eyes off Joey so he had time to summon one of his dragons.

"I summon the Water Dragon, Sofia to me." Joey called. Before he knew it he was air born, on the back of the water dragon, Sofia. He aims for the girls to pick them up, but the yellow demon saw and knocked him into the roof of the labyrinth, making the dragon to go to the floor.

"It was a great try, but know this; guardians. You are playing by my rules. So I will not a loud you to combine your powers together to stop both my pets." General Amos was laughing as he reappeared.

"So you choose to come back, and face us." Joey said standing back up with his water dragon next to him.

"Not at all, but you are in my labyrinth, so it is my rules for which you follow. If you can beat both my pets, then the entrance will open letting the villagers and you good free. I will still be waiting for you at the temple, but just to keep you in line I will put up a barrier to keep you from flying to the two guardians. SHOW ME WHAT A TRUE GAURDAIN IS!" General Amos said while disappearing again.

"It looks like we will need a new plan." Sue said.

"Yeah, so let you and I deal with this one. Defeat it, and hopefully the barrier will come down so we can help Joey." Lady Autumn said.

"Joey; are you okay with dealing with that demon on your own?" Sue yelled and asked.

"Yeah, I can take care of this ugly thing and get the hell out of here. It looks as if I might have to pull out the heavy guns." Joey yelled back.

"What do you mean by the "heavy guns"?" Lady Autumn yelled at Joey.

"Watch and see." Joey said with a smile on his face. As Joey was looking at his cousin and Lady Autumn; he smiled at them and before they knew it; he was doing another summoning.

"I SUMMON THE KING SPERENT; LEVIANTHAN!" Joey called. As the summons came, Joey was holding a weapon, not his normal pike, but a Lance that was in his hands, he was on the back of a huge snake like animal, and he threw the Lance of the King Serpent at the demon. As it hit; there was a huge wave of water knocking the demon off it's' legs. As the demon fell Joey pulled the Lance out and his water Dragon, Sofia finished off the demon with a water attack so powerful that it shook the whole labyrinth and some of the roof fell down by his feet. As this was happening Levantine had disappeared. Joey was on his water dragon's back floating just above the floor. The girls yelled with glee, and looked at Joey with huge smiles on their face. As they looked at Joey, he look almost drain of power.

"Joey are you okay?" Sue yelled.

"Yeah, just used way to much power. Hurry up and get rid of that damn demon so we can get the hell out of here." Joey yelled back.

"You got it. I guess it is my turn to pull out the power." Sue said smiling.

"Then let us use our powers to save everyone and finish this because if we don't we will never get out of here." Lady Autumn said smiling at her fellow guardians.

"SUN DANGERS; DANCING SUN!" Sue called; as she did she pulled out two dangers the color of the sun. These dangers are not the same as she normally uses. She moved with so much power and speed in a like dance cutting at the tentacles on the demon causing it to fall. When she was done she was down on one knee breathing hard, but happy with herself for not passing out with using a new power and weapon.

"Well done Sue. Now it is my turn to finish this." Lady Autumn said smiling.

Chapter 9

Lady Autumn had stood up looked at Joey and Sue. She is smiling from ear to ear. Glad you two are on our side. Knowing that they have a chance to win this and free her people, and to find the Star Princess to bring peace to all the realms. As she did she knew that it was the time to push her to the limits that she is so aware of. As she did she knew that it will take some major power to get rid of these demons.

"I think it is time that I put some more effort into this fight and stop doubting myself." Lady Autumn said.

"You can do it. We are here with you." Sue said.

"Yeah, show this ass hole who is boss. Give him a taste of his own medicine." Joey said laughing and barely able to stand. He knew that she could do it; they all can as long as they are together. They are the true guardians that have been chosen to protect the Star Princess, The True Prince, and all of the realms as one.

"HEAVEN'S CRESENT MOON DANCE!" Lady Autumn yelled. As she did it hit the demon and making it fall to the ground? The attack was powerful but not enough to get rid of the demons. So she knew that it was time to use an even more powerful attack.

"SPIRIT SHOCK WAVE!" Lady Autumn had said using her bow and arrows. The shock hit the floor, and the demons causing them to fall into the floor and disappear into dust and then the floor begun to shake. As they were able to get on the back of the dragon a door opened up, and all the village people was safe running out of the Labyrinth. They were happy to see the sun light on their faces.

"Well done guardians. You are as powerful as I have been told. I a wait for you at the temple in Heaven's Gate." General Amos said reappearing and looking down at the guardians.

"So have you chosen to face us or do you plan on running away again?" Joey said.

"Not in the least Guardian of Summoning. I wanted to see if what I have heard was true. You guardians don't disappoint at all." General Amos said smiling.

"What does that mean? Why are you doing this, have you had enough fun toing with people?" Sue asked with anger.

"Not at all, the fun is just beginning. I still a wait for you at the temple in Heaven's Gate." General Amos said. Then Amos had disappeared again this time back to the temple to see how far his fun could go. The guardians were very tired and worn out from the hard battle they just had, but they felt good with learning a new skill. Sue and Joey gain their true weapons, and Lady Autumn learned to trust her friends and in the peace that once was.

"Well I have to say you two did very well, as well as gaining your true weapons through your powers. Let us use this new power to save this realm, and find the Star Princess." Lady Autumn said with a smile.

"Thank you, very much." Sue and Joey said together.

"Excuse me my ladies, and sir. Thank you so very much for getting us out of that dungeon. If you need to rest you can rest at my house which is on the out skirts of the village." Emery said.

"That would be most welcoming." Lady Autumn said.

"I promise that you will not have to worry about being trick, and have a nice hot meal to fill you up before heading to the temple tomorrow." Emery said.

"Then please show the way good sir." Joey said with smile on his face, then he clasped. Sue ran to him and Emery helped her pick him up.

"He must of used way to much power during that fight." Sue said.

"Yeah, it looks like it. It must have taken a lot of power to summon Leviathan and still have a dragon stand by. Let us take him so he can rest and eat. We all could use the sleep after this long night till morning." Lady Autumn said. So they all head to Emery's home which took the rest of the morning and midday to get to. Joey being out cold made it hard for them to move fast. Even though they took a while they made it without any problems from General Amos. As they stepped into the house they walked into a kitchen that had dishes in the sink, then they took Joey into the front room and laid him down on a loveseat. The house was not very big; it maybe had two rooms, a small front room, and a small kitchen. It felt good to be somewhere other than a dungeon.

"I know it is not much to what you are used too. I hope that it is good enough for you to rest, clean up, and eat. What I have is not much, but what is mine is yours. Please help yourselves." Emery said with a smile.

"It is very wonderful, it is enough to let us rest, clean up, and eat. Thank you for the help." Lady Autumn said.

"Yeah, without your help we might not have made it out of that fight with just a few cuts, burses, and scratches." Sue said.

"I'm glad I can help in some way. I had lost my wife, children to those demons. So if I can help in any way I want to. Meeting all you guardians has given me more hope than I have had in the last few years." Emery said.

"Yeah, we are glad we can give you that hope. I am sorry for the loss of your family." Sue said.

"It opened my eyes to the lies that the Dark Kingdom Zodiac has been telling." Emery said.

"We are glad at least a few people believe in us, and can see the truth for what it is." Lady Autumn said. As the girls set talking to Emery way into the night they finally get some rest after getting cleaned up in the bathroom, and going to sleep on the floor in the front room, even though Emery had offered his bed to them, they had to decline because they didn't want to wake him when they leave first thing in the morning. As the girls slept along with Joey, they dreamed of a kingdom so wonderful that they didn't want to wake from the peace, happiness, love, and warmth of it all. Joey was shaking Sue awake, as she looked up at him, she was still somewhat a sleep but started to move, and walked over to Lady Autumn awake. Lady Autumn looked at her and smiled. It was the first night that they all have any kind of good rest and sleep.

"Is it time to go?" Lady Autumn asked.

"Yes, Joey is awake and looking good and well rested." Sue said.

"I'm glad to hear that." Lady Autumn said.

"Yeah, it was a great sleep, but do you two want to explain where we are at and how we got here?" Joey asked as the girls walked into the kitchen.

"We had to carry you. You had passed out after the fight with those two demons, and Emery was more than happy to help us out." Sue answered Joey.

"Okay, so he is staying here, so that we can get a move on? I will summon a dragon and if we can fly even most of the way to the temple in the South then we could cut the time in half." Joey said.

"Yeah, that would help considering all the time we have lost dealing with battle and fight after battle and fight. We could use some luck on our side." Sue said.

"Yeah, we need to get moving. It looks like that Emery has left us some food to take with us on this journey." Lady Autumn said closing the fridge door. So the guardians got up from the table and started to head out the door when Emery came running, he was yelling at them to wait.

"Wait every one; I want to go with you." Emery said.

"Emery it is too dangerous for you to come with us. You can help by making sure that the villagers are okay." Lady Autumn said.

"I want to help if I can; this is the same people who took my family from me. I want to make sure that they pay for it." Emery said.

"Revenge is not the answer to this. Your family would not want you to do this. They would want you to live your life to the fullest, smile often, laugh as much as you can, and keep moving forward for them." Lady Autumn said holding his hands.

"How do I do that, knowing I lost everything thanks to them? I want to help in any way I can." Emery said.

"You have done more than enough to help us out. Now I need you to be strong for the people of this realm, because after we defeat this enemy; I will be leaving this realm to do my duties as a true guardian of this realm. You can help my younger sister Lady Julia make sure that those who were affected by this issue are well taken care. There are children and other families feeling the same way as you. So please keep on living for me at least. Can you do that?" Lady Autumn said.

"I can. Please be safe my lady. I know that it is very dangerous. Please come back to us safely. Take care and I will do my best to help where I can." Emery said.

"Thank you very much. You can go to the village to where my younger sister is. Just tell her I sent you to help. Head to the village of Spirit. This was the very first village attacked by General Amos and the Dark Kingdom Zodiac. You can find that you will be need there. Okay?" Lady Autumn said.

"Yes, okay. I will do my best to help." Emery said. As this conversation was over the guardians headed a few miles away from the home so that Joey could summon one of his dragons. As the guardians makes plans to summon a dragon to help them something started to become really weird and it felt as if they were getting heavy. As they looked around they notice that there was someone coming near them. Emery was running to them as the person approached them.

"Well if it isn't the famous guardians; we generals of the Dark Kingdom Zodiac have been hearing so much about." Dark General said.

"What is going on? How do you know who we are?" Lady Autumn asked with shock.

"Well you see I have been watching you three for a while now without my co-workers knowledge of course. You see I'm the Dark General Jilana, I will be waiting for you in the next realm, so I thought; that I would introduce myself beforehand." General Jilana said.

"What do you want with us?" Sue asked.

"The same as all the other generals that have come before me. Your heads on a plate, and for the Majestic Star Kingdom to never be reborn again. So I will be waiting for you in the next if you can survive this one. "General Jilana said laughing. Emery was standing in front of them when General Jilana had disappeared into darkness. The guardians were able to finally stand up.

"It looks to be a new enemy from the Dark Kingdom Zodiac. At least she was not shy to show herself here." Lady Autumn said.

"Yeah, it looks to be another problem we have to deal with to be able to have peace again." Joey said.

"Well let us finish here, and then head to the next realm." Sue said.

"Just one thing, how do you get to another realm from one realm?" Lady Autumn asked.

"I can open a light portal that only true friends can enter and guardians of the Majestic Star Kingdom." Sue answered.

"Oh, I see. That is one of your powers as a guardian of Travel and Light." Lady Autumn said.

"Yeah; well let's get moving." Joey said. So the guardians and Emery got on the Wind Dragon, Emily. So they flew as far as the wind dragon could carry them without using too much power. They were almost there when a group of huge demons attacked them. These demons looked worse than the ones they faced in the Labyrinth. They were also a lot bigger, stronger, and even more-uglier than those last two where.

"Emery, since you did not have much of a choice to come with us. We are going to land and I want you to hide somewhere while we take care of these demons. Okay?" Lady Autumn said.

"Okay, deal with those demons so that we can get to that temple." Emery said.

Chapter 10

So the guardians got off of the Wind Dragon, Emily, to take care of the demons. As the demons have notice the guardians and the dragon they were not concerning themselves with them. So this was a good time to snick into the temple to stop Amos. As the guardians were approaching that is when the demons attacked them.

"Man couldn't have them damn demons not ever notice us because this is getting out of hand. Amos is such a coward." Joey said.

"We'll let us deal with these demons and finish him off. So we can save the people of this realm and find the other guardians." Sue said.

"Agreed!" Lady Autumn said.

So the guardians stepped up to the plate and used their powers to finish off the demons which seem to be way to easy, but then there is nothing easy about dealing with demons of any kind. As they deal with the demons and keep them from entering yet another place of joy and happiness. They stopped the demons approach and turned the demons to dust.

"It looks that they might be done for...." Sue said.

"Maybe, but DO NOT LET YOUR GUARD DOWN!" Joey said.

"Agreed, because we have no idea if this is all of them. We need to get to that temple and finish this." Lady Autumn said. So the guardians ran for the temple they seen from where they landed.

It was not that far to run only half a mile of a field and track. As they reached the bottom of the temple another swarm of demons came for them. As they are using their powers while trying to go up the long stairs that seemed to go on for miles. They had to dodge many demons' attacks to keep from getting hit.

"This is way too much. We can't even get up these stairs to the temple without demons using powers to keep us from advancing." Joey said.

"Yeah, what is the deal with them? They are really trying to keep us from entering the temple of this realm." Sue said.

"Yeah, but we must. If Amos gains the powers from within we might not even make it out of this mess and save the people of my realm. We have to at least try." Lady Autumn said. So the guardians still trying to get up the stairs to enter the temple before Amos can take what power lies there. If this happens then it would mean the end of the Healing and Spirit Realm. It would also mean the end of the Majestic Star Kingdom along with the alliance between all the realms. That would also mean that the Dark Kingdom Zodiac would rule for all times. Which might lead up to a revolution, that which would mean taking arms up against the Dark Kingdom? As long as there is that chance that they could lose all the peace they have and the people losing their lives is not an option for the guardians. They need to stop the mad man from taking control of this realm. So they rush and push themselves to get to the top of the stair, spit the demons trying to stop them. They knew they have to at least try and push until they are on the break of death to overcome this evil. It may take everything they got, but it will not stop the guardians from doing all they can to make sure that Amos is gone for good. As the guardians run up the stairs to the temple to stop Amos from gaining more power for himself and the Dark kingdom Zodiac, the guardians are almost to the top of the stairs when another demon stands in their way. This demon is way bigger than the demons they fought in the labyrinth. As the guardians approach they feel the ground started to shake and they feel to their knees try to keep from being knocked back down the stairs. Before they knew it Lady Autumn had pulled out her twin katanas.

"HEAVEN'S WAVE!!!" She yelled hitting the demon straight into the chest. Sue followed suite.

"DANCING SUN!!!Sue yelled after pulling out her twin sun dangers. As the girls hit the demon knocking it back Joey summoned Levantine along with his Lance of the serpent king.

"TSUGNAMI WAVE!!!!" Joey yelled as Leviathan left along with the holy lance, taking the demon with them. As they did the guardians bust into the temple. As they did something started to spell out into the air like it was poison. They had to cover their mouths to keep them from inhaling the poison smoke. Lady Autumn put her katanas back and pulling out her bow knocking an arrow to it. The arrow started to glow purple. Then she released it calling out the power that goes to that arrow.

"PURFING ARROW!!!!" Lady Autumn yelled to purify the poison smoke. This worked making it easier for them to breath. They knew that this was just one trap that Amos has set for them in the temple, jut to slow them down as he gets the power of the temple, elders, and gods. So the guardians ran down the hall fallowing Lady Autumn. She had turned right just to be stop by a net of demons; Sue took over and used her powers.

"SUN BLAST!!!!" Sue yelled. Making the demon net to turn to dust and the guardians continue on their way to the temple center were Amos is. As they reach a dad end that only gives you to choices right or left. Lady Autumn took the left turn this time only to find that it has been blocked off. So the guardians turned around and went the other direction. As they were reaching the end they ran into another set of demons. Joey stepped in and summons one of his dragons.

"FIRE DRAGON!!!!" Joey summoned. The fire dragon, Ifrit, used fire storm and cooking the demons to death. So the guardians finally reach the final turn just to be stopped by a bunch of demons preventing them from moving forward. So they put their powers together making a new attack among the guardians. First it was Joey who called his powers, Lady Autumn called her powers second, and then Sue called hers.

"FRIE DRAGON, USE FIRE STRIKE!!!" Joey called.

"HEAVEN'S ARROW!!!" Lady Autumn called.

"SUN BURST!!!" Sue called.

"LOTUS ARROW!!!" All three guardians called together. As the attack hit the demons turning them to smoke and dust. They can finally reach the center of the temple where Amos is at. The turn they took turned into a very long hall to the open area of the temple. As they are reaching the center they can see the double doors to the main area. As the guardians bust though just to be thrown back against the way with an attack from Amos.

"It took you guardians long enough to get here!!" Amos said laughing. As the guardians start to get back up, just to be knocked down again.

"You are a coward. Face us head –on Amos you demon..." Lady Autumn says standing back up along with Joey, and Sue.

"Why would I give you a chance to face me if you can't even fight against my barrier?" Amos said laughing.

"If that is the case. Spirit Arrow..." Lady Autumn said letting her arrow fly. Breaking Amos' barrier and the arrow just missing Amos' head. The guardians now can stand up without getting knocked down again. As the guardians started to Amos, the ground started to move. Coming out of the ground was a dragon of bones with a very powerful attack.

"Please let me introduce you to my favorite pet. The dragon of the dead, with an attack of poison slim." Amos said.

"So we kill or send that thing back to be ever it came from." Joey said.

"You can try; it won't be so easily done." Amos said.

"Let us deal with this thing, and then deal with him." Sue said.

"I'm with you both." Joey said. As the guardians gather their powers for the attack to stop the Bone Dragon. The dragon let out its' first attack hitting Sue in the arm causing it burn.

"AHHHHHHHHHHHHHHHH!!!!" Sue yelled. Joey had run to her pulling her away. Lady Autumn ran to her and tried to heal her only to be hit in the back by the dragon's tail. As she was hit getting knocked out for a few seconds only to come to with a daze.

"We have got to do something about that damn dragon." Sue said though gritted teeth.

"You are right; we do need to get rid of that dragon. So let us use our powers right after each other, me going last because I can purify the poison." Lady Autumn suggested.

"Okay let us do this thing." Joey and Sue said together.

"SUMMON THE WATER DRAGON, SOPHIA. WATER BOMBS!!" Joey called.

"SUN BLAST!!!" Sue called.

"HEAVEN AND SPIRIT ARROW!!!" Lady Autumn called. All three powers hit one after the other turning the Bone Dragon to dust.

"YOU WILL PAY FOR THAT YOU DAMN GUARDIANS!!!" Amos yelled with furry.

"Then let us put an end to this. Guardians let us combine our power to get rid of Amos for good." Lady Autumn said.

"YOU WILL NOT WIN! DEMON KING SWARD, DEATH BREATH!" Amos yelled. Lady Autumn put up a barrier to protect them. The attack was strong, but not strong enough to destroy the barrier. It did knock her on her ass, but getting back up and ready to deal with Amos.

"You got it." Sue said.

"Summon Fire Dragon, Ifrit, and FIRE STRIKE!" Joey called.

"SUN BURST!!!" Sue yelled.

"HEAVEN'S ARROW!!" Lady Autumn yelled.

"LOTUS ARROW!!!" Joey, Sue, and Lady Autumn yelled together. As the attack hit Amos straight in the heart turning him to dust, and disappearing. As the guardians was able to save the Healing and Spirit Realm, and the people are protected. Finally the guardians can breathe fresh air. At least they thought they could, until someone came out of the dust.

"Well done guardians, let me see if you are even stronger in the darkness. Come to the realm of the Crystal Star of the Darkness Realm. The prince there will be waiting." Dark General Jilana said.

"So you returned, just to watch your partner get beaten by us. That is even low for the Dark Kingdom Zodiac." Joey said.

"Well I never said we were close. If you use the portal in the other room you can go to the Crystal Star of the Darkness Realm." Jilana said.

"Why are you helping us?" Lady Autumn asked.

"I want to test your strengths. Then destroy you." Jilana said laugh while disappearing into the dark portal.

"Lady Autumn, are you okay with going with us?" Sue asked.

"Yes, as promised you helped my realm, I will and use my powers for the greater good. My younger sister can take of this realm without me." Lady Autumn said.

"Well, welcome aboard. We guardians can use someone like you on our team." Joey said.

"Thank you, but if I'm going to start a new life, please just call me Autumn. I'm equal to you all now." Autumn said.

"You got it." Sue and Joey said together.

"Then let us use that portal in the next room." Autumn said. So the guardians walked to the other side of the center room of the temple. As they did Sue can see the door to the portal? As she walked over to the portal touching it with her hands. It began to shimmer and a Light Portal opened up. As the guardians walk into the portal, and out on the other side it is like standing in the dark with clouds over head but there is hardly any light. But you can see as if it was day, in more sense it was about mid-morning.

Crystal Star of the Darkness Realm

Chapter 11

So the guardians started to walk down a road at least that is what they thought it was. As they walk wondering why it is always dark and that it looks like it is going to rain every minute or any second. As they walked they start to notice that they hear birds, some other animals in the distance, but could not make out what they might be.

"Welcome guardians to the Crystal Star of the Darkness realm. Isn't it a beautiful place?" Jilana said.

"So Dark General you find the darkness to be welcoming. We find it depressing." Autumn said.

"Don't say it like that; it is a wonderful place if you could see what it used to look like." Jilana said.

"Maybe we will get that chance once we get rid of you and your dark kingdom." Joey said.

"HAHAHA, I would love to see you try, guardians I will give you time to find the prince of this realm, and make your way to that dark castle in the distance. I will give you that time, but your journey will not be so easy." Jilana said laughing and disappearing again.

"I'm beginning to hate those damn generals of the Dark Kingdom Zodiac." Autumn said with anger.

"We know how you feel, so let us try and find a town, village, or something to start looking for the guardian of this realm." Joey said.

"Okay, I will take my anger out on her next time we see her." Autumn said.

"That is good; we should be able to find something before night fall." Sue said.

As the guardians continue walking down a dirt road with gravel they notice that it was getting darker as they went on. So they started to stubble over things like cracks, stone, and small holes that was in the road. As they started to feel their way on the road something up head caught their eye.

"What do you think that might be?" Sue asked.

"I'm not sure but we need to figure it out before we reach it." Autumn said.

"Agreed." Joey said. So they kept watching whatever it might be. As they got closer they notice that it was some type of animal. So they moved slowly so not to get its attention. But it was to late the animal had already seen them moving down the road ages ago. It ran at them and making them all jumps to the side of the road to keep from being hit with its claws. It did not stop there it came at them again. This time they could see that it was a Lynx with poison claws and some kind of slim coming out of its mouth. The slim hit the ground and started to sizzle making a small hole where it hit.

"Well I guess this is the welcome community." Joey said with a little laugh.

"That is not funny cuz. We need to get rid of this damn animal or we are going to be its' next meal." Sue said.

"You both are not funny, let us stop it before its friends show up and help it out." Autumn said.

"Okay." Sue and Joey said together. So the guardians get ready for the Lynx to attack again, only to be hit with its' slime coming out of its' mouth and spit it at the guardians causing them to jump back again. Only thing that kept them from being hit is Autumn's barrier which helps to purified the slime. So the guardians armed themselves with their weapons of choice. Autumn had pulled out her bow, Sue pulled out her draggers, and

Joey was using his pike. As the Lynx jumped to attack again it hit the barrier making it shake its' head, to get unfazed. As the Lynx is circling the guardians getting ready to attack again, and looking for an opening.

"Now is our chance while it is trying to figure out how to get around the barrier." Autumn said.

"Let us do this." Joey said.

"I'm with you." Sue said.

"Light Arrow!" Autumn called.

"Sun Burst!" Sue called.

"Iron Dragon, sword attack." Joey called. As the guardians' attacked the Lynx turning it to dust. They were glad it was over for now.

"Well done guardians." Jilana said.

"Well at least you were watching. Now you know that we are not some teenagers that have special powers. That we are strong and we will stop you and the Dark Kingdom Zodiac." Sue said.

"You have showed that you have skill. I will give you that. You are still some teenagers playing heroes." Jilana said.

"We are not teenagers playing hero, we are guardians given a mission to save our Star Princess, and the Majestic Star Kingdom." Autumn said.

"Do you think that I can be bitten so easily?" Jilana said.

"We know you are no push over, but that will not stop us from freeing this realm, and stopping the Dark Kingdom Zodiac." Joey said.

"Show me your powers guardians!" Jilana challenged.

"Fine we will fight you here and now. When we stop you, you will live this realm without any more problems." Sue said.

"We will see how far you guardians can get. ARROW OF QUAKE!" Jilana said laughing. As the arrow hit the gourd where the guardians' are standing causing them to fall into darkness.

"HEAVEN'S LIGHT!" Autumn called into the darkness casting light in the hole they have just fallen into.

"Iron Dragon, Jamaal!" Joey called, making the dragon to catch the guardians from falling to their death. Also flying them out of the hole just to see that Jilana had disappeared again.

"It would figure she would take off the minute we fall to our death." Sue said.

"At least she is making herself known." Joey said as the guardians are still on the back of the iron dragon. They could see that there is a town nearby.

"Let us go there and see if we can get some answers, and maybe some place to sleep for the night." Autumn said.

"Good idea. Jamaal fly as close to that town as you can. So the iron dragon did as Joey asked and flew them just to the outskirts of the town. It was not even an hour walk away. So the guardians walked into the town to see people walking around with light colors on and lanterns in their hands to light their way. As a woman walked by with really black hair that it looked as if it could blend into the darkness.

"Excuse me miss, can you tell us where we are? We are not from around here." Autumn said.

"Yes, ma'am, you are in the town called Twilight Moon." Woman said.

"Thank you very much." Autumn said.

"Your are very much welcome. Can you tell me where you came from?" Woman asked.

"We came from a faraway place." Autumn said.

"Oh, well welcome. If you need a place to stay the night; there is an inn right down the street off to your left called Twilight Inn." Woman said.

"Thank you again, that does help out a lot." Autumn said.

"Welcome. Also there is a celebration starting tomorrow, our Prince has found himself a bride. She is not from here but, there is something very off about her. Our Prince also has changed which is causing us to have all this darkness. It is the Crystal Star of the Darkness Realm, but there were days when we could see the light from the moon, and our two suns." Woman said.

"Oh, well congrats on the new bride and princess to your realm." Autumn said. Then the woman continues on her way to do her earns; walking away from the guardians.

"I don't like it. Something is really off here." Sue said.

"Yeah, I feel a very uneasy and think that this new bride might not be who she is claiming to be." Joey said.

"I feel uneasy as well. Let us go to the inn, get some rest, and then figure out what is going on around here." Autumn said. So the guardians headed to the inn that was down the street and off to the left, seeing all kinds of stuff. Mostly that people seem to be in a depression state and that they carry lanterns with them everywhere. As they are walking and stopping at different booths to see what each person had. Autumn kept walking to the next booth and ran into someone. As she looked up, all she could see was golden eyes and short white hair, but a face that was very good looking, with that bad boy image he had going on, she felt her face turn all shades of red.

"I', I', I'm so sorry." Autumn said. He looked at her and smiled as if it was something he didn't do often enough, but he felt good to smile at a woman that is as beautiful as she is. Eyes the color of light brown to a honey, light brown long hair to her waist and skin that smelled of passion flower, and vanilla. There was something about her that just mad his heart skips beats. Her touch was light, but comforting, compared to his soon to be bride, which is cold and hard. She was full of life, but she seemed to be very shy.

"It is okay, you are not from around here are you?" Mystery guy says.

"N, N, No I'm not, I come from a faraway place called the Crystal Star of the Healing and Spirit Realm. My name is Autumn Williams." Autumn said.

"It is very nice to meet you miss, I'm Alvaro Sky. You here all alone? Or did you come with someone?" Alvaro asked.

"I'm with friends, but I think we got spilt up somehow. We were looking at the booths on our way to the inn; Twilight." Autumn said.

"Well let me walk you to the inn so that you don't get lost, or hurt. Okay?" Alvaro said.

"Okay." Autumn said with a smile that could reach the moon. She did not know why she felt as if she was floating on clouds with him, but it felt so good even though she knew she was smiling like a crazy person.

He just kept taking peeks at her, he never felt this way about the common people, but there was something about her that made him want to protect her from harm of any kind. He felt as if her life kept him from the darkness that was taking over his realm, and making his people questions who and what they are. With her it felt if her life was to end now his would too. So he walked her to the inn to meet her friends and make sure that she would be okay. There are many women in this realm that was very beautiful, and even his bride to be are pretty, but no one could match her beauty no matter what.

Autumn started to notice that her heart rate had speed up when Alvaro took her arm and touched her skin. He looked like a fantasy from a movie, anime, book, or cartoon with Golden Eyes, White Short Hair with sliver highlights, and Cappuccino skin that smelled of trees, plants, and oceans, with just the right amount of that bad boy image going on that she could not stop looking at him. Being with him, she felt as if she could move mountains, that her life was protected, and that she could do almost anything as long as he was around, but would she be able to see him again after they find the guardian of this realm? She wanted to; she knew that if she didn't she would never feel this way again. She also knew that finding the Star Princess and restoring the Majestic Star Kingdom back was her main mission. Could she have a mission after she fulfilled this one? All these question going through her head that she didn't know which way was up or which was down.

"We're here." Alvaro said taking Autumn out of her dazed mind, and looking around to see where she was. When she noticed that she was standing in front of the Twilight Inn.

"Umm, thank you very much." Autumn said looking away from him.

"You are welcome. Are you and your friends staying for the celebration tomorrow? If you are, would you mind hanging with me?" Alvaro asked.

"I'm not sure if we are, we are looking for someone who is very important. I would love to; maybe if we find this person then we could hang out for a while." Autumn said.

"Well, I'm sorry to hear that. Well I will leave you here. You can go on in. Good Bye." Alvaro said feeling as if the realm had fallen from under him. So Autumn had walked into the inn where her friends were waiting for her. She had a smile on her face that could go for miles. But she knew that there was more to do than google over some random guy. So her smile started to fade into a fawn because she knew that her heart would not stop beating like a mad man. She felt that everyone around her could hear it just as much as her and feel it.

"So where did you disappear too?" Sue asked.

"I'm sorry; I started to look at all the booths and then got swallowed up by the crowd that was moving in all directions." Autumn said.

"Well at least you are okay." Joey said.

"Yeah. Where you able to get us a room for the night?" Autumn asked.

"Yeah, the inn keeper said that we can have a room as long as we help out at the celebration tomorrow with all the customers." Joey said.

"Cool that will give us a chance to talk to everyone. Then maybe we might find the guardian of this realm." Autumn said putting a smile back on her face.

"What is up with you girl? You went from frowning to smiling like a crazy person." Sue asked, Joey was not paying attention at this point.

"I meet someone very nice. He is got that bad boy look going for him; he is very handsome, and kind. He walked me to the inn so that no one would mess with me. Isn't that sweet?" Autumn said.

"Girl you have that crush thing going, he could be your soul mate. I know how that is, I felt the same way when I met Andrew. A smile that could go on for miles, and days." Sue said.

"It looks like we both have it bad." Autumn said.

"Don't let Joey fool you, he has someone special as well." Sue said laughing.

"Really, who is it?" Autumn asked.

"She is another guardian from the Crystal Star of the Fire Realm. Her name is Lola. You will met her soon enough." Sue said.

"I can't wait to meet her, and the other guardians." Autumn said.

"You will like them all. There is Alena which is the guardian of the Crystal Star of the Water and Ice Realm, Richard of the Crystal Star of the Wind Realm, Andrew of the Crystal Star of the Earth Realm, Lola of the Crystal Star of the Fire Realm, and Leroy of the Crystal Star of the Elemental Realm. You know Joey and me." Sue said.

"They all sound like really great people." Autumn said. So the girls continue talking late into the night before heading to their room for the night. The girls will wake up early in the morning to do the morning rush of customers before everything gets started.

Chapter 12

༄═─◦─═༄

The girls got the wakeup call in the morning to start their shift at the inn where they will help the customers, take their orders, and delivery the food that they order. It also gives them an excuse to talk to the people of this realm to find out who, where, and what the guardian of this realm might look like. So the girls started to talk to many customers about the realm, the people, and what the celebration is all about. So Sue took the first table to fill up with people and walked over to them.

"Hello, what can I get all of you to drink?" Sue asked. Everyone at the table gave Sue their drink order and she went a put it in to the bar tender. As Sue is waiting on the drink order for table 13. She walks over to her other table where she sees' a guy with white hair, gold eyes, and cappuccino skin. Not bad looking, just in her eyes' not in the lead as Andrew. So she smiled at the customer and waited for them to stop talking and notice her after she had cleared her throat to get their attention.

"May I take your orders?" Sue asked.

"Yes, we would like some coffee and orange juice to start with." The guy said.

"Okay, I will put your order in and be back to take the rest of your order." Sue said.

"Okay, we will be waiting for your return." Guy said. Sue went back to the bar to get her drink order for table 13, and took over to the table and handed everyone their drink.

"What else can I get for you?" Sue asked.

"We would like over easy eggs, toast, fruit, bacon, and pancakes." People at table 13 had said. So Sue took the order and turned it in to the cook; and walked back over to the table 20, where she had taken her next drinking order to finish up the order.

"What can I get you two?" Sue asked.

"Hello, we would like pancakes, sausage patties, scabbed eggs with cheese, and wheat toast." Guy had said. So Sue took the order and turned it into the cook and delivered the food to table 13. As Sue went back to the bar to get her next order and take it to table 20. As Sue had delivered her orders Autumn had enter the bar/restaurant to do her shift, she had been working in the garden with other customers when she walked by table 20 and froze when she seen who was sitting at the table. She walked over to Sue at table 15 when she pulled her to the side and started to talk to her.

"Why is he here?" Autumn asked Sue.

"Who are you talking about?" Sue asked.

"The guy at table 20; that is Alvaro, he is the one who walked me to the inn yesterday." Autumn said.

"Oh, the guy that you were all flushed about." Sue said smiling and laughing.

"That is not funny, but yes he is most definitely a good looking guy." Autumn said.

"Yeah, he is cute, but Andrew is cuter." Sue said. Autumn could not agree with Sue, she felt that Alvaro was the best looking guy in the whole bar. So she looked at him and smiled before he could notice her staring at him.

"Sue who is Alvaro with?" Autumn asked Sue.

"I'm not sure, maybe his wife, girlfriend, or fiancé." Sue said. Autumn could not believe her luck, was so charming when walking her to the inn and felt that he cared what happened to her. Then watching him from across the bar/restaurant getting sick to her stomach whiling watching Alvaro and his date. Sue had gone to check on her table 13.

"How is everything?" Sue asked.

"It is great; we would like the check now?" Guy said.

"Sure let me get that for you." Sue answered. Then she walked over to table 20.

"Hello, sir, how is everything?" Sue asked.

"It was really great and good. Could we please get the check we are in a hurry?" Alvaro said.

"Sure let me get that for you." Sue answered and walked away from the table. She went and got the bill for both tables. Autumn walked up to Sue and started to talk to her.

"Let me take the bill to table 20 please." Autumn asked.

"Sure that helps me out; it looks like it is going to get very busy. We might have to have the bar tender call Joey down to help out." Sue said.

"Sure, I will take it." Autumn said with anger in her eyes as she walked over to table 20. As she is holding the bill out the guy looks up and his face went south and sour. As if he had been caught doing something wrong.

"Hi, Autumn I thought you would be leaving?" Alvaro said with a sad face on him which did not suit him at all.

"Hi Alvaro, we were supposed to leave, but we ended up working in the bar/restaurant to pay for room and board. At least you look like you are having fun. So that flirting with me yesterday was just that flirting." Autumn said.

"Autumn it was not like that. This is my fiancé; we are getting married in about two weeks and today are our engagement party." Alvaro said not happy with the way the conversation was going.

"So, I was just a last flirt before you get married. That is a way to make a girl feel really special and good about herself. So just let me clear it up, I was just your last stop and that you wanted to make at least one more girl fall for you. Well just for your information that did not happen. Thanks for walking me to the inn; I hope that this is the last time that I ever have to see you're lying, cheating face again." Autumn said with anger, and threw the bill at him; and walked away crying. She kept running until she could not breathe again. She found herself out in the garden where she was working and delivering food. So she went around to the back of the inn just to get some air and try to breathe through what she just saw. How could she have been so dumb, and fall for the first guy that helped her out. Why did she have to feel so hurt from what she saw, how could she fall so quick for the first guy she met when she did not feel that way about Joey. He was so cute, nice, even gentle why can't she get his face out of her head, most of all out of her heart. She felt hurt, lonely, and still loved him. Now she could not be with him because he is not free to be with her. She sat down on a log that was out back of the inn and just wanted to die and not feel this bad. How can someone you just met make you feel so alive and happy? How can, how could you feel so hurt when you just met that person. As she was sitting there someone came around the building but she did not look up to see who it is.

"Are you okay?" Alvaro asked. Autumn looked up with blood shot eyes and crying. Alvaro looked at her and his heart felt like it was sinking deep into an ocean of hurt.

"Why do you even care? You have a fiancé which is waiting for you in the bar/restaurant; who is very pretty. Prettier than me. So what do you want? Leave me alone and go about your life." Autumn said with anger. Alvaro stepped back looking very confused and wondering why he even came out here to check on her.

"I do care, but we can't be together. I'm, sorry. I can't stand to see you hurt." Alvaro said.

"You should have thought about that before you flirted with me, walked me to the inn. You should have told me when you first met me that you were taken instead of asking me out." Autumn said.

"Look I wanted to make sure you where okay. I felt that there was a connection between us. I know you felt it too. I can't change what is happening; I sure can't make it right. I didn't want you to find out. I hope that you can forgive me and move on." Alvaro said.

"Thanks, you can leave now. I don't need you, or your damn sympathy." Autumn yelled at Alvaro.

"Fine, I will leave you alone. I hope that you will be okay out here by yourself." Alvaro said with anger in his eyes.

"I will always be fine because unlike you I have friends who will always be there for me and won't hide or lie about the truth." Autumn said. Alvaro had held back a retort, turned around and went back into the inn. Then there was a low growl in one of the shadows and then came out was a loin that had black fur, and green eyes with drool that smoked, and turned anything it hit to dust and crumbled to the floor. She got up to run but her feet would not move. So she turned to screaming but nothing would come out. She was frozen in fear, but Alvaro didn't want to leave things the way they were. So he turned back around only to see what was going on. It was a Darkness Fear Beast making its' way around Autumn so he ran at her grabbing her around the waist just time to knock her out of the way.

"What the hell were you doing just standing there and not running?" Alvaro had said still with anger in his voice because he felt that the world would end if she was not in it; even if they are not together. Autumn still could not speak because she was still scared because she has never come up close to a creature like that before. Then she came to her senses and she was mad at Alvaro for what he said. She knew that there was work to do.

"Thanks for helping me, but I can take care of this thing on my own without you or your help of any kind." Autumn said.

"It looks like it to me; that you can use my help weather you want it or not." Alvaro said.

"Even if you are here to help me. Why would you even pick up a figure to help me out?" Autumn said.

"Look I am not going to let anyone get hurt because they are to stubbed to ask for help or accept it." Alvaro said.

"So you are going to help me even if I don't want it." Autumn said.

"We don't have time to talk about this when there is this beast trying to eat you for lunch." Alvaro said.

"I can handle myself, thanks very much." Autumn said. As they argued about everything the beast was coming close to them. Autumn moved even further away from the animal by backing up and pulling out her bow and arrow as Alvaro had turned about she was knocking an arrow to fire it at the beast. Alvaro could not believe his eyes. Who is this woman and how did she get the bow and arrows? Alvaro was wondering how she got it; as he was his own sword was in his hand. His sword was passed down by his father to son and it would pass down to his child.

"Arrow of Light." Autumn called.

"Sword of Darkness." Alvaro called and their powers combined creating a rainbow of white power hitting the loin turning it to dust. Autumn had fell down to her knees holding her bow and arrow and breathing hard.

Chapter 13

Alvaro looked at her and could see that she had amazing power; that could be used to help others. He notice that she was strong willed and caring. This is the type of tract that his mother had when he was a young child. She cared about her people, what happened to them, and made sure that they had what they needed. He hoped that his soon to be new bride would be just as loving as her. Even though she had passed when he was young, he remembered her caring hands, loving heart, special smile, and every one of his people loved her. His father had died two years after his mother and he was forced to be made king at a young age. He knew that it was no easy task that he had taken on. Now that he has been king for a while he was being pushed by his advisors to marry as soon as possible. So he jumped at the first woman he met a few weeks before. Wondering if this was the right move or if the right girl is in front of him but keeps losing her to certain problems, most of from a strange energy that seems to sucking the land dry and taking over all the animals in his realm. It seemed that darkness had taken over the land and that it was swallowing up everything. Alvaro seemed to being drain of all energy all the time since he met his soon to be bride. So he walked back into the restaurant of the inn and took his seat by his soon to be bride. The big announcement about being engaged to his soon to be queen.

So; Autumn was still sitting outside of the inn crying and catching her breathes. After the attack with the lion, she had to recover some of her own energy so that she could go back to working. Letting Sue deal with her table and Alvaro so that she does not have to see, talk, or breathe the same air as him. She knew that the festival that was going was for him and his new bride. She got up from where she was sitting and walked back into the inn not noticing anyone. Went back up to the bar, and got her order and took to her table and finished out her hours for working. Headed back to the room she was sharing with Sue, and joey and went an laid down on her bed and feel a sleep, hoping after this nightmare was over that she could move on with her life helping to protect the Majestic Star Princess and all the realms.

Back in the inn Sue was taking orders to tables, taking over Autumn's tables to let her rest after what happened today in the back alley behind the Twilight Inn.

Autumn went upstairs to their room to rest and she had passed out from the drain of using her powers. She fell into a deep sleep; she was walking in a field of flowers that seemed to be so familiar to her. They smell so good with the natural of the land. This land was so beautiful, peaceful, love, and warmth of happiness. It claimed her and she felt as if her energy was returning to her, it felt so good. Then when she turned around she saw someone walking toward her. She just knew that it was a guy, but his face was in shadows so she could not make out who it was. She knew that he was handsome, she could feel. As she started to walk near him she jumped up from the bed with a bang on the door. It had startled her out of her sleep; she ran over to the door and opened it. As she looked there was a woman standing in the door with a cart of food.

"The Inn Keeper asked me to bring you something to eat." Waitress said.

"Thank you, but I didn't ask for any food." Autumn said.

"I know ma', but the Inn Keeper saw you earlier, and felt that you could use this. He also asked me to tell you that the celebration is about to start for our Prince." Waitress said.

"Yeah, I have heard. I'm just not feeling well right now. I might be down later to see everything. Just give a little bit and I will be down. Thank you for the food, could you please let my friends know that I'm just feeling up to anything right now." Autumn asked.

"Yes, I can do that. Get some rest and maybe you will feel better real soon okay." Waitress said.

"Will do." Autumn said back. As the waitress was walking back down the hall to the elevator pushing the cart in, and listening to the ding of the doors closing. Autumn heard it and went back into the room and sat back down on the bed trying to remember the dream she just had. What was that? It is like I have been there before and it felt so nice and claim that I didn't want to leave it. It is like a pass life or something. As she was sitting there wonder about the dream, it started to fade away from her memory. Then her smotch started to rumble. So she got back up and went over to the food that waitress had brought her to eat. It was mash potatoes, carrots, steak, and a roll. She had some type of liquored to drink that looked orange with a hint of brown to it. It tasted really good when she took a drink and the warmth went down her throat. It started to make her feel a little better with everything that has happened in the last few days. As she started to eat her diner she realized that she was really hungry today for some reason. It must be from her using her powers and being up-set with Alvaro. Finding out everything that was going on. It made since that she would feel the strain because with emotions they can be even more draining than using her own powers to different a rouge lion that was being controlled by the Dark Kingdom Zodiac. Which she had no doubt about this? She knew that she would have to face the music sooner or later. So she got up and went and got in the bathroom got undress and turned the shower on, for a hot shower to help her relax after the attack today in the back alley behind the inn. Why did Alvaro want to protect her if he had someone already? She could not wrap her head around that. So she stood in the shower taking in the heat of it to relax and claim herself before she made an appearance outside for the celebration of the prince. So after about an hour in the shower and bathroom getting and dreading the festival of the Prince. She walked out of the room and down the hall to the elevator to go down stairs. The hall looked like something out of space the wallpaper had what looked like stars on it, but was only a dark midnight blue with glitter on it. It shines in the hall lights and it made a claiming affect to the guest that walked down any hall in the inn. The rooms where no different. As the elevator ding letting her know it had averred to take her to the first floor of the Twilight Inn. She stood in the elevator with a few other people from the other floors heading down to the festival for the prince's engagement. The people were looking at her giving her smile after smile making her feel very uneasy. Then she noticed that it was her clothes they were looking at not her. She was wearing a black pencil skirt, red dress top that was off the shoulders somewhat, black flats, and her hair pulled back in a half bun with curls hanging down. This is the reason it took so long in the bathroom up in her room; because her hair was so long. She did not have much of a choice on the clothes considering that the inn keeper gave Sue and her clothes to wear while they were working to pay off their own rooms. It had been so long it seemed that she had not had much fun since the Dark Kingdom Zodiac invaded her realm.

The elevator had come to a stop on the first floor of the inn. Autumn had stepped out with everyone else and someone came up behind and tapped her on the shoulder.

"Excuse me?" Guy said. She turned around and looked at the guy standing behind her. He was not bad looking for a guy she had never met. He had light brown eyes, green hair, mocha skin, and he looked kind and handsome.

"Yes, can I help you?" Autumn asked kindly.

"Yeah, I was wondering if you would like to join me for the festival tonight." Guy said.

"I would love to, but my friends are waiting for me. What is your name sir?" Autumn asked.

"I'm Wyatt Sky; the prince that is engaged to be married in the next couple of days is my older brother and the rightful heir to the throne of this realm." Wyatt said.

"It is nice to meet you. Are you just getting to town?" Autumn asked.

"What is your name miss? Thank you." Wyatt asked.

"My name is Autumn Williams. I think that we could just hang out with my other friends; if that is okay with you?" Autumn asked.

"I think that would be wonderful. I'm not too happy with my brother's choice of bride. She seems to be cold all the time, I think there is darkness in her that he can't see." Wyatt said.

"I met her early today when I was working in the restaurant. She did seem to be off somewhat." Autumn said.

"At least I'm not the only who can see that. Yes, I'm just getting into town tonight. I wasn't sure if I wanted to come. I don't approve of this marriage in the less." Wyatt said with hurt, hatred, and anger in his eyes. Autumn put her hand on his shoulder and he started to claim from her healing touch her mother always called.

"I understand what you mean. It is hard to look at someone you care about and see that they are making a huge mistake, but won't listen to you at all. The reason is because they are blinded by love or something else altogether." Autumn said.

"Yeah, that is how it feels with his soon to be new bride." Wyatt said. So they continued their conversation walking out the door.

As they are walking out the door Alvaro was standing in the door watching his younger brother and Autumn walk hand and hand from the Inn. He could not believe it. How could his own brother do this to him, how could she do this to him. He was so mad that his true powers started to show for which he always kept under wraps and under control. Something broke in him watching them walk together. They were laugh, talking, touching, and everything thing he wanted to do with her. He was doing with her. He felt betrayed by both of them, when a woman walked up to him and watch as she seen where he was looking at. Her eyes turned red, so the guardians survived that attack by the lynx, and the lion she sent at them, mainly her guardian of the Crystal Star of the Healing and Spirit Realm. She knew that if they found out that the Dark Kingdom Zodiac was trying to take over this realm they were interfere with their plains mainly hers. She was not going to let that happen. Not a chance in hell was she going to let the guardians find the guardian of this realm to add to the others.

"My dear Prince Alvaro, what are you looking at my love?" Jilana asked. Alvaro looked at her as if he didn't see her or know her, when he realized that it was his soon to be bride.

"Sorry, I thought that I seen my brother with that woman over there." Alvaro said.

"I think that is him. I thought he wasn't coming to our engagement festival because he did not approve of me." Jilana said.

"Same here. He told me before we left the castle that he was not coming, and that he could not give us his blessing for our marriage." Alvaro said.

"So what are we going to do if he makes a big since in front of the whole village?" Jilana asked.

"I will stop him. I will go and talk to him, if you don't mind waiting here." Alvaro said.

"Not at all my love." Jilana said. So Alvaro walked away from her as she watched him leave. She started to get anger and knew she had to keep it together before they knew what she was up to. She also could tell that Prince Alvaro did not know that Autumn, Sue, and Joey are guardians' that are to protect the Star Princess and the Majestic Star Kingdom. Is there a chance that Prince

Wyatt is the guardian for which they seek out? If so she had to get rid of him before they could discover he is their next guardian.

So she started to make her plains to stop the guardians at this festival before they could find any more guardians'. As she watches the prince walk on it; was almost time for them to show themselves to the people of this land who will be their next princess, than their next queen if everything goes well with the plan of the Dark Kingdom Zodiac. So she goes a gets ready for their grand entrance to the festival.

Alvaro was still walking toward Wyatt and Autumn wanting to know what they are doing together. As he got closer he stopped a little ways away to see what happens and Autumn walks' up to Sue then smiles at her trying to hide the pain she is feeling.

"Hey girl, how you feeling?" Sue asked.

"A little better, still a little out of it. This is Wyatt Sky. He is the brother of the prince of this realm." Autumn said.

"Really, I guess we have a new friend here. So Wyatt what is it like to live in this realm?" Sue asked.

"It feels good, I grew up here and when my parents passed not too long ago my old brother has been taking care of me. Then he goes and gets engaged to this woman I can't stand and do not trust at all." Wyatt said.

"Damn man, you sound like Autumn. I have been sensing some really dark things here that have nothing to do with the realm itself." Joey.

"So you all can sense things in other realms." Wyatt said.

"Yeah, man we are all worriers from our own realms. By the way my name is Joey. Since Autumn forgot this handsome face here." Joey said laughing.

"You are not that handsome to me, and I did not forget, you just never gave me a chance to introduce you to him. His brother is the one getting married in a few days' time. As well as this celebration or festival is for his engagement. I got this really bad feeling that something is going to happen." Autumn said.

"You know, now that you mention it I have been feeling uneasy since we cross the portal from the Star Crystal of the Healing and Spirit Realm too." Sue said.

"It all seemed to start right after my brother got engaged to this woman he never met before. That is when everything thing seem to be really off. That was about a week ago." Wyatt said.

"Well let us enjoy the festival while we can before anything bad happens. Wyatt thanks for inviting me to come along, I'm glad I did. I do feel better now that I'm with my friends." Autumn said.

"You're welcome. Thank you for introducing me to your friends, I see we can be some really good friends here." Wyatt said.

"You know it man." Joey said giving Wyatt a fist bump. As the three guardians' and their new friend look on at the stage waiting for things to get going Alvaro was still staring at Autumn and thinking how beautiful she looks tonight. Then before he knew it he was heading back to the Inn to take the center stage to introduce his new bride.

Jilana and Alvaro head up to the stage as the announcer was talking to the people and telling them how in love they were and how it was love at first site.

"Now no more further introduction, no further due. I give you, your prince and his soon to be new bride. Prince Alvaro and Jilana." Announcer yelled to the crowd. There was yells of joy, whistling, hands in air, and so on. As he walked out on stage Autumn's mouth dropped and so did the other guardians' when they saw who was going to be the new princess of this realm. They could not believe it, how could she have missed it, how could they not notice that this was who was going to be the bride of the prince and the Crystal Star of the Darkness Realm.

"Wyatt we have to stop your brother from marring that woman. She is no princess; she works for the Dark Kingdom Zodiac who is trying to take over all the realms, which destroyed the Majestic Star Kingdom." Autumn said.

"What wait a minute, who are you guys? How do you that Jilana is working for the Dark Kingdom Zodiac?" Wyatt asked.

"We are the guardians' of the realms that helped protect the Majestic Star Kingdom and the Star Princess." Sue said.

"Your brother might be the guardian of this realm or you could be? Have you been able to use any types of power that comes from this realm?" Joey asked.

"No, I wasn't born with the power of this realm, my brother was that is why he has to take the throne and save our realm from this darkness invading it." Wyatt said.

"The woman your brother is going to marry is a general in the Dark Kingdom Zodiac's army." Sue said.

"Then let us stop this now." Wyatt said. So they ran to the stage to get to Prince Alvaro and Jilana before they knew something hit them hard in the backs, causing people to scream and run in all directions.

Chapter 14

Joey got up looking around to see what hit them, still unsteady on his feet because the attack was so hard. As he turned around he seen it a cheetah that was moving at a fast pace as well as something green dripping from its mouth. Alvaro stood on stage stunned at what happened, he ran for his brother and Autumn who were next to each other getting up; but not making much of a difference. Alvaro lifted Autumn up, helping her to her feet, but she was still unsteady on her feet. Wyatt and she had taken the full force of the attack, but it hit them all. Sue started to get up and felt her head, she had pulled her hand from her head and it had blood on it. She must have hit her head really hard, but she could see what was happening in front of her. Everyone that was at the festival was running in chaos in every dedication they could go. Some running for houses and slamming doors shut locking themselves inside to protect themselves and those they loved.

"Is everyone okay?" Joey said with a splitting headache.

"I'm okay just got this splitting headache." Sue said.

"Autumn isn't able to stand she is still unsteady on her feet." Alvaro said.

"Alvaro that woman is an enemy of our realm and all realms. She did this to us and now Autumn is really hurt." Wyatt said.

"You have no proof it was her, you can't just blame anyone because this happened. You never approved of her from the beginning." Alvaro said.

"He is telling you the truth. She is a general in the Dark Kingdom Zodiac's army. She is the general of Venom. That cheetah is her pet and she is controlling it." Autumn said through raps of breathe trying to breathe through it all. Alvaro looked at as if she was someone she didn't know, but his heart was breaking all the same watching her take deep breathes. The cheetah made another attack this type right at Alvaro and as it did Jilana jumped down off the stage and the cheetah made another turn and went at Joey who was now steady on his feet. Sue was starting to become steady as well. Wyatt was so scared he did not know what to do. His friends were hurt, and Alvaro was not listening to them. Autumn started to stand but went back down on her knees with Alvaro's arms still around her. She started to stand and he tried to stop her but she pushed him away.

"If you won't listen to your own brother or us please just leave." Autumn told him.

"I can't leave you like this, you going to get hurt if I just leave." Alvaro said.

"I don't care, take care of your soon to be bride, believe what she is saying not those who truly care about you. JUST LEAVE PLEASE!" Autumn yelled at him.

Alvaro got up; helping her to her feet before letting go. She held on to his strong arms for just a second before letting go. She had to get ready for the next attack, just as she was getting ready the attack came and before she knew what Alvaro jumped in front of her using his true powers.

"DARKNESS REFECTION!" Alvaro called sending the attack back at the dark cheetah. Causing it to be thrown off all four legs. It got back up, but Alvaro could not move again with using the attack he never tried before. So Joey, Sue, and Autumn all jumped in the way calling forth their own powers.

"COME WATER DRAGON, PERSIDION, WATER CYCLONE!" Joey yelled. As the dragon Presidion appeared it let a very loud screech, and then a lot of water started to fall in balls, it was like having a shower but with lots of water that could drown you.

"Sun Blast!" Sue called. As the sun blast hit the cheetah after the water attack did throwing it across the square and into a booth that was selling balloons for the festival causing the cheetah to stagger.

"Heaven's Arrow!" Autumn called. The light arrow hit the cheetah and it turned to dust causing a big venom attack and making the air toxic to breathe. The guardians' knew that if they did nothing it would be devastating to all the people who are here to celebrate Prince Alvaro's happiness.

"Autumn, do you have enough power to use your healing power to clear up that toxic before it kills us all?" Sue asked.

"I might, it just that I also used my powers earlier today to fight a darkness lion in the back alley when I went out there after noticing Alvaro in the restaurant." Autumn said.

"Can you please at least try." Wyatt asked with fear in his eyes at what just happened and at what he just saw his friends do.

"You can do this. You are a strong guardian." Joey said encouraging her to at least try.

"Okay, I will try, but I might pass out after this. So make sure that you catch me so that I don't hit my head again please." Autumn said with a shy smile and a forced giggle from her mouth.

"You got it!" They all said together. They moved around her to catch her if she fell.

"HEAVEN'S DOORS!" Autumn called. As she used her powers; the doors appeared and opened up, as the doors opened the toxic was purified and the people were safe for now. As Autumn finally released her powers she went down as if she was falling into the sea of time. As she could see, there once was a beautiful place that was full of warmth, happiness, love, and peace. This place was a place worth protecting from darkness that might one day take it over or at least tries.

"So this is where I can find you?" A woman said.

"Do I know you?" Autumn asked.

"Yes, silly we are best friends after all." The woman said. The voice was familiar to her as if she heard it before. She just could not place where. So she turned around and facing her was Sue, but not Sue. This Sue was a little older, just as pretty, and just as confident. She was really there, it was as if she was in a dream world of some kind, but didn't want to leave.

"I'm sorry Sue, I was just day dreaming." Autumn said.

"It is alright, I know the feeling with the darkness slowly approaching." Sue said.

"Yeah, it seems to be getting stronger. It is hard to face everything. Just want to have some peace and enjoy this night with our princess and prince. It is a big deal." Autumn said.

"I know what you mean. Andrew is waiting for me in the ballroom to dance. How are you and Alvaro doing? Have you two made up yet, because you know if there is frication among us guardians' it can become our weakness and that can be a problem?" Sue said.

"I will try, but I am not sure about him." Autumn said feeling the dread in his heart. Then she woke up in the Twilight Inn in her room with Sue sitting in a chair next to the bed asleep. Autumn just looked at her and she could feel their friendship as if it had been there the whole time. She could feel the love that is being given by her friends knowing that she can count on them for anything.

Sue started to wake up and coming too. Her eyes saw Autumn and knew that she was going to be alright.

"Hey girl, you did wonderful yesterday night. You saved everyone." Sue said with tears in her eyes.

"Glad to hear. It is okay." Autumn said looking at Sue with different eyes.

"So you seem to be back to the swing of things. Also just so you know Alvaro and Jilana went back to the castle, and we have to start heading that way. We have to save him from her and the Dark Kingdom Zodiac. I know you don't want to, but think of the people of this realm like it was your realm. Wyatt needs his brother to be safe also we need to save him and this realm." Sue said.

"I know it just gets under my skin that he can be so blind to her and the power she has over him." Autumn said.

"I know that, it just that we told him when we were attacked last night. She looked at me and smiled like she had already one. How do we stop her?" Autumn said.

"We do what we are supposed to do. We get Alvaro to help us. He has a really big thing for you. He seems to be really into you. It is a connection that two people have between them that they can only understand. For an example for Andrew and me we connected on a level that can't be understood by someone else. If we want to reach him, and really reach you are going to have to do it. Do you understand?" Sue asked.

"Yes, I understand well. We need to get moving, is Joey and Wyatt ready for us to go? How does the inn keeper feel about us bailing on our deities in the restaurant?" Autumn asked.

"He gave the room to us for free after what we did last night, and most of all what you did last night. They are almost ready, we leave in one hour. This gives us time to stock up on food and drink as well so that we can eat before we leave." Sue said.

"Okay, and Sue thanks for being a great friend." Autumn said.

"Always and forever no matter what happens we will get through this and bring him back, and defeat the Dark Kingdom Zodiac." Sue said. So the girls got up and got dressed after showering and headed to the elevator to go to the restaurant were Joey and Wyatt was waiting with food already on the table. The girls sat down and started to eat their breakfast of waffles, eggs, bacon, orange juice, and coffee.

"Glad you could join us." Joey said with a smile. The girls smiled back at because they knew that he was just trying to make them smile and not think about what they had to do to stop this woman and her dark plans.

"I was able to get us a ride to the castle, which we will be able to proceed with collision." Wyatt said.

"Thank you for your help. What are you going to do when we get there?" Sue asked.

"I'm not sure yet. I know one thing that he does care about you, Autumn, by the way he reacted last night during the fight with the cheetah. Also I could see it in his eyes that he would rather die than not have you on this realm." Wyatt said.

"Thank you." Autumn said but her smile didn't reach her eyes like before. So the friends ate their breakfast in quit until they were all done and full. Getting ready to head out, when the inn keeper came up to them and hand them a wrapped gift.

"Please take this; it will help you all on your way. Thank you for helping out in the restaurant and saving us all last night. This is a gift of thanks from everyone." Inn Keeper said.

"Thank you for giving us a room to stay, and thank you everyone for the gift, we will use it wisely." Sue said. Everyone looked at them as they went outside of the inn. As they stepped outside waiting for them was a carriage and horse.

"This is the only way I could think of for us to get into the castle. The wedding is supposed to happen in a few days and they order a carriage for the wedding and I guess we could use this to get into the castle." Wyatt said.

"Well if it gets us there and in the castle without a second look or questions, is a great idea." Sue said.

"Thanks, it is the east I can do." Wyatt said.

"Well let us get a move on it. The wedding isn't going to wait." Joey said. So they all got into the carriage. Wyatt was the one who was driving the carriage to the castle which would only take them the day to get there. Also they had to figure out how to deal with Jilana and the Dark Kingdom Zodiac. So they sat in the carriage wondering how they could get rid of her and free this realm from the dark kingdom.

The carriage had dark curtains that was slick in the color of dark gray which seemed to match this realm well, the sits were soft and comfortable for long rides in the realm, the sits were embroider with a cross pattern in the color of god. It matches his eyes, Autumn thought. It looked great and went well with the dark gray curtains to stand out.

Autumn was looking out of the carriage windows; the scenery was different from her own realm. Which seemed to be different from wondering around in fields; of her own realm, this realm seemed to so interesting, festinating, it was just amazing. It was midafternoon when they reached the castle which was tall, beautiful, and it looked wonderful. The realm was worth saving, but only if Alvaro could see what everyone else could see. Jilana had a strong hold on him, she wanted to save this realm, and him very much. As they pulled up to the gate it was made up of wood that looked very old, but strong. It had a boar on it to scare the enemy away; it also looked strong and protected just like the prince. The gate operator came out to investigate the carriage when Wyatt got down to talk to him, the operator stopped and looked at him than told him to go ahead on in. Wyatt got back up in the driver's sit and moved the carriage forward.

Chapter 15

As the carriage moved forward into the gates of the court yard where the wedding was supposed to take place; Autumn looked up at the castle and she fell in love with how it looked. It had statues of angels', goblins, gargoyles, and other things that she could not see. It was something out of a fairy tale she had read as a child. She grew wondering about her dreams and what they met, she only seen a place that was so beautiful she could not take her eyes off it. This was no different, there was something about it that made her want even more to save this realm and their prince from the darkness the Dark Kingdom Zodiac has put on everyone. As they approached the finally stop where the carriage would have to be there was a side door they would be able to get into.

"Well this is where we get off. We can go inside through that door over there without being spotted because that is the servants' entrance." Wyatt said.

"Let me guess you use to sink out that way when you were young." Joey said. Wyatt smiled at him and shack his head at Joey.

"This is no time to crack jokes cuz." Sue said.

"Well it helps, and it is fun. I guess you are right we have worked to do." Joey said. Autumn looked at them two and just shacked her head and moved to Wyatt.

"Did you really do that?" Autumn asked Wyatt.

"Yeah, but not just me Alvaro also did it too. He is the one who showed me we could go this way without being spotted by the help." Wyatt said with a smile from remembering the fun and good times with his older brother. So the guardians' just smiled back at him. They knew all too well what it feels like to leave family behind, and they started to remember the good and fun times with their family and friends. It made them feel great and even more powerful than they felt before coming here.

"Are you all ready to go in?" Wyatt asked them.

"Yes." They all said together. Smiling at him.

"Let us go then." Wyatt said opening the door and letting them in as he followed behind.

As they stepped in the door; what they see in front of them is a long stairway leading up to the main part of the castle, most likely the kitchen area. So they started up the stairs and something really seemed off. It was hard to breathe, it felt like the air was being sucked out of their lungs, and they garbed their chest. Autumn felt as if the air was toxic, and that anyone without the antidote they would either die or go into a very long sleep. So she did the best things she could think of at the time.

"Shield of Spirit!" Autumn called. As she did this the air around them cleaned and they could breathe again.

"What did you do that for?" Wyatt said now breathing normal not heavy.

"So that we could breathe. My powers are of healing and light, I am a high priestess in my own realm. So the powers I have are of the healing type. It is like a healing touch you could say." Autumn explained to Wyatt.

"Well, good thinking. We can at least move with your shield around us." Joey said.

"Yeah, that was a fast move. Thanks a lot." Sue said.

"Thank you all. We need to keep moving, I'm not sure how long my shield will hold down here." Autumn said.

"Do you think that we might have triggered a trap when we came in here?" Wyatt asked.

"That is a really good chance. With the Dark Kingdom Zodiac you could never know what tricks or traps they have set up for us." Joey said.

"Okay." Is all Wyatt could say?

"So we have to be on our feet when they are involved." Joey said. As they moved up the stairs and into the kitchen they saw a huge stove with boiling water, bread strove had fresh bread being made, other types of food for that day's lunch, dinner, and lots of food. There was a storage space that had extra dry foods' in it like grains, cans of fruit and vegetables, and other foods' that were dry. Some was different from what they were used to seeing. This was a site that looked like it is used all day. There was another door off to the left that lead out into the hall way.

"Let's go this way." Wyatt said. So they followed him out the door and into the hall way which was very long, and had all kinds of doors off of it.

"Which door would we go into to get to Alvaro?" Sue asked.

"What door leads to the throne room?" Autumn asked.

"We also need a door way to lead to a portal to the next realm after this one." Joey said.

"First of we need a plan, second is to find were Alvaro might be in the castle, and third of we need to stop Jilana." Wyatt said.

"Then let us ask a servant that is working today." Joey suggested.

"Good idea, but lets' head down the hall and to the fourth door on the right, which is my room. That way we can ask around after we change into something a little more formal. Okay?" Wyatt said.

"Okay." They all said together. So they headed down the hall to Wyatt's room so they could change and call a servant to the room, so they could find out where Alvaro might be. They ran down the hall and got to the fourth door on the right and went in. As they went in they notice that the old style of design even went in the room. It was just a nice and beautiful as it was on the outside of the castle.

"Man, this is your room?" Joey asked with his mouth a little opened.

"Yeah, Alvaro's room is a lot better and bigger than mine but the designs are the same, but with angels' instead of gargoyles which seem to fit this room just right. Autumn and Sue looked around the room which had a couch, a small kitchen in with an icebox, small strove, and a small wall that separated the bedroom from the living room. The bed had the same smoke gray color as the carriage window curtains, and golden comforter which had a different pattern almost like a leaf pattern. It was a really big bed it could most likely sleep eight or nine people comfortably. There was a canapé over the bed which made the interior look even older. It was really beautiful in its own way. There was also a few dressers, walk in closet, and full bathroom with a bath tub that was really big.

"I will call a couple of servants for some food, clothes, and answers that we are looking." Wyatt said. So he went over to the night stand and picked up the receiver of the phone which looked old fashioned as well and called down to the savants quarters requesting a couple servants to bring women's clothes, and men's clothes so they could change. Also a hair styles to do the girls' hair for lunch. As he hung up the receiver and looked around at everyone and noticing that they all needed to be cleaned up.

"Why don't you two ladies go ahead and get cleaned up while Joey and I wait for the servants' to come in and start to ask the questions. Okay." Wyatt suggested.

"Okay, as long as you wait for us to finish before you start to ask questions, please." Sue asked.

"You got it." Wyatt answered.

"Joey keeps an eye out for anything that might be off or feel off." Autumn said.

"I'm wide awake and you got it." Joey answered back. So the girls went into the bathroom leaving the boys alone.

As Joey looked around he noticed that there was some huge windows in the room that let light in to bright the room up. Still making the room look accent, but it was really net in his eyes, he could see why Autumn was so into this type of thing because it is not seen very often. There was a knock on the door as the girls' started to come out of the bathroom with towels wrapped around them to help keep them covered.

"Come in." Wyatt answered. As a girl servant enter the room no older than at least 20 years old with a smile. She bent over bowing to the second prince and looking around at who was in the room. Than her smile started to faded.

"Thank you for coming on short notice. Please don't look so unpleased to see us. These three people are friends of mine. We met in town a little while ago. So what have you brought for us?" Wyatt asked.

"Your highness, we were warned not to trust these people, because they work for the Dark Kingdom Zodiac my load." The servant said.

"You have been given wrong information about these people. They are the good ones and the bad one is Lady Jilana." Wyatt said.

"My load, can they be trusted?" Servant girl said.

"Yes, now please what have you brought us to ware?" Wyatt said starting to get upset with his servant.

"My load, I have brought a couple of formal sundresses, and a couple formal suits for lunch today with your brother out in the court yard. "Servant girl said. The dresses were pink and yellow; the suits were of a dark and light gray color. She handed them over to the prince and left the room leaving the shoes by the door. There was a pair of heels in the color of gray, black dress shoes for men, and a pair of wedges in the same color as the heels. For which the girls both grabbed. Autumn put on the yellow formal sundress, Sue put the pink formal sundress on, while the guys went into the bathroom one at a time to take a bath to clean up coming out looking really good. After everyone had a bath and clean clothes; they looked at each other.

"Well we didn't get a chance to ask where your brother is." Joey said.

"No your wrong Joe, she told us where he will be, the question is how are going to go about this lunch thing without having eyes come our way?" Autumn asked.

"We could pretend that I invited you all for the lunch dinner, and brought dates." Wyatt said.

"Good idea, Joey and Autumn can pretend to be on a date for which you invited your friend, and I could be your date Wyatt; that way we don't look to out of place; because Joey and me are cousin's." Sue suggested.

"Okay, that will work. So let us head to the court yard, after the girls' get their hair done." Wyatt said. There was another knock on the door, and the hair dresser came in and pulled Autumn's hair into a bun with hair hanging down which she curled. Sue had her hair pulled up half way, put into a bun and her hair was flat ironed. After the hair dresser left they head for the door holding onto each other for support. They went out into the hall and looked up and down the hall wondering which way to go.

"We go to our right and continue down the hall to the main stair well, which will spilt into two sections which you would go the stairs and make a left turn down the bigger stair well which leads to double doors that lead to the court yard." Wyatt said. So they went right and down the hall until they reach the double stair case that leads further down the hall and then the one that goes left to the double doors to the court yard; which is the way they want to go.

So they start walking down the stairs when Alvaro came out of the hall to the left and went to the double doors and turned and looked up at them coming down the main stairs. He spotted Autumn right away looking very beautiful and making his heart skip a beat. She was very pretty and he could feel that pull she had over him, making him question what he was doing. They notice him and stop mid-way down the stairs before going any further.

"Please don't stop, come join us for lunch guardians' and my dear younger brother." Alvaro said. It seemed to be off his own natural talking as if it was forced out. Autumn had notice that his voice was sweet and soft when he ever spoke to her, but now it seemed to be hard and cold. There was something really bad going on, she could feel it, she also knew that the other could as well.

"Okay, brother we will join you in the court yard for lunch. Please tell me who else will be there with us?" Wyatt asked.

"Why, my soon to be bride Lady Jilana, by the way we moved the wedding up to tomorrow at 8pm." Alvaro said.

"Why would you do that? What does she have on you? Why can't you see pass her evil?" Autumn said with a sad and hurt sound to her voice that she didn't even know was possible.

"I have no idea what you are talking about guardian of Healing and Spirit. You have not been honest with us either." Alvaro had said with an evil smile on his face that did belong there. Autumn had nothing else to say because she knew that this was the evil of the Dark Kingdom Zodiac making him talk like that.

"Don't worry we will get him back." Autumn said more to Wyatt than Alvaro. Everyone looked at her, but she was determined to stop them and save this realm and Alvaro from their evil. So they all started back down the main stair well, walking toward the double doors when Alvaro stepped in their way.

"What is it now brother?" Wyatt said with anger.

"I will escort the guardian of healing and spirit to the court yard if you don't mind brother." Alvaro said with an evil smile that was not his own.

"She has a name and it is Autumn. She is my date not his, so you should be asking if it is alright with me first." Joey said.

"Guardian of summoning let me put it this way, I will escort the guardian of healing and spirit not a request but a demand." Alvaro said.

"It is alright Joey, he can escort me if he would like." Autumn said keeping a fight at bay the best she could. So Joey let go of her arm but he stayed right behind her when they walked out into the court yard to a table waiting for them to show up, with Jilana already sitting there with what look like another pet of hers. Joey did not like this, something was way off and he knew what will be coming next.

As they approached the table Autumn went to sit in a seat far away from Jilana and Alvaro, but he pulled her along to a sit right next to his. She could not believe what she was seeing or what was happening. She knew something was way off, as she looked at everyone's face they felt the same way.

"Welcome, to our castle guardians', and Prince Wyatt." Lady Jilana said.

"Well thanks for the welcome, but we did not come here for small talk, we came to finish what we started last night." Sue said with anger.

"Well, guardian of light and travel you are in luck because I will make sure you will not leave this place a live." Jilana said with an evil laugh. It made the hairs stand up on all their necks.

"What is the meaning of this? Why are you so bent on destroying this realm, and all realms?" Wyatt asked.

"Because it is my job. Now we could do this the easy way or the hard way?" Jilana asked.

"We would rather do it the hard way." Joey said with a smile. Before he knew it something hard hit him in the chest and knocking him backwards. Sue stepped forward and started to call her powers when they same thing happened to her. Autumn went to help but Alvaro grabbed her and held her so she could not move.

"Let go of me!" Autumn screamed.

"I can't do that, my dear. I was granted one thing and that is your safety." Alvaro said with a sad note to his voice.

"Why me? Why not your own brother or the people of this realm? Why me?" Autumn asked him.

"Because I feel that if something happened to you I would lose my mind." Alvaro said.

"I don't care." Autumn said as she hit him in the face with her elbow knocking him backward from her.

"ARROW OF HEAVEN!" Autumn called before Jilana knew what hit her; an arrow made up of white light so bright that she feel backwards giving Joey and Sue time to get up.

"I SUMMON THE DRAGON OF FIRE, IFRIT. FIRE STORM!" Joey called. This dragon was so big that Alvaro and Wyatt could not take it all in. Jilana was getting up after the attack from Autumn's arrow still hurting her she sent her pet at them again and this time they could see what it was. It was an eagle that had green wings and venom coming off it with teeth the size of razors. Sue was not going to let that thing hit her friends again.

"SUN SHIELD!" Sue called as the eagle got close hitting the shield and been thrown back. These made the eagle disappear; making Jilana really mad. She aimed an arrow at Autumn that was putting off some venom which was very toxic that if that arrow hit her it would kill her. Before she knew Jilana let the arrow go aiming at Autumn when something knocked her out of the way. She looked up to see that Wyatt had taken the arrow in the shoulder, causing Alvaro to come out of the trace that Jilana had on him. Making him so mad that he let all his anger go and he felt the power of his realm come to him.

"DARK ARROW!" Alvaro called.

As the arrow hit Jilana turning her to dust and sending her pets back to where ever they came from; the Dark Kingdom Zodiac no longer had a hold on his kingdom or realm. That was not all Wyatt was gasping for breathe when Alvaro came to. He ran to his brother holding him and tears fell from his eyes and his heart hurt.

"I'm so sorry Wyatt, I didn't mean to let this happen. Can you please forgive me?" Alvaro said through tears of sadness.

"It is not your fault we all were blinded by her. There is nothing to forgive. I love you big brother." Wyatt said. As the others looked on, Sue had tears in her eyes while Joey was helping Autumn up, then walked over to her and held her tight. Autumn looked at Wyatt and knew what to do. She walked over to him and touched Alvaro's arm, he looked up at her than looked away. He didn't want her to see him like this.

"Please look at me, I can help. Wyatt thanks you, please hold still, Okay." Autumn said as Alvaro looked at her, he moved over so she could bend down and touch Wyatt. Wyatt was too weak to talk so he shook his head yes. Autumn went to his left shoulder and put her hand on it.

"Spirit Healing!" Autumn called as a white light came and healed Wyatt's shoulder and removing all the poison from him. He sat up right, and looked at her with new eyes and smiled. Autumn looked at Wyatt and knew it had worked and then she passed out from using her powers to much in one day. Alvaro let go of Wyatt and caught her.

He held her for a long time it seemed before anyone said a word.

"I'm sorry about this, but we need to know if you have a portal we could use? Also Alvaro we need to know if you will come with us and be the guardian of the Crystal Star of the Darkness realm." Sue asked looking at them and at Autumn; who was out cold still. Wyatt was the one to answer Sue.

"Yes, we have a portal room. Why do you need it?" Wyatt asks.

"Remembering me telling you that Sue could use portals to get to on realm after another. Well we need it to send Autumn and if Alvaro comes with us to the Crystal Star of Water and Ice realm." Joey said.

"I see so you need to leave this realm with her, and me." Alvaro said.

"Yes, that is right. We also need to know what realm this one is connected to as well." Sue said.

"We are connected to the Nature Realm. Also I would be coming with you. I am the guardian of this realm and my parents have been trying to figure out a way to bring back the Majestic

Star Kingdom. It is our duty to help protect the Star Princess with the other guardians'." Alvaro said.

"Brother you are going to be king soon; you just can't leave like this." Wyatt said.

"I'm not because I'm leaving the realm in good hands. Yours', you will make a fine king. This is what I really want; please protect this realm and the people here better than I did. Also you earned it." Alvaro said.

"Are you sure about this?" Wyatt asked.

"Yes, very much so." Alvaro said. Wyatt shook his head at his brother and got off the ground. Alvaro stood up as well picking Autumn up and planed on carry her to the portal room.

"Please come this way, the portal room is straight up the stairs into those double doors that you didn't notice earlier guardians'." Alvaro said pulling out a key from inside his pocket at the same time still holding up Autumn. He picked her up under her legs and head, a started to carry her into the main lobby of the castle. The others followed him going back through the double doors coming from the court yard, and heading back up the main stairs.

They notice that the door was there and before they knew Alvaro and Wyatt had the double doors open waiting on Joey and Sue to go through. As they walked through the doors Sue saw a lot of portals before but none like this. She knew which portal would lead to the Crystal Star of the Nature Realm and which would lead her to Alena on the Crystal Star of Water and Ice Realm. She turned to everyone as Autumn started to come to. She looked up at Alvaro holding her and she smiled turning her face deep red. Sue started to laugh and that is when Alvaro, Joey and Wyatt a notice that she is a wake.

"You can put me down now." Autumn said still red and smiling.

"I would love too, but I like holding you like this." Alvaro said smiling at her and his heart felt great. She was the one, she was the one, and she is the one he kept saying in his own head. He knew that if he married that evil witch Jilana he would have mean very unhappy, but with Autumn he knew that she was the one he wanted all along. Now he has his chance and is going to take. So he bent down and his lips met hers and he kissed her, no matter who was watching them. Sue's face turned red think back to when Andrew did that to her. Joey cleared his throat and they pulled apart. Autumn was trying to get her breathe but could not help but smile at Alvaro. She knew in her heart that he is the one for her.

"Okay, now he is the kicker for you two." Sue said pointing at Autumn and Alvaro.

"What will that be?" Alvaro asked.

"I can send you two back to the Crystal Star of Water and Ice or you can come with Joey and me to the Crystal Star of the Nature Realm?" Sue had asked.

"We will go with you two. That way we can help you out if both of you need it." Autumn said.

"Okay than, let us head to the Nature Realm." Sue said. So they head for the portal at the very top of all the portals and touched it. It shimmed under her touch opening up to the Nature Realm.

Wyatt stood back to see the portal shimmer as Joey walked through it, then Autumn, Alvaro waited a moment and walked dover to his brother.

"Wyatt please takes care of you, and of our home." Alvaro said slapping Wyatt on the shoulder.

"I will do my best brother. I will become a king you are proud of and proud to call brother." Wyatt said slapping his brother on the shoulder. Alvaro walked away from him and stepped into the portal, followed by Sue which then the portal closed up, leaving Wyatt in a dark room with tears on his face from watching his older brother leave. He walked out of the portal room taking the key and putting it into his pocket for safe keeping. Until he can see his brother again and there is peace in the entire realm someday.

"GOOD LUCK BIG BROTHER ALVARO, GOOD LUCK GUARDIANS' OF THE MAJUSTIC STAR KINGDOM, WE WILL BE WAITING FOR YOUR RETURN." Wyatt said to the dark room hoping and praying his brother and his new friends heard him.

Crystal Star of the Nature Realm

>┼≻─⊙─≺┼≺

Chapter 16

As Joey stepped out of the light portal made by Sue, he notices that they were no longer in the Darkness Realm anymore. Behind him came Autumn, Alvaro, and then Sue who was closing up the light portal she made. It is so bright; that they had to put their hands in front of their eyes to block the sun from beaming down on them.

"So this is the Crystal Star of the Nature Realm?" Alvaro asked.

"It looks that way." Joey said.

"Let us hope so." Autumn said.

"Don't worry it is. We made it through the portal safe, because the Dark Kingdom Zodiac can't enter the portals I make, because of the love, peace, and happiness they have." Sue said with a smile on her face. She could tell that they all were getting stronger now, but so is the dark kingdom. They had to find the last two guardians' before the dark kingdom can turn everything around on them.

Sue, Alvaro, and Autumn all started to look around when Joey was trying to figure out what their next step would be. They would stand on the edge of a creek not far from a small water fall of crystal clear water, in the middle of a rain forest of some kind. They did not know the name of this forest but could sense that there was power here somewhere.

"So what do we do?" Alvaro asked still turning his head in every which way he could. He had never seen anything like this before.

"I'm not sure, but we need to start moving before night fall, or an attack happens." Autumn said feeling familiar with this place; it reminded her of some parts of her own realm.

"Your right, we need to get moving. Which way should we go?" Joey asked. He was looking for the best route to take so that they could still keep their barriers around them. Then he noticed that to the East there was a safe way to go for now.

"How about we go east until night falls?" Joey asked.

"Sounds like a plan to me." Alvaro said, grabbing Autumn's arm making her blush even redder then the fire. Sue laughed at the site; Joey just rolled his eyes and took lead. Alvaro went behind Joey with Autumn right on his side. Sue herded up and caught up with Joey to help take lead. So they lead them through a lot of trees, plants, and animals they couldn't see.

It had become mid-day before they stopped and rested, Joey and Alvaro went looking for food so they could eat, and came back with coconuts, mangoes, bananas, and star fruit. They had spring water for them which they used the trees to break open the coconuts and drank the water or milk out of the coconut. Alvaro had never seen these types of fruits before and they were really good. He ate a lot because he just could not stop eating the fruit. Joey had packed some fruit so they had it for later when it started to get dark and they needed to set up camp. That was still some time away before they would stop. It was late afternoon when it started to rain in the forest but they kept on walking hoping that the rain would stop soon. As it came to a light mist my mid-evening, they stopped and rested a few minutes than continue to walk some more, that is when they heard a really big nose and turned around to see what it was, but nothing was there. They started to get that feeling that something was about to happen. As night got closer they choose to stop near a ridge by a bigger waterfall than the one they had seen earlier in the day.

They had to have traveled a few miles before stopping, it felt like that at least. They may have went 10 miles maybe a little more. They started to set up camp, they took out the tent, some clothes to change out of the dresses, and suits they had been wearing for lunch the day before, without having a chance to change. The dresses were cut, and ripped up from walking the forest all day; the suits were in no better shape.

"How are you able to set up camp, and have a tent if we didn't come here with any supplies?" Alvaro asked.

"It is simple; my light and travel dragon can carry it for us. She has had it this whole time. She has clothes, food, and place for us to sleep for the night. We need to take shifts each." Joey said.

"Okay, I get it. Well how about Sue and you rest first. Autumn and I will take the first night shift after we eat, drink, get cleaned up, and change our clothes. Okay?" Alvaro asked.

"Sounds great to me. Is that alright with you, Autumn?" Joey asked.

"Yeah, that is fine. Sue you don't have a problem with that do you?" Autumn asked Sue.

"Not at all, be my guess." Sue said with a smile. So they all took turns getting cleaned up, changed, ate, and drank before Sue and Joey headed off to bed. Autumn went outside the tent and sat in front of the entrance with Alvaro just looking up at the stars wondering how everyone was doing. She didn't know what to say to him, or how to even start a conversation with him.

"You, know I would not have let her hurt like that." Alvaro said.

"What do you mean? Are you talking about Jilana and what she had done?" Autumn asked.

"Yeah, I just could not image not having you in any of the realms. That day I met you in the street during my engagement celebration to Jilana, I felt as if time had stopped. I could not breathe without you near, and thinking that you might just get hurt was one thing I didn't want. So please forgive me?" Alvaro said.

"Like, Wyatt said "there is nothing to forgive" I liked you the minute I met you that day, my heart felt light as a feather on a bird. I was in love before I knew it. In trust when I say this, I don't trust so easily, it was so hard growing up and having special powers so strong that you couldn't control. That was the way it was for me, if not for my young sister, I would have felt alone all the time. She had powers too, just not as powerful as mine. Now I know why, I can use them to protect those I care deeply about." Autumn said.

"I felt the same way, there was Wyatt did make some of the loneness go away, but he was not like me. My mother had told me that I got all the powers and was blessed by our realm that there was none left for him. I didn't want life to be like that, but he seemed not to mind. He still wanted to be with me. When I first met you I wanted the same thing for the first time in my life, I did not feel better about myself as I feel for you." Alvaro said.

"It is just a matter of time before you met someone who is like you, and someone you want to protect more than anything in all the realms. I protected my people, I wanted nothing more, but there always seemed to be something missing in my life an now I know what that was. Thanks to you." Autumn said with a smile on her. That is when Alvaro had turned and kissed her again and this time it was deeper, sweeter, and more love than anything she had felt before. That is when it happened; something came flying out of the sky aiming at them, and before she had a chance to react Alvaro had already called his powers to him.

"SILENT WALL SHIELD!" Alvaro called, putting up a shield so strong that it even protected the tent; were Sue and Joey was sleeping. It was a meteor that hit them, than it was gone, and they heard this rough laugh as if someone was watching them and the fun they were having at their benefit. As they looked around to see who was there, but could not find anyone. Then Joey came out of the tent yawning, looking at Alvaro and Autumn wondering what they were doing.

"What is going on? You two look as if you have seen a ghost or something?" Joey said.

"well if that is what you want to call it that. It was like an illusion of some kind." Autumn said.

"That might be the Dark Kingdom Zodiac messing with us or another general from their ranks." Joey said. Sue was just starting to a wake up when another attack came this time Joey was standing with Autumn and Alvaro and huge Black Widows came running at them.

"I SUMMON THE QUEEN DRAGON OF ICE, SOFIA. ICE SPEAR ATTACK!" Joey called. The Ice Dragon hit the Black Widows with spears of ice killing them, at least that was what it looked like, but they just disappeared. Sue came walking out of the tent, then looked at the others wondering what is going on.

"Um, guys what are you looking at?" Sue asked.

"Well if you consider huge Black Widows something to look at than yes we are." Alvaro said.

"Well I think that we might want to find out who is doing this." Sue suggested.

"Well whoever it is, it can't be a friend it might be a general of the Dark Kingdom Zodiac's army." Sue said.

"Then let us find out who is welcoming us here tonight." Joey said.

"Okay, than let us get ready for a fight we know is coming." Autumn said.

"So show yourself? Who are you? What do you want with us?" Sue asked.

"Well; guardians', I guess it is only right that I show you who the strongest general is in the Dark Kingdom Zodiac's army!" Mystery person said.

"So; who are you then? Oh, thanks for the welcoming party it has been fun." Sue said.

"My name is Jomo; I'm the general of Illusion! The strongest general you will ever meet. I can take your worst fears and make them reality." General Jomo said laughing.

"Then give us your best shot!" Alvaro said.

"In due time guardians', I will be waiting for you. Until then have fun with this illusion." General Jomo said.

"Bring it on!" Autumn said.

"Illusion of t-rex, megladon, and ocean floors!" General Jomo called while disappearing into the darkness of night. As the guardians' looked around it looked as if they had been put in the ocean and that there was a megaladon and t-rex coming at them. Autumn started to panic and losing her breathes due to the illusion. Alvaro grabbed her hand to claim her. She felt him and the others around putting their hands on them. So they all got close to each other to keep from losing their heads. Then it came to Sue what they had to do.

"Guys we need to use our powers to get out of this. We can't let the Dark Kingdom Zodiac win. Our friends are counting on us." Sue said.

"Okay, you got it. Let us show them, what we as guardians' can do!" Joey said.

"I SUMMON THE DRAGON OF WATER, WANI. WATER CYCLONE!" Joey called. This caused the water to disappear, taking the megladon with it before it could attack them.

"DANCING SUN!" Sue called. Hit the t-Rex, which just stagger backwards.

"DARKNESS OF HEART!" Alvaro called making the t-Rex to disappear as well.

"HEAVEN'S RAYS!" Autumn called to heal everyone at once to give them more strength so they could move on from where they had set up camp. It met moving in the early morning before dawn appears, but they had to move because of the attack and the problems it caused.

"Is everyone okay?" Autumn asked.

"Yes, thanks for healing us and giving us energy." Sue said.

"Glad I could help." Autumn said.

"Yeah, nice move Alvaro; that attack did the trick to that damn t-Rex." Joey said with a smile at his new friend.

"Thanks, we should pack-up and get moving before that general wants to come back to finish what he started with us." Alvaro said.

"Good point." Joey said. So they all gather up everything and packing the tent back up, giving it to the light dragon to carry, so they would be able to move faster in the forest east.

As the guardians' continue on their way through the forest the sun started to rise making it easier to see what was around them. They had come to a waterfall with a field of flowers that was really beautiful. They smelled really sweet for this time of day, and the dew that was on them from the rain yesterday just gave this realm a look of mystery and adventure. Autumn liked what she could see with Alvaro right next to her holding her hand to make sure that he will never lose her again. He never wants to feel like he did with Jilana ever again and with Autumn he had a great new start with his true love. So he was not going to let her go for nothing. Spend as much time together as they could. They looked around and seen vines of flowers that were starting to bloom in the morning. These flowers are so beautiful that they all wanted to see.

"So which way should we go now?" Joey asked.

"Not sure man, maybe you could summon one of your dragons' and fly up and have a better look around and let us know which way we could go." Alvaro suggested.

"That is a great idea." Sue agreed.

"Do you have enough power to do that?" Autumn asked.

"Yeah, thanks to your healing and the little rest I got." Joey said.

"Okay, go for it." Alvaro said.

"I, summon the dragon of wind, Jade!" Joey called as a green dragon appeared and he climbed on top.

"Please take me as high as you can, so that we can see which way to go." Joey said to the dragon. The dragon was willing to do as Joey asked.

So the dragon, Jade flew as high as she could go and Joey had one heck of a view from the back of the dragon. He could see for miles on miles, he spotted a small shack about 5 or 6 miles from where they are located in the direction of Northwest. It was maybe a few hours walk as long as they don't run into any trouble like the new enemy they have. If so it would take them half of a day or longer if the fight takes too long. So Joey flew back down to his friends to let them know which way to go.

Chapter 17

"We need to head Northwest from here, I seen a shack from up there. Someone might live there that can help us at least find a small village or something were we can get information from about who might be the next guardian of this realm." Joey said.

"Okay!" Everyone said together. So they headed in the direction that Joey had suggested. As they kept walking and end back up in the forest again after the clearing they were just in about two hours ago. Something was wrong, as if they have been going into a circle this whole time. So, Alvaro started to mark trees with his swish army knife that was given to him from his late father for a birthday present. He started to notice that he had marked the same trees before.

"Wait up, everyone stop please." Alvaro said.

"What is it?" Sue asked.

"We have been going around in circles for the past two hours maybe longer." Alvaro said.

"What do you mean?" Autumn asked this time.

"What I mean is that someone or something has put us into a dream or illusion of some kind." Alvaro said.

"So what you mean is we fell into the enemies trap again." Joey said.

"Yeah, that about sums it up." Alvaro said.

"Great!" Joey said. Then they all started to hear laughing, and this time it was coming from a tree of some kind. As they looked around they notice that a weeping willow started to disappear and there stood a man that looked as if he was a part of the forest. His eyes dark green to a burnt green, skin light brown, hair was the same color as the leafs on the trees. He was wearing some kind of armor that could have been made from bark. That is what it looked like anyway.

"You must be General Jomo." Autumn said.

"Well, guardian of healing and spirit you are very smart and very pretty. I don't see what the Dark Prince sees' in your one friend, but you are breathing taking." General Jomo said with smile.

"Well, she isn't for you." Alvaro said getting very angry.

"Oh well, guardian of the darkness. You should have thought about that when you tried to tie the knock with my co-worker Jilana. She was smart and pretty too, but her well she don't come close to the guardian of healing and spirit. Now does she?" Jomo said.

"She would never come close; too her. That is also over. So what do you really want?" Alvaro said.

"I want you all to die, but I will spare you three if the guardian of healing and spirit, gives herself to me without hatred. If not I will take her by force. She is very strong and I could use her, and her powers to my advantage." Jomo said laughing making Autumn feel sick to her tummy.

"Over our dead bodies!" Sue said.

"Well, guardian of light and travel, that can be arrange." Jomo said getting very angry.

"We will see about that." Autumn said.

"Autumn, is that your name guardian. I'm I right?" Jomo asked her.

"My name means nothing to you or your dark kingdom, so let us get this over with." Autumn said started to feel angry.

"As you wish my beautiful guardian. Illusion of stampeded of Rhinos!" Jomo said as a really huge stampede came at them making them all jump out of the way. Causing Autumn and

Alvaro to be spilt up, as well as Joey and Sue being spilt up. Both on different sides of the forest. Alvaro watched as Jomo ran over to grab Autumn, but Joey was there before he could summon yet another dragon.

"I summon the FIRE DRAGON, RUBY; FIRE BOMB!" Joey called. The fire hit some of the rhinos, and Autumn had pulled out her Katanas' which Alvaro had never seen her do before.

"ANGELS' WING!" Autumn had yelled. The attack hit the other rhinos; on Joey's and her side of the forest. The attack was like feathers' being sent in a spear like attack. As the wings hit causing more light, other than the sun's light rays; but beautiful, wonderful, amazing light of power. So Alvaro and Sue knew what they had to do.

Sue had pulled out her twin daggers of the sun for the second time. Only to have a new power with them.

"DACING LIGHT!" Sue yelled. She looked as if she was dancing to her type of music; that she was the only that could hear it. So, Alvaro felt it was time he used his own weapons for once instead of hiding them from everyone.

"I guess it is my turn." Alvaro said.

"Yeah, now is the time to show us your powers guardian of darkness." Jomo said laughing. Alvaro pulled out his sward of accents' to help his friends and his true love.

"DARKNESS STAR DANCE!" Alvaro yelled, as many star attacks happened at once; when he brought down his sward splitting the veil between darkness and light. As these stars hit the rhinos they all started to disappear into dust a long with the illusion.

"You will pay for this. You can't save this realm as long as I can keep you from finding the other guardian." General Jomo said with an angry look on his face as he was disappearing again. Alvaro was happy; with himself, but felt weak at the same time.

"Come back you coward, and finish what you started." Joey yelled at him.

"HAHAHAHA, another time guardian of summoning." Jomo said still disappearing. The illusion started to fade away, and the guardians' realized that they were closer to the shack than they thought. So they headed in the same direction they had been before walking into the trap. Alvaro still felt weak and feel to his knees, Autumn ran over to him, but he got back up and started to walk only to go down once more, but this time she caught him before he could hit the ground again.

"Are you alright?" She asked him.

"Yeah, I will be fine. Just weak from using a strong power for the first time." He said. She yelled at her other friends to stop.

"Guys', wait. Alvaro is weak from the fight just now. He needs to rest. Would you like me to heal you?" Autumn asked Alvaro.

"No, we don't need you passing out from over using your powers too. You must think I'm weak?" Alvaro said.

"No, we don't, because it happens to all of us." Sue said coming back to them.

"So, you have either passed out or feel really weak from over using your powers." Alvaro said.

"Yeah, I had passed out when I'd forced open a portal when we feel off a cliff, and landed into water. Yeah, Joey and Rich helped me out and made a fire to keep me warm. So that is why we are asking you to take it easy, let us help you out." Sue said.

"Sue is right Alvaro, I know how it feels to lose control of your powers, because it happened to me when I first met Joey and Sue, Joey kept me from hitting the ground and Sue was gentle to help me come too. They took care of me, so let us do the same for you." Autumn said.

"Thanks, you are really great friends anyone could ask for." Alvaro said.

"SPIRIT OF HEALING!" Autumn called. As her healing took effect on Alvaro making him heal and getting his strength back. Autumn was not feeling weak like use to when she used her powers a lot, but she knows that she is the only one right now that can help heal everyone. So the guardians' took another break so that Alvaro could gain some more strength and rest, even with the healing they all still needed to eat and drink something to keep moving in this uneven landscape of the forest which still makes them very tired. So they all sat down in a clearing of wildflowers so beautiful that it made them forget about what is going on in the entire realm with the Dark Kingdom Zodiac, even for a short while there is still some peace in this realm.

The field of wildflowers had so many different flowers and colors. Each flower seemed to be different some looked like bells, tulips, roses, mini roses, and other flowers they could not think of the names of. As the guardians' sat in this very wonderful place they made a picnic lunch with what they had in reserve for their trip before they moved on. Alvaro was resting next to Autumn; when they felt something seemed to be off, as if someone was watching them from a distance, but could not make out who or what it might be. As they finished their lunch they packed up everything sending back with the Light Dragon to carry. So they started back on their way. They left the clearing and went back into the forest for which they had to go through to get to the hut or shack they had seen a while back.

So they walked into the forest even though they felt that something or someone had been watching them for a while when they were sitting in the field of flowers. They just shook it off as Deja via, and continue on their way. It was already getting late afternoon by the time they had reached another clearing and in front of them there was the shack that Joey had seen earlier in the day on the Wind Dragon, Jade. So the guardians' looked around before exiting the forest this time, and walked really fast, like almost running to the shack hoping that someone was in there that can point them in the right direction they needed to go to get to at least one town or village. As they approached the shack being very caution, they slowly opened what look to be a bamboo door on the shack which up close looked more like a hut, but bigger. The roof had straw or leaves on it; the door was made of bamboo rods, the circle of the hut looked to be made out of mud, grass, or maybe even clay of some kind. It looked like something from a story of some kind. So they knocked on the door, but no one answered. They slowly opened the door, just in case there was a trap everywhere. Then it hit them like a forced wind that came out of nowhere knocking them back out the door, only just to look up and see a huge Bald Eagle that seemed to be out of this world because they have never seen an eagle that big before it was as big as the roof of the hut if not bigger.

The eagle came in for another attack, the guardians' had jumped out of the way just time where it had landed and started to take a different shape. Autumn held her breathe and where the eagle had just been was a woman wearing a two peace skirt outfit that looked to be made out of leaves or hid from an animal. She was really different and in her hand she held a whip that was made out of rose thorns. She had green hair shoulder length with pink highlights, really dark brown skin like an Asian woman, with yellow eyes that looked like cat eyes. Everyone looked at her as if she was not of this world and that she was an alien or something. Before they knew she had attack them again but this time she used powers that where of a guardian.

"ROSE PETAL SHOWER!" She had called; the attack was of rose petals that turned into thrones as it hit you. It had knocked Sue off her feet, knocking Joey to the groud with blood coming from cuts on his arms, legs, neck, and check. It hit Autumn with just as much force as it hit Sue, but she managed to stay on her feet with just as many cuts as Joey had. Alvaro had no marks on himself, they could not understand why.

"SILENT WALL SHIELD! Alvaro called; as the attack hit them, because they were all spread out it only protected him. The Rose Petal Shower attack was like a rain storm, but a lot worse. After it had stopped and most of them had some type of cut on them from the attack, they could barely stand; Alvaro got to his feet and ran to Autumn who was holding her arm that had blood coming out of the cut. Sue had gotten it the worse because she was knock to the ground without any protection of any kind because when the eagle had did the whirl wind attack to knock them out of the hut she was in front and got the most of the attack and so her cuts where a lot worse than the others. Joey was getting to his feet when he seen Sue down for the count and ran to her. Alvaro and Autumn did the same with Alvaro's help to walk. Another attack came again.

ROSE PETAL SHOWER! She called again and this time it was stronger than before so Autumn did what she had to do to protect her friends from this woman.

"BARRIER OF HEAVEN!" Autumn called as a huge shield had protected them all, but it was too much for her, the attack was strong, but she was already hurt and this just made it worse causing her to fall to the ground unconscious. Alvaro got up and went to her, he held and was crying because he thought he lost her again, but she heard her breathing which was a good sign.

"Alvaro, Autumn will be fine. She just over did it a little; with the wounds she has and her power." Joey said.

"Okay, what can we do if both Sue and Autumn are out for the count?" Alvaro asked.

"We need to talk to her, that woman over there; to get her to stop the attacks." Joey said.

"Okay, I will try. You stay with them." Alvaro said.

"You got it. I can try and summon the healing dragon, Ariel to help with these wounds we have, but it might be much of a success because of the barrier, Autumn out up." Joey said.

"Okay, you try that and I will try talking her to her. Even if it means by force." Alvaro said.

"Okay, I summon thy, DRAGON OF HEALING, ARIEL!" Joey called, but the dragon did not come and then Joey started to feel really weak and almost passed out, but stays conscious, while Alvaro left the barrier and went to talk to the woman in green.

Chapter 18

⊱───◯───⊰

"Please stop, we are not the enemy. We come in peace, we need help and we are looking for someone. My name is Alvaro Sky; I'm the prince of the Crystal Star of the Darkness Realm." Alvaro said. As the woman began her attack again, but stop when she saw that Alvaro was holding up both hands in front of himself pleading with her to stop. So she lowered her hand and stopped the attack on the others and looked at him; as if he was something strange.

"What do you want with my realm? Why have you come here Prince Alvaro of the Crystal Star of the Darkness Realm? What do you have to gain by entering this realm without permission?" Woman asked him.

"I enter the realm with these people right here. The girl with blonde hair that has on jeans, a graphic t-shirt, tennis shoes opened up a light portal for us to travel here in search of the guardian of this realm. We need that person to help protect and find the Star Princess and Prince of the Majestic Star Kingdom." Alvaro said.

"The Majestic Star Kingdom has been destroyed a thousand years ago, along with its' star princess and prince." Woman said.

"You're wrong, if us guardians' are being woken up to protect her than there is a chance that she was sent to the present time and reborn to a different family. That is the same with the prince as well." Alvaro said.

"YOU'RE LIEING! The star princess was taken by the Dark Kingdom Zodiac and killed." Woman said.

"No, you're wrong again, she was sent to the present time with the rest of us. We need to find them so that the Majestic Star Kingdom can be reborn again." Alvaro said.

"ENOUGH OF THIS, ROSE PETAL SHOWER!" Woman said.

"SILENT WALL SHIELD!" Alvaro called as the attack hit him making him lose his balance and knocking him down which caused him to drop the shield. So he ended up with cuts all over his body, but he got back on his feet pulling out his sword of accents'. She was still looking at him as if he was not of this world and she was done with them already.

"This is it Prince Alvaro, you have come here of your own free will, and in that I can't have you destroying my realm or taking it over, here is to goodbye. ROSE PETAL SHOWER!" Woman called again, but this time she missed Alvaro because he moved so quick that she could not see it. Before she knew it he was right behind her with his sword out, and ready to attack.

"I'm truly sorry for this. DARKNESS STAR DANCE!" Alvaro called as he let the attack go against the woman who had been attacking them. The Star attack hit her dead in the front and knocked her far back causing her to go unconscious. Alvaro walked over to her and touched her. She was still breathing, when he looked over to his friends, Sue and Autumn was coming too. Joey got to his feet and walked over to Alvaro putting a hand on his shoulder to let him know that he did what he had to, to save them all.

"You did good; she will be fine. We need to get her inside the hut before she wakes up again and thinks that we are the enemy again." Joey said.

"Yeah, still I wish I never had to do that. But there seem to be something wrong with her, it was as if someone had taken her over and was using her body. It felt like another person was in control. Is that even possible with this enemy we are against?" Alvaro asked with sad eyes.

"Your guess is as good as mine. We don't know how this enemy can work, or does work. Illusions are a big problem because everything can seem real to you, so we need to keep our gourd up better, than what we have been doing." Joey said. Then they heard it. I evil laugh coming from above them. As they looked up they saw Jomo the general of Illusion.

"Well guardians' that was fun, thank you for entertain me for a bit. It is sad though that your own guardian went against you, because she thought you were with the Dark Kingdom Zodiac. Too bad, she didn't kill you four guardians'. That would have been better for us, but I guess you can't control everybody when their heart is against it. But, remember this guardians' next time you won't serve." General Jomo said while disappearing and laughing.

"Listen you coward, come and fight your own battles." Joey and Alvaro said together.

"At least we know that she is the guardian we are looking for, but can we trust her?" Alvaro said.

"I'm not sure, but if her heart was hurting when she was attacking us, then maybe she can be. We will have to see." Joey said.

"Yeah, but how was he able to control her like that?" Alvaro asked.

"Maybe, she has been so hurt that it caused him to take some control of her, but not all control." Joey said.

"I guess we will have to see." Alvaro said. As the guys were starting to stand, Alvaro picked up the woman as Sue and Autumn came over to them holding on to each other for support. Alvaro looked at Autumn with sad eyes again, and she knew why. He felt he could not protect her again, but that was not the truth at all. He did protect her; he protected them all this time. She looked at the woman in his hands and felt a little jealous of her. She could not figure out why, but she did feel that way.

As the guardians' walked up to the door to the hut, they entered with conation to make sure that there are no more traps.

Joey looked at Sue and Autumn as they both were holding on to each other for support he had to ask her.

"Sue, can you use your powers to detect if there is any more traps inside the hut, please?" Joey asked her. She looked at him, and shook her head no.

"I'm sorry Joey, but no I can't use my powers to detect if there are any more traps inside, I'm just too weak to even master enough energy to hold myself up without Autumn; I would be face down on the ground because of that attack hitting me." Sue said.

"It is alright, I know you would if you could. We'll just have to take that chance for more damn traps. But you do look like you have been through hell and back again." Joey said with a smile lifting her spirits just a little.

"Joey this is no time to crack a joke. But thanks for the laugh, it does help a little. So let us move in slowly to the hut. Now that she is knocked out for the count." Autumn said. Joey smiled again, but this time he went first to the door, and pushed it open slowly and looked around to make sure that there was no more traps for them. As he walked in he realized that all the traps have been undone with her being out cold for now. So they all walked into the hut looking around. It had a small kitchen, a bed that was at least a queen size where Alvaro walked over and laid down the girl. Alvaro looked at her as if seeing someone really different, but she did not look like she was any older than 16 or 17 years old. The others were still looking around the hut; they did not see any photos of her family or her, to tell them who she might be. There were a couple of windows that looked out into the forest, some stairs that lead up to the top deck which Sue and Autumn had went up. Joey could tell that she lived alone. She must have been on her own for a while. He went to the stairs while Alvaro was still staring at the girl on the bed. She was pretty in her own way, but to him she did not match Autumn, Sue, Alena, Faizah, or most of all Lola, but she was pretty.

"Alvaro if you keep starring at her Autumn might get the feeling you are looking for someone new, other than her." Joey said with a smile. Alvaro looked at him with disgust in his eyes.

"Man, no one can compare to her. She is pretty, but she is not up my lead. I like Autumn, might even love her. She knows that, but I get the feeling that this one is not like the other two. She is different that is true, but she seems to be heartbroken. I could tell by her eyes. I feel sorry for her." Alvaro said.

"Yeah, I know that feeling. Maybe when she finally comes too we can talk to her. Then maybe she won't feel so alone. I'm going to go to check on the girls. They went upstairs. Why don't you look in the small kitchen and see if you can find some food and drinks for us all. If you also could make a small in the fire place over there in the living room please. Stop starring you are creeping me out dude!" Joey said with a laugh.

"Okay, yeah I can do that. I will start us a fire and some food and drinks." Alvaro said heading to the kitchen as Joey went upstairs to find the girls looking out into the forest. Joey could see that it was a huge forest and that they have a long time before they find out where they are going from here. Alvaro started to look in the cabinets for some drinks and food. He spotted an ice box and opened it to find some frozen fish, fresh vegetables, and drinks inside. The drinks looked like orange soda or juice, and the vegetables looked like they have been picked just recently. So, Alvaro pulled them out and went over to the fireplace a seen that there was still wood in the fireplace. On the mantel there was a thing of matches and to the side of it some more wood that had been cut into small pieces. So he put some small wood in the fire and went out the door to see if he could find some died leaves for the fire. He spotted some just on the left side of the hut. He grabbed some and went back inside and put them in the fireplace, lite the match and put it on the dried leaves and then there was a fire going. Which felt good because it had started to get dark, and then it started to rain again some more, but this time it was pouring down like a waterfall over a cliff?

He went over to the door to notice that there was a small pouch and small rood over it, for which none of them had notice at first or the second time they came inside the hut. He looked out into the rain waiting for the fire to die down a little so he could put the fish in, and vegetables on. He had found some herbs to put on the fish, and a pan to put water in which he had notice was to the side of the ice box. The water was clear as day and must have been fresh from that day before everything happened. Then he held Sue, Joey and Autumn coming down the stairs. He turned around and walked away from the door and went over to the fire. Started putting the fresh vegetables, and fish in the fire as they all came into the small living room of the hut. Autumn walked over to him and put her hand near the fire to warm. Sue and Joey had did the same thing to warm their hands as well. He looked up at her. He notices that she still had the cuts from the attack not too long ago.

She looked down at him and saw the pain in his eyes. She knew that he was hurting from not protecting her from the attack by the woman.

"Alvaro, please don't look so hurt about earlier. It couldn't be help, she was very powerful. She was also tricked into doing it as well by the Dark Kingdom Zodiac." Autumn said to him in a low voice that he barely heard. He looked back up at her and could not put a smile on his face.

"I should have been able to protect you; a lot better than I did. Instead you damn near gave your life to protect us. I know that I couldn't be much help, but please I want to protect you with my own life." Alvaro said.

"No, you are wrong in that thinking. You protected us all from her attacks when you had to face her. If you had not stopped her, we all might be hurt, or worse dead. So please stop blaming yourself for what happened. If you don't have faith in me then there is no chance for us or the guardians', prince or for the Star Princess. So please don't think like that. I'm begging you to stop blaming yourself for what you don't have control over." Autumn said to him. He looked at her as if she had just punched him in the face. His mouth was open before he realized it, than closed. Joey had looked at her as if she was someone different from the first time he met her. Sue could not believe she was getting mad at him for wanting to protect her from harm. She looked at her and was wondering "why?" she would be upset with him.

"Autumn, why are you upset with Alvaro?" Sue asked when both Joey and Alvaro had walked away.

"I'm not upset with him for wanting to protect me, I'm upset with him because he keeps blaming himself for not being able to protect me, but he protected all of us. Also I'm upset with him for not having faith in me to be able to help and also protect the Star Princess and Prince." Autumn said.

"Oh. I see why. It happens, he is blaming himself for what happened in his own realm, because he didn't believe us and you got hurt. So he blames himself for what happened there." Sue said.

"I know that, but I wish he would just have faith and trust me some. I can take care of myself, but I also depend on my friends to also help." Autumn said.

"We would always be there for Alvaro, you, and the other guardians' as well." Sue said.

"I know you both would. I know all the guardians' would be there. I just want him to have trust and faith in my abilities that you guys do." Autumn said.

"I know you do. It is going to take him a while before he can forgive himself. It happens to the best of us." Sue said.

"You are right Sue. I will give him the time he needs." Autumn said. As Sue and her finished talking Joey and Alvaro came over to the fire place from the kitchen to check the fish, and vegetables. When Alvaro took the food from the fire place and put it on the small table in between the kitchen and the living room to eat. They heard thunder outside the hut. Hoping that the hut would hold though the night's storm; because it looks like they would be staying the night. Sue looked over at the sleeping woman on the bed wondering when she might wake up. When she does, they are hoping that she can give them some answers.

Sue turned back to the table with the food. Autumn had been watching her and looked in the same direction she had and then back at Sue understanding what she was thinking because it showed on her face. They continue to eat their dinner which was very good considering it was fish, vegetables, and an orange drink that tasted like soda to them. When they had finished eating they all went back to the fire and sat on the small couch that was in there just relaxing. Then they all started to fall asleep, the only ones that could stay up was Joey and Alvaro. They felt bad about eating the food without the woman's say so, but they had planned on asking her to come with them once they learned some more about her.

As the night got later and later, Joey and Alvaro felt that it would be okay to fall asleep for a little while without being attack by the General Jomo, for at least the night considering they had went up against him earlier in the day. They needed rest, and maybe in the morning can heal them all before heading out again. So Joey fell asleep on the couch, while Alvaro went over to where Sue and Autumn had fallen asleep to lay next to her. They got lucky after dinner to find a couple of blankets to use as mats and cover up with to stay warm next to the fire place.

Chapter 19

Someone had kicked Alvaro in the foot to wake him up. As he looked up it was the woman from yesterday. She looked down on him then walked over to the small couch where Joey was sleeping and smacked him to wake up. Joey jumped up ready for an attack before his notice that he had been wakened up by the woman from yesterday.

"Can I ask you why are you people in my house?" Woman said feeling angry.

"Do you remember us from yesterday?" Alvaro asked her.

"You are the people who attacked me, than turned and almost killed me." Woman said.

"It was you who attacked us first!" Sue said getting up after hearing them start talking. Autumn followed immediately after Sue had wakened up.

"I'm sorry, who are you people and what do you want?" Woman asked started to feel a little unsure why she wanted to be nice to these people she had never met before.

"Well, my name is Sue Stang; this is Autumn Williams, Joseph Ryan, and Alvaro Sky. We are guardians' that is given the mission to protect and find the Star Princess and Prince of the Majestic Star Kingdom." Sue said with a smile.

"So you really believe that the Star Princess and Prince are alive and kicking it." Woman asked.

"Well to answer your question we know who the Prince is. His name is Leroy Addams. The Star Princess we still need to find." Joey said.

"I see so the rumors are true. From what I hear the Dark Kingdom Zodiac has returned to finish what they started a thousand years ago." Woman said.

"Yes they have. They have also entered your realm and took control over you." Autumn said.

"I'm sorry about yesterday, but I don't remember much of it. It was like I was in a whole different place. By the way my name is Exie Green. I'm the guardian and Princess of the Crystal Star of the Nature Realm, welcome to my home." Exie said with a smile.

"It is nice to meet you Exie." Sue said.

"Let us talk over some breakfast. Do you mine helping me make the food?" Exie asked.

"Sure we would love to help. Considering it is the least we could do after eating your food without your permission." Sue said.

"It is okay, I own you at least that and shelter, for saving me from the Dark Kingdom Zodiac." Exie said with a huge smile.

"You are welcome. We didn't want General Jomo of Illusion that works for the Dark Kingdom Zodiac has you. So, Exie how old are you?" Sue asked.

"I'm 17 years old. I have been on my own for a long time now. Since my parents have been taken from by the darkness; by that terrible kingdom." Exie said with sad eyes.

"So, I can that you have had it very rough for a long time now. Sorry to hear that, we understand pain, lost heartache, and other things that go with that feeling." Sue said.

"Yeah, ever since that damn Dark Kingdom Zodiac showed up here in my realm, there has only been trouble." Exie said.

"Yeah, it seems no matter where they go or touch they destroy everything. They tried it in my realm, and others. So we are going to be your friends and get through this all together. If we do, would you join us as one of the guardians' that protect the

Majestic Star Kingdom, help find our Star Princess, as well as our prince." Autumn said.

"I will help you, if you will help me take back this realm and the people here? Can we bring them peace and not hardship?" Exie asked.

"Yes, we can. We will help you and the people of this realm." Alvaro said. So they all talked a little longer as it was still raining outside from the storm last night. Exie made them all something to eat. As they talked then was a really big bang outside of the hut.

"BANG!" as lightning hit a tree near the hut as everyone ran outside to get a better look another lightning strike took place, this time near all the guardians' making them all jump out of the way.

"What the hell is going with this lightning?" Exie asked.

"It seems to be control by something or someone." Autumn said too her.

"Who in Gods' Name could do this?" Exie asked again.

"The only ones we can think of is the Dark Kingdom Zodiac." Joey said.

"Yeah, they are the only ones that could bend this lightning to hit us." Sue answered.

"So it looks like we are going to have defiant this enemy before we can even relax for a minute or we might be turned into dust by that damn lightning." Joey said.

"So let us show them that it is not fun to mess with the guardians' of the Majestic Star Kingdom. Are you with us Exie?" Autumn asked.

"I'm with you. I'm tired of these good for nothing dark enemy messing with my realm and the people here." Exie said.

"So, show yourself?" Alvaro said.

"Well guardians' it would seem that by making lightning, it let you know I was here. So how about I give you something to be scared of." General Jomo said.

"So you show yourself. You still have not learned from that last few encounters we have had with you." Alvaro said.

"This time you guardians' won't make it out alive." General Jomo said.

"Bring it on then!" Exie said.

"DARK ILLUSION BLACK PANTHERS; DEADLY STRIKE!" General Jomo called as many black panthers' came out of nothing but light.

"ROSE PETAL SHOWER!" Exie called as many rose petals had turned into many thrones that caused a lot of damage.

"HEAVENS' ARROW!" Autumn called as she released an arrow into many panthers' taking out many at a time.

"DARKNESS STAR DANCE!" Alvaro called as his strikes turned to stars hitting many panthers' at once.

"DANCING SUN!" Sue called, as she looked like a whirl wind of light taking out as many panthers' as she could with her hits.

"I SUMMON THE ICE DRAGON, SILVEA; ICEBREG ATTACK!" Joey called as the attack hit the panthers' with huge blocks of ice, taking out the rest of the panthers' that had been summon into reality by General Jomo.

"You damn guardians', why don't you just give up. I can call forth as many illusions as I want. But if you want to save this realm from more destruction come to me at the castle in the forest of Dreams." General Jomo said to the guardians' as he was disappearing, but not all the way when he heard them call back.

"We will stop you. We will meet you at the castle in the forest of Dreams!" The guardians' called back.

"How do we get to the forest of Dreams Exie?" Sue asked. Exie looked at her with sad eyes, but she seemed to not hear her.

"Exie, can you hear me?" Sue yelled at her. That is when she looked at Sue and seemed to be out of it. But she answered her with the best she could.

"It would take at least two whole days to get to the castle in the forest of Dreams' from here. Just to warn you; that place is very dangerous. It can take your worst nightmares and make them reality. So if we go, and I do me we. I'm coming with you. We need to make sure that our hearts and minds are as one and there are no nightmares, hatred or anything along those lines to enter the forest, or it could kill us all. So let us rest today and tonight while we prepare for the journey to that damn forest. The castle is called the Light Rose Castle which once belonged to my family." Exie said as she started to pass out. She feels to the ground, but before she hit the ground Joey and Alvaro caught her, to keep her from hitting her head.

So they carried her into the hut and laid her on the bed to rest after using her attack so soon. She still had not recovered from using it against the guardians' when they first showed up the day before. So they let her rest and went about getting things ready to go for the next. They made some lunch of fruit, salad, and coconut milk to refresh them as the night was coming close. So they collected some firewood from the pale on the side of the hut to start the fire so it would be at least warm in the hut as it had started to rain yet again.

"I don't believe it, it is raining again." Sue said with a sour look on her face.

"It is like a damn rain forest in the Wind Realm, but if we go to the top of the hut we can see how pretty it is considering this is the Crystal Star of the Nature Realm." Joey said.

"Yeah, and the rain can be peaceful, even when you sleep. I was listening to it last night before I fell asleep. It made me feel claim." Autumn said with a smile.

"Yeah, it is different from what I'm used to. We didn't see as much rain in the Crystal Star of the Darkness Realm at all. When we did it was like black in color or gray. This rain is peaceful; it belongs to this realm as one of the things to like about besides the people, animals, plants, trees, and Exie which is another guardian." Alvaro said.

"Well said Alvaro, but there is something that Joey and I need to talk to Autumn and you about. If you two will please come down to the first level and sit at the table so we can talk." Sue said with a sad look in her eyes.

"Okay." They both said together as they all went down to where the light was dim, but nice and peaceful. Joey had pulled out some more candles and lite the wick. He sat one on the small table that barely sat four people at once so they could at least see each other. As Autumn and Alvaro looked at Sue and Joey they was wondering what was going on.

"So what did you need to talk to us about?" Autumn asked with a smile on her face but it didn't reach her eyes like the others have.

"Remember when I asked if you wanted to come here with us? Well the thing is that when we leave this realm at least two of you will have to by portal to the Crystal Star of the Water and Ice Realm, where Alena, Leroy, Rich, Andrew, Faizah, and Lola are. I can only take four people at a time with my portals. So if Exie choose to go with us to the next realm after this to find the last guardian, I need to know if it will be okay with the two of you if you go there." Sue asked them.

"To make it easy on you and your powers I think that we could do that. Do you agree Alvaro?" Autumn asked.

"Yes, I agree. At least I won't be going alone, and that I can be with you. I know that I might miss out on some action, but that is okay with me." Alvaro said.

"That is not true. You won't miss out on too much action, because the Water and Ice Realm is still being attack by the Dark Kingdom Zodiac. They keep trying to take our strongest guardian Alena of the Crystal Star of the Water and Ice Realm. The dark prince has already taken her once. He also has tired with Sue in the Crystal Star of the Fire Realm, and now the General Jomo wants Autumn for his own benefit. SO you still have to keep your guard up even there. So are you still willing to go?" Joey asked him.

"So it looks like I might not be missing out on any action at all." Alvaro said with a smile.

"Great then it is settling. Now we all need to get some sleep before we leave in the morning. Let us eat and then relax by the fire and try and rest the best we can." Joey said. So the friends ate some diner, finish getting things ready to go, as Joey had called his light dragon to help carry the stuff for them. They all settle down by the fire to relax, and Autumn was sitting in front of Alvaro, while Sue sat next to Joey just looking at the fire. Both Alvaro and Joey had fallen to sleep before Autumn and Sue did. So the girls got up and did more work, while also checking on Exie to make sure that she didn't drain herself to much from the battle they had that day.

"Sue, do you think that we will ever have peace again?" Autumn asked while wondering if that was the right thing to ask.

"I think that if we can find all the guardians', the Star Princess, along with the Prince we can have peace once again." Sue said.

"Did you ever want this type of life?" Autumn asked her.

"When I first found out I had powers was when I was very young. My parents always told me that I was very special that maybe one day someone like me would become my friend. Well that fall a new girl had started at my school, and she was very pretty that everyone looked at her like she was some kind new thing they could have. But she walked over to me and introduced herself. It was Alena Patches, we became friends quick. At the time I didn't know she had powers like me. As time went on she let her guard down around me and I knew she was who my parents had been talking about. Many years later while we were just starting middle school she had lost her father. He had been working and something really bad happened and he didn't make it. Anyway, she became somewhat distance, but in the end she still was my friend. She has the heart of gold. When we started our second year in second dray school she bet this boy name Leroy Addams. Any way we all became friends and they are also guardians. We don't choose this life for ourselves, but destiny has, and we embrace it the best we can. I would not have chosen this for me, but since I have become a guardian, I have mad friends that I never thought I would ever have. You are one of my best friends." Sue said.

"I see, so if you hadn't become a guardian you might not have met all of us. So how did you react when you first found out that you are a guardian of light and travel?" Autumn asked.

"Well, the funny thing with that is, I reacted really badly. Because I did react bad Alena had been taken because I couldn't take it. Now I would not give it up for nothing, because I am doing something others are not doing." Sue said.

"Thanks that make me feel really good. Because when I first came into my powers, I always felt alone until I met all of you. So now I don't feel that way. I feel that I'm doing something that really matters, and I can help out those who need my help and those who have less than me." Autumn said.

"I'm glad you feel that way." Sue said smiling.

"I'm glad too. I have friends now, and I don't feel so alone any more. Also I think I might be in love with Alvaro. He is so handsome, and he makes my heart skip a beat every time I look at him, or when he looks at me. Even more; when he smiles at me. Well, Sue it has been fun, I'm heading to bed now, thank you for the understanding." Autumn said.

"I'm glad that we had this time together again. It feels wonderful to be able to talk in peace before all hell breaks loose. HAHAHAHA!" Sue said while laughing. Autumn started to laugh as well making the guys to move in their sleep. So the girls head to bed on the floor, and Autumn looked at Alvaro once again and felt her heart skip and speed up as he breathed in and out. She smiled and was falling into a deep sleep.

Chapter 20

When morning had arrived Exie was standing in the door way looking out into the forest while every now and then she would look back at her friends sleeping on the floor, on the couch and really early in the morning she had woken up; and went over to Sue and woke her up having her move to the bed. She had done the same with Autumn, but she had refused to move away from Alvaro who was also a sleep on the floor next to her. She smiled at them letting them sleep some more. She knew that they had been up late last night getting everything ready to go, while she was passed out from over using her powers for two days in a row. After standing there for what seemed like hours, she headed out side and looked once again at how everything seemed to be different after a heavy rainfall. She went and got some more fire wood, and went back around to the front door of the hut to see that Alvaro had woken up and was standing in the door way to the hut. He smiled at her and went out to help her with the fire wood.

"Here let me help you?" Alvaro had said not waiting for an answer and took the fire wood from her. So she went back around to the side of the hut and grabbed some more so that the fire would really good, because she felt that this might be the last time she gets to stay in it, and wanted to remember what it was like to have friends over and share things, and food with. She that the journey she has in front of her was going to be a long one. She was ready for it. She knew the legend of the Majestic Star Kingdom, the Star Princess, and Prince that would someday be married a rule over them all with happiness, love, laughter, warmth, and peace. She also knew that she was born for this, and her parents did raise her to do so as well. She was going to make them proud of her no matter what.

Alvaro came around the hut looking for her, and he notice that she had grabbed more firewood and went over to take it from when she saw him heading her way she came out of her ravine and smiled at him and headed for the hut.

As she enter Autumn was awake now, but Joey and Sue are still a sleep. She had notice that the hut was warmer than it was when she first went outside. Alvaro had started the fire while she was thinking to herself. Autumn had started to cut potatoes to cook, some eggs, drinks where on ice, and some other foods that looked really good. She smiled at her and walked over to the fireplace, and put the wood down and went to help her out. Before she knew they were laughing, talking, and getting along, when the others' finally woke up.

"Did you two sleep well?" Exie asked. Sue looked at her and smiled. Joey got off the couch and went over to see what was cooking in the fireplace, and turned then smiled at her.

"Yeah, I slept well considering your couch isn't that big. The food smells really good. Is there still some left for us?" Joey asked.

"It is just getting done. There is enough for all of us. After we eat and clean up, we need to head out on our two day journey." Autumn said.

"Thanks you guys. Yes, I slept great as well." Sue said waiting for the food to get done. As she looked around the hut, she notice that what she had said to Autumn the night before was right on the nail head. Because without her friends she would not be right where she is now, and she might not have as many friends then what she has now. She smiled to herself, thinking that "if she had not been a guardian, she may not always been in danger which isn't true, with what the Dark Kingdom Zodiac was going to do if they have their way. But still, she could not help but be thankful for being who she is. She would not have Alena, Leroy, Exie, Autumn, Rich, Andy, Lola, Faizah, Alvaro, as well as Joey even though he is her cousin; any other way because she has made many friends on this journey which soon will come to an end and the really battle for all the realms will begin.

Joey looked at Sue and was wondering why she was smiling at everyone. He looked at her and then smiled himself.

"So little cousin what you smiling about?" Joey asked.

"I'm happy because of all the friends we have made. Also I know that in the end we will find the Star Princess, and Leroy will be happy to be with her. I know how he feels about Alena, but if that means the Star Princess and Leroy can save all the realms then it would have to be like that." Sue said feeling sad for what she just said knowing it will tear Alena apart because she truly loves him. She also made that comment because of the look on Joey's face.

"You know, I feel the same way. But I feel even more for our friends which finally admitted they liked each before we left for the Fire Realm. I do feel bad about that only because it would hurt me to no end if I could not be with Lola." Joey said.

"You know, you're right. So what are you going to do when you see Lola again?" Sue said with a smile than a giggle. That is when everyone looked in their direction. Joey's face turn beat red, and got up from the table not answering his cousin, not because he couldn't. It is because he wasn't sure how to act around Lola after being gone for a while. He had to be turning spring or summer in the Crystal Star of Water and Ice Realm now. Because they have been gone for over a year. Each realm seems to be longer and changing all the time. As he returned to the table to sit down, he looked at Sue and said nothing. The food had finished cooking after he had gotten up from the table to cool his head from that embarrassing moment with his cousin. So he ate his full and heading out the door to wait for the others to finish.

The next one to join him was Autumn, which was a change because she is usually after Sue when she eats. He looked at her and started to smile, he was glad that they are friends. He missed Lola very much, and wanted nothing more than to hold her, kiss her beautiful lips, and never let her go, that he was much temped to go with Alvaro, Autumn, or Exie back to the Water and Ice Realm. But he knows he can't until Sue and his mission was over to find the rest of the guardians'. So he started to count them off one by one to see how many was left for them to find.

"1. Autumn, 2. Alvaro, 3. Leroy, 4. Faizah, 5. Andrew, 6. Sue, 7. Lola, 8. Richard, 9. Exie, 10. Alena and 11. Himself. So they have found almost all of them. That only leaves one left to find, then we can return back to the Water and Ice realm to find the out what to do next in finding the Star Princess." Joey said as Autumn walked over to him.

"One what is left?" Autumn asked him.

"We need to find one more guardian than we can return to the Water and Ice Realm; Sue and me. Then we all can work together to find the Star Princess." Joey said.

"You mean the Star Princess and the Prince, right?" Autumn asked a little confused.

"No, we just need to find the Star Princess, because Leroy Addams which is the guardian of the Crystal Star of the Elemental Realm is the Prince for which we seek." Joey said.

"So you have met the prince who will marry the Star Princess and bring peace, happiness, love, and kindness to all the realms. Who will also bring the Majestic Star Kingdom back?" Autumn said to him.

"Yes, I do mean the one in the same." Joey said starting to laugh when the others finally joined aspect Exie she was still inside the hut taking everything in before leaving. So the guardians' waited for her to finish before heading into the forest again. She walked over to them and was ready to go when she felt as if she was doing the right thing.

"We need to head east from here to get to the castle I told you about and the forest of Dreams. Please watch where you walk because it can get really bad with footing and stuff. So if you are not use to this kind of travel over forest floors please stay next to someone." Exie said looking at her new friends and then smiled.

"Okay, I will stay next to Autumn that way we can make sure to use healing if it is needed with me being her support." Alvaro said smiling at Autumn.

"Thanks, but I think you need me to be the support because I'm use to this type of walking." Autumn said while smiling back at him.

"Sue and I are used to it as well. Because we go hiking all the time back in the Water and Ice Realm with friends and family all the time. But still it is good to have a support no matter what." Joey said.

"I agree with him. So it is safer that way as well." Sue said.

"Okay than. Shaw we go then?" Exie asked.

"Yeah!" All they said together.

So they all headed in the direction that Exie had pointed them in. She joined them to the forest of Dreams. She knew that it would be a trap considering it was the Dark Kingdom that was behind everything. She wanted to trust these people and believe that they are as good as they say they are, but it was just too hard to trust just anybody after what happened when she was younger. It seemed to be a whole old life that she can't remember. But still, it was something about them that made her what to trust them. She had to see if their hearts where pure, and if so they could overcome everything. It was a test even she needed to do herself. It was that type of test that would help you face your worst fears. Hers were over whelming to the least. So they walked on, it would take a few days to get there. Joey would not be able to summon any type of animal where they were heading. She hated doing this, but it was the only way to see her family again. That is what he had said to her, when she first met him. But she did not trust Jomo very much if at all. There was something about the way he had said it to her. "If you stop those people from the Dark Kingdom Zodiac, you will be able to see your parents, friends, and etc. again really soon. You have to kill them first; if it doesn't work even with my help then you can always take them to the Forest of Dreams where their worst nightmares come to life. Just remember you can't trust them, but you can trust me." But still there was something in his voice that made her not want to trust hardly or not at all. With these people she knew that they were kind and nothing like the people she heard of from the Dark Kingdom Zodiac, but still it was even hard to trust them a little. As she kept walking and thinking about what has happened in the last 48-72 hours of her life that there was something sticky in the air she did not like.

As they walk she looked around to see where they were at. It was the forest just before the Forest of Dreams. This forest was no better than that damned forest of Dreams, because in this forest your dreams can become reality, it is just as dangerous as the Forest of Dreams which bring your worst nightmares to life.

"Everyone listen up, as we enter the next part of this forest it is just like the Forest of Dreams, but it can make your heart's true come to life and you will not want to leave it behind, but you must stay focus on your mission and where we are heading. You don't want to get caught in this forest wanting something that is not true. Please remember this." Exie said. As she turned from the others.

"Okay." They all said together. Alvaro grabbed Autumn's hand and turned to her. He pulled her in to his arms and before she knew he was kissing her on the lips, and after words smiled at her.

"You are my dream; I thought would never come true." Alvaro said to her. She started to tear up from what she felt as the warmth of his lips and hands started to leave her. She looked at him and smiled, she leaned in and kissed him harder this time and wrapped her hands around his neck and kissed even deeper and longer to let him know her own feelings.

"You are all I ever wanted in my life. I have never had a dream like this before, but you are my dream which is my reality so let us get through this forest and be on our way to finding the Star Princess and Prince, okay?" Autumn asked him still smiling.

"You got it my love." Alvaro said, as he grabbed her hand and held on tighter than before, and then they moved through the forest after Exie. They both looked back at Sue and Joey to see if they were still behind them and realized that they both had moved away from each other and seemed to be in a dazed.

"EXIE WAIT! IT IS JOEY AND SUE; THEY SEEM TO BE IN A DAZE!" Autumn yelled at Exie she stopped looked back and saw that they do look to be in a daze. Then they started to here laughing, she came running to Alvaro and Autumn and grabbed them by the arms and pulled them behind a tree.

"What do they truly want?" Exie asked them both.

"I am not sure; we just met before coming here." Alvaro said.

"I know what they both want. I have been with them long enough to get to know them and their feelings. They both have someone they had to send back to the Water and Ice Realm where the other guardians' are meeting up. Sue had told me once that she had fallen in love with another guardian. That guardian is the guardian of the Crystal Star of the Earth Realm, Prince Andrew. For Joey it was with another guardian of the Crystal Star of the Fire Realm, Princess Lola. That is what they truly want right now because they miss them so much." Autumn said with a sad look on her face.

"How can we help them?" Alvaro asked as he heard laughing again.

"We will have to fight who ever might be forcing them to see what their hearts' true desire is." Exie said.

"I can try using my Slight Wall Shield to put up a barrier." Alvaro said.

"Okay that might help somewhat with the air here." Exie said.

"I can use my power to make them open their eyes to reality. The thing is you both would have to stay behind them, me and out of the way so that my powers have a chance to work on them. It won't hurt you, but it might make you blind for a few hours for which we don't need right now. Not only that, I keep hearing laughing which I do know the voice of that General Jomo of Illusion. He could be adding his powers to the forest power to incest them. What is the name of this forest anyway?" Autumn asked.

"It is the forest of Nightmares." Exie said.

"Okay let us get started." Alvaro said.

"Alvaro will use his powers first, I will use my powers second, and Autumn, you will use your powers last. I will use my Spring Dance; which is like healing the heart and the head. It only works if they both are under the powers of Illusion; from both the forest and General Jomo. It is like a warm tender rain. It won't affect you two which I am not sure why; you are both not under the illusion of the Forest of Nightmares. Okay." Exie said.

"Okay!" Autumn answered.

"We are not under the illusion is because our hearts have what it desires. Okay." Alvaro said.

"I see, okay then let us save our friends." Exie said. As they ran over to Sue and Joey that is when an Illusion hit them so hard that it knocked them all three on their asses. They could see the illusions clearly as day comes and night falls. It was just like they had said to Exie that their hearts desires those guardians. So the guardians got back up, and this Alvaro ran around to the back of Joey and Sue to use his powers' Exie ran behind them as well so that she could use her powers, while Autumn ran around the front to use her powers.

"SILENT WALL!" Alvaro called as a shield was put up around them.

"SPRING DANCE!" Exie called, and then there is a rain so warm full of love and it did start to clear their heads and hearts. Sue and Joey both started to come out of the Illusion when someone started to laugh again.

"SHOW YOURSELF GENERAL JOMO!" Alvaro called.

"Well guardian of Darkness Realm, it would seem you all are trying to wake those two up from their most wonderful dream. How cruel you are." General Jomo said.

"It is not cruel for what you are doing. They are just being shown what they truly want. This is cruel of the Dark Kingdom Zodiac." Autumn said.

"Well guardian of Healing and Spirit, what will you do about it? You were also given a choice between yourself and your friends. Do you still feel the same way as before?" General Jomo asked with a cruel smile on his fac.

"Yes, she stands by what she said before. You will not have her. She belongs to no one. But she has my heart." Alvaro said.

"Well, it looks as if your friends don't matter to much to you both." General Jomo said.

"Y-O-U A-R-E W-RO-O-NG!" Autumn said.

"Then prove me wrong guardian." General Jomo said.

"You got it! AUTUMN YOU'RE POWERS!" Alvaro called to her over the rain now coming down harder. Exie just was standing still calling the rain and listening to what is being said.

"HEAVEN'S DOORS!" Autumn called as four doors appeared with oak wooden doors, with Angel Wings on them. With gold emboldening in the feathers of the wings. Then as the doors opened up releasing bright white light of healing and energy. Exie and Alvaro had to turn their heads to keep from looking into that light so tense. Making General Jomo disappearing, while coving up his eyes with a smirk on his face.

"I WILL BE WAITING FOR YOU GUARDIANS IN THE FOREST OF DREAMS. THEN I WILL HAVE YOUR LIVES!" General Jomo called as he had to disappear back into the darkness away from the light of healing and spirit.

As the light and the doors started to disappear back into the light of healing and spirit, Sue and Joey was shaking their heads wondering why they had just seen some bright light. It felt warm, kindness, love, and happiness. They looked around wondering what just happened.

"So explain what is going on?" Joey asked.

"You fell under the illusion of the forest of Nightmares, and General Jomo." Autumn answered. They just looked at her, and then realized what she was saying. Then feel to their knees to grab themselves and hold on to what they had seen.

"What were you seeing?" Exie asked.

"I was seeing Lola and holding her in my arms again. Wanting to kiss her, hold her, and started to believe that this mission was over. I also was seeing my other friends, I miss them very much." Joey said.

"How about you Sue?" Exie asked her.

"I was seeing Andrew again. He walked over to me pulled me into his arms, kissed my forehead, hand, and then on my lips. He held on to me as if, he would never see me again." Sue said with a sad look in her eyes.

"Look you two, you will see them soon enough. We just have to get through this and to the forest of Dreams. Then to the castle in that forest. We need to keep moving. We will rest for a little while so you can get your heads on straight. As well as eat and drink." Exie said.

"Your right. We need to get our heads on straight. We need to eat as well as drink something. Let us rest for now." Sue said. As they all set down to rest for a minute and get their heads on straight. So they ate and drank something. Then they all got back up and started to move to the forest of dreams. They knew they had to rest before they reached the forest of Dreams. They all moved faster this time, they managed to get out of the forest of Nightmares before night fall. They enter a clearing and set up camp there. It was filled with dandy lions, tulips, daisies, and whipping willow trees. So they set up the tent and found a fresh water spring near by the camp site that they had brought some back to the camp to cook with, and drink. As everyone got some wood for a small fire to cook over, Exie had pulled out of her rucksack some cut up vegetables, some already cooked meat, and some can fruit for them all to share. Alvaro had started the fire; Joey put some water in a bottle for everyone, so they have something to drink the next day. Sue opened the can fruit because it had one of those pop open tops and Autumn helped Exie cook dinner. It turned out to be a stew of some kind. Everyone enjoyed the small but really good meal. As they all were setting around the fire just watching it, they all looked up at the stars which were shining brightly at night. So they all just relaxed and rested before heading to bed.

"I will take first watch." Joey said.

"Are you okay to do that?" Exie asked.

"Yeah, I think I have everything set in my head and heart. I can look forward to her smile when this mission is over." Joey said.

"I will take next watch." Sue said.

"Okay, then I will take the third watch. Everyone can get some rest tonight. We can leave at first dawn." Exie said.

"Okay, then Autumn and I can take the early watch before we head out. We can also get some food ready to eat and drinks for morning." Alvaro said.

"Sounds great to us." Everyone agreed on. So Joey took first watch for a couple of hours.

As he was on watch he started to think of all his friends old and new. He felt that he had come very far. He let Sue sleep a little longer, then went and got her up. Sue got up a little sleepy, but still got up. She took her watch, she knew that her friends are worried about her, but she also knows that she can count on them any time. So she took her watch and felt that they could do this as long as they are together. Sue got up and went to get Exie to find that she was not in her cot in the tent while everyone was sleeping she must have went outside, but Sue looked all over for her without going too far from camp. Still she could not find her. So, Sue took the third watch, then went and got Autumn and Alvaro up for their watch and morning duty. Sue went back to sleep, she did not say anything to the other about

Exie disappearing, but maybe she will come back in the morning before they leave.

Autumn went and got things to eat; they still had water from the night before. She just filled up the water bottles some more to make sure that they had enough. Alvaro had kept watch at the door to the tent while the others slept. As soon as the sun broke the day light Autumn went and got everyone.

She got Exie up first, but to discover that she was not there. "EVERYONE PLEASE GET UP, EXIE IS MISSING!" Autumn yelled as Sue jumped up and Joey fell out of the cot he was sleeping in.

"What is going on?" Alvaro asked as he ran into the tent.

"Exie isn't here. Does anyone know what happened to her?" Autumn asked.

"I'm not sure; she was here when I got Sue up for watch. Sue was she here when it was time for her watch?" Joey asked.

"When I went to get her up, she was gone. I didn't say anything, because I was thinking she might be looking around the area for enemies. I was thinking she would be back by now. Maybe she went ahead of us to the forest of Dreams?" Sue answered.

"Maybe, so let us pack up and start heading to the forest of Dreams. It should not be far from here. Maybe by mid-morning we will be at the forest of Dreams." Autumn said.

"Yeah, and maybe on the way we might run into her." Sue said.

"Okay." Everyone said together. So they all headed out of camp and headed east to the forest of Dreams. They knew that General Jomo would be waiting for them; this time might just get what he wants. So they needed to hurry on their way. The guardians' had to make haste because they also needed to find Exie on their way, there is the chance without her they could get lost. So they headed in the way she had said. As it hit mid-morning almost noon, for it was only a few minutes before noon. So they stopped to rest eat, and drink quickly, they sat in a nearby tree line so they could keep watch on all sides. As they were watching Autumn notice that there was a lot of trees in the direction she had been guarding. Then she realized that, that was the forest of Dreams.

"Everyone look the forest of Dreams. Don't ask how I know, I just do." Autumn said.

"It looks like we made it. Maybe Exie is in there?" Sue said.

"Maybe, but we need to head to it. So let us get moving." Alvaro said.

"Then let us go." Joey said. The guardians' headed to the forest of Dreams. As they enter the forest they could feel the power of the illusion which the forest puts on the people who enter it. So they all took a deep breathe then headed in. They started to walk as if the ground started to shack them to their knees, but they were able to keep their balance. The forest has a lot of weeping willow trees, one tree, oak trees, maple trees, walnut trees, and all kinds of fruit trees. There were many different kinds of flowers that they could not see all at once then they ran into something hard. Autumn reached out her hand only to be pushed back by some dark power.

"What do you think it might be?" Autumn asked out loud what she was thinking.

"It might be a shield or barrier." Joey said.

"Let me she if I can get through it?" Sue said as she walked over to touch it. As she reached out her hand she was pushed back so far that she lost her balance and hit the ground hard. She got back up holding her left hand; she was looking around then realized that it was some dark barrier, keeping them all out of the forest.

"It is a barrier, maybe if I open a portal for the other side we can get through." Sue suggested.

"The only way, is to at least try." Alvaro said.

"Be careful, we don't need you to get hurt in the meantime. We also need to find Exie." Joey said.

"Okay here goes nothing." Sue said.

"Good luck." Autumn said.

"PORTAL OF LIGHT AND TRAVEL, OPEN US A DOOR TO GO THROUGH THE DARK BARRIER!" Sue called as a portal opened up for them to past safely through. Before they knew it the barrier started to disappear, and before them was not only General Jomo, but also Exie. Too all their surprise that she was with him, but not by force.

"What is going on here?" Sue demeaned.

"Can't you see guardian of Light and Travel." General Jomo said while laughing.

"I can see clearly, what is going on. What did you do to her to; make her believe a word that comes from you?" Alvaro said.

"You are wrong. He isn't the enemy. YOU ARE!" Exie said.

"No that is wrong. We are the good guys who help to protect the Prince, Star Princess, and the Majestic Star Kingdom." Autumn said.

"Prove me wrong then." General Jomo said laughing really loud.

"What do you think we are here for?" Joey said.

"What did he promise you Exie?" Alvaro asked getting very mad.

"He told me if I would find the Star Princess, Prince, and then I can see my family again." Exie said looking even sadder than she did days ago.

"What if we can tell you who the Prince is? Then would you believe us?" Autumn asked.

"If you know who the Prince is. Why didn't he come with you?" General Jomo said with a huge smile on his face.

"That is none of your business Jomo. We are going to finish you off here and now." Autumn said.

"I like it when you get angry. Show me how you plan to defeat me guardians' of the Majestic Star Kingdom." General Jomo said smiling even more.

"WHAT? WHAT DID YOU JUST SAY?" Exie said as she heard what the General Jomo said.

"Never mind that. We have work to do. If you ever want to see your family again you will take care of them." General Jomo said.

"I'm not sure who to believe. Them or you?" Exie said grabbing her head. She fell to her knees and started to rock back and forth holding her. Crying not sure what to do.

"You are worthless, to us now guardian of the Crystal Star of the Nature Realm." General Jomo said.

"YOUR WRONG!" Sue said.

"DANCING SUN!" Sue called. As two dangers came out of nowhere. Sue looked as if she was covered in sunlight, she moved so gracefully, that it looked as if she was dancing. The attack hit General Jomo, as it hit it looked as if he had been struck more than once by the draggers. Before he knew what happened he had been knocked back many feet.

"I SUMMON THE KING SERPENT, LEVIATHAN, AND TSUGNAMI WAVE!" Joey called. As a huge wave of water came at General Jomo, and out came a huge snack like dragon with Joey riding on his back carrying what looked to be a Holy Lance. The wave and holy lance hit the Dark General making him fall to the ground.

"DARKNESS STAR DANCE!" Alvaro called as his attack hit the Dark General head on. Hitting him with a thousand stars.

"HEAVEN'S ARROW!" Autumn called as an arrow of holy light hit the Dark General Jomo causing him to fall even more making him weak, but still not enough to stop him. Exie was still holding herself and crying, hurt that she had been tricked into doing mean and bad things to these people. But the arrow of Heaven did more than cause harm to General Jomo it created a light and in that light there was people who were looking down on them.

"Listen to me, my dear daughter you have never been alone. We have always been with you." A voice said from the light.

"Mother?" Exie said looking up and still crying. She could see people looking at her.

"Listen, the people that have been felling your head up with things like to trust, love, or believe that you could never love again. They are wrong, the people you need to put your trust into now and believe them is the guardians' that you have become friends with." Shianne said.

"How can I love, trust, or even believe in them if I can't do that for myself. I have betrayed them so much." Exie said.

"Listen to what she is telling you my love." Another voice said.

"Is that you, my love, Darla?" Exie asked.

"Yes, there is another you will love even more than me. Trust in the guardians here and believe in yourself." Darla said.

"I will try. It will not be easy to do." Exie said.

"That is why you have us." Sue said.

"We are your friends." Autumn said.

"We will always be here for you no matter what." Joey said.

"You can do it. Believe in yourself. Please trust in us, as we trust in you, and believe in you." Alvaro said.

"Listen to them. They will not lend you down a wrong path. They will lend you down the right one." Darla and Shianne said together. As they did the power of the Heaven's Arrow started to disappear just as General Jomo was getting to his feet.

"I CALL FORTH THE POWER OF ILLUSION, DARKMARE COME TO ME; PUT THESE GUARDIANS' OUT OF THEIR LIVES!" General Jomo called as a dark shadow had appeared.

"NOT A CHANCE! SILENT WALL SHIELD!" Alvaro called as he jumped in front of all the guardians' protecting them from the darkness that was about to take them away.

"I HAVE HAD IT WITH YOU AND YOUR DARK KINGDOM ZODAIC. YOU HAVE TAKEN MY FAMILY, MY LOVE, AND NOW YOU ARE TRYING TO TAKE MY FRIENDS FROM ME. NOT HAPPENING!" Exie said.

"WHAT WILL YOU DO GUARDIAN?" General Jomo answered her back.

"STOP YOU! ROSE VINE WHIP, ROSE THONE ATTACK!" Exie called. As the attack hit General Jomo making him turn to dust with a million thrones at once. A light opened up and as the guardians' stepped though it they were in the Rose Castle of the

Crystal Star of the Nature Realm. Sitting on the throne was her mother and father.

"You have done well my dearest daughter, but your journey is just starting. Darla had given her life to protect you all this time since you left at the age of 15 years old. You are now 20 year old. You are very beautiful. Please help these guardians' to find the Star Princess, Prince, and Majestic Star Kingdom so that there is peace once again in the entire realm. Guardian of Light and Travel there is a portal here in the wall next to the thrones, the one on your right lends you to the Crystal Star of the Unknown Realm, and on your left lends to the Crystal Star of the Water and Ice Realm. Please be careful from here on out." Queen Shianne said.

"Okay, Joey, Exie, and me will head to the Unknown Realm. Autumn and Alvaro this is where we part ways. Is this okay with everyone?" Sue asked.

"Yes." They all agreed on. So Autumn and Alvaro held hands and walked through the portal to the Water and Ice Realm, and Joey, Exie after hugging her mother and father bye, and Sue walked through the portal to the Unknown Realm.

Crystal Star of the Unknown Realm

Chapter 21

As the three of them had stepped out of the portal into the Crystal Star of the Unknown Realm, they had stepped into a town of some kind. Not sure what kind just some kind. They see people walking around them, but they had stepped into an alley where the portal had opened up for them. It was different from all the other towns they had been too. Sue looked like she was in the twilight zone. Which is not normal for her because she has never seen that type of show before? It did seem that way though. It is going to take a lot of planning and thinking before they can go any were. So they stepped out of the alley and got into the flow of the people. It was a busy place, there was a lot of people, many inns, many shops, and so on. It was like living in a really big city. This place also had some wired color; it would be one color then change to another. It was a rainbow changing from red, to purple, to white, to pink, to blue, to green, and so on. You could see almost all colors at once as well.

As the guardians' stepped out from the alley too go look for either an inn or restaurant, they looked around the realm they were in and notice many different things. As they looked around they choose to go left in search of at least an inn, if not they would try and find a restaurant.

So one of the first things' the three guardians did was look for an inn to at least eat and rest up before heading out to look for the last and finally guardian. The guardians had been walking around the small city for a few hours before they came across a restaurant and inn in one. It looked to be a really big inn with many nice things like more than one restaurant in it. The inn they came across was called the Breaking of Dawn Inn; it was more like a hotel than any inn they had ever seen. So they walked into the inn through the routing door. As they stepped inside of the lobby to the inn; Breaking of Dawn. It had a marble floor the color of white sand, Cream to a tan color, chairs, couches, and tables to sit at while waiting to go to their rooms, or for customer service to be free to check in. So they all walked over to the counter that stretched almost the whole lobby which was really big with a dorm shape window to see the starry sky outside in the evening. The counter was made up of the same marble as the floor was, just had added plants to give it that home feeling. There was lady, and a couple of guys helping other customers to check in for the night, so they waited on the couches until someone were free to help them. Then Joey's stomach started to growl because he was hungry. People had started too looked their way when a little girl said something to them.

"Hey, mister there is a really nice restaurant to your right through the door over there by the steps and shops. It is called the Crystal Palace, it has really great food." Little girl said as she was being pulled by her mother away from them.

"Thank you for the help!" Joey yelled at her as she was going through the routing doors to the inn. She looked back at them and smiled waving bye as she was leaving the inn with her mother.

"So, we have some place to check out to eat at, after we get a room to stay in." Joey said to the others.

"Yeah, but just one question? Does anyone have any money?" Exie asked.

"I have some, not much. It should be enough to get a room for the night and get something to eat for dinner and breakfast in the morning." Sue said.

"But will your money work in this realm?" Exie asked.

"Not sure, but I have notice that whenever we change realms, our money changes with it as well." Sue said.

"Where did you get money from?" Joey asked.

"From the Darkness Realm, when Autumn and I was working in the Twilight Inn. It was from our tips we got. Which we were able to keep." Sue said.

"Oh, so how much do you have?" Joey asked.

"I have enough for a room and to be able to eat tonight and tomorrow morning. That should be good enough for you. I also have enough money so that we can get supplies if we need to." Sue said.

"Okay." Joey said.

"It looks like the counter is free from people. Now maybe we can get some help." Exie said.

"Okay, let us go up there and see if we can get a room." Sue said as she got up from the couch she had sitting on with Exie. They all got up and went over to the counter, but no one was there. So Joey rang the bell on the counter for someone to come help them. A woman had stuck her head out from the back room to see who was at the counter.

"Hello there, give me a minute. I will be with you soon." Counter woman said.

"It is okay; please take your time we are not in a hurry." Exie said smiling. The counter woman looked back and smiled at her to let her know that she herd her. After about 15 minutes the woman came from the back and met them at the counter.

"I'm so sorry about that. We had stock that needed done and it had to be done before we leave for the day and the next shift takes over. So how can I help you young folks?" Counter woman said.

"We would like a room for the night?" Sue answered.

"Okay, let me check to see if we have some still open." Counter woman said.

"Okay." Sue said waiting for her to check to see if there is rooms open for them.

"It looks like we have two rooms open. One has a double bed and the other is a king size bed with a couch in the room. Would you like both rooms or just one?" Counter woman said.

"How much are the rooms per night?" Sue asked.

"It depends on what you are looking for. Our starting rate is $75.00 per night for the king sized bed. For the double bed; it will be $55.00 per night. We are having a special going on this week with each room. So the rates are lower, but we are also offering a free breakfast to our guest." Counter woman said.

"Okay, we would like to have the double bed just for one night stay. We will need a wakeup call in the morning around 9am if that is possible?" Sue answered.

"Yes, we can arrange that for you. I will need a credit card, photo ID, and the payment." Counter woman said.

"Okay, here is my master card, my ID, and we will be paying cash for the room. Is this okay?" Joey said.

"Yes, that will be just fine sir. Name please?" Counter woman said.

"It is Joseph Ryan; here is my ID and my Master Card" Joey said.

"I also will need your ages and names, please." Counter woman asked.

"Sue Stang, age 16 years old, Joseph Ryan, and 17, and Exie Green age 20." Sue answered the counter woman. As Joey was handing her his credit card, master card.

"Oh, sir it looks like you are just 17 years old. Are you with a parent or guardian?" Counter woman said.

"I'm their guardian. Here is my ID. My name is Exie Green; I am on a field trip with them for school. The rest of our group is staying at another inn in the area. They were full so we had to come to a different inn for the night until a room opens up for us. We will also need a wakeup call in the morning around 8:30am please." Exie said giving her ID to the woman at the counter.

"Okay, this will be fine. All I need you to do is sign that you are their guardian, and sir I need you to sign for the master card.

Please enjoy your stay with us. The cost will be $59.13 with tax and all." Counter woman said.

"Okay, here is the money for the room." Sue said handing her the money for the room.

"Okay, it is processing, and it has been approved. Your room number is 1645 which is on the 16th floor room number 45. Yes, we can set you an automotive call for 8:30am." Counter woman said; handing three key cards to them all for the room. Joey had finished signing the paper for the credit card, as Exie had finished signing the check in papers for them all.

After receiving their key cards, they headed to the elevators to head up to the 16th floor to room 45. As the elevator had arrived, they all stepped in and pushed the number for floor 16. As they looked around the elevator to see if anyone else had stepped in, notice that they were the only ones. The elevator looked just like the lobby. It had a marble floor, with wood designs for the wall; it also had gold rails on it too. So that you could hold onto just in case you might fall, or if you are scared to ride the elevator. It took the elevator to get to the 16th floor about 10 minutes. There was no stop in between the first floor and their own floor, which they all was very glad, because they got tired of being starred at by people.

Finally when the elevator stopped at the 16th floor, they all stepped out to see that; on this floor there was carpet of the color of golden-brown, and the walls was the same as the elevator, which made the carpet stand out which was really great. They needed to head to their room, so they looked at the signs to which way they needed to go. As they looked at the sign it turned out that the sign read "to your left rooms 15-30, and to your right rooms 31-45" so they all turned right to head to their room. Their room was all the way down to the end of the floor which was a good few minutes' walk from the elevator. So they all head in that direction which met that the room might be big or could be small.

"When we get into the room, let us put our stuff away, and take a shower before we head to dinner. So that we are clean." Joey said.

"We agree with you." Sue and Exie said together.

So as they reached the door to their room, Exie inserted her key card to open the room. As they opened the door they looked into the room to find that it was in between big and small. It was enough room for them to sleep, and it did give them some space. So they all settle in their room, and they all choose to take a quick shower before heading out for dinner. Sue went first because she had the most dirt on her from the battle before they enter this realm. She also knew that if they were not attack going to the inn, it was sure to come when they step out for the night. The bathroom looked very nice it had the same color marble floor as the rest of the inn did. In the bathroom had a different type of wall paper, the wall paper had sun flowers and other colors of different flowers though the wall paper? Then Exie went after Sue, she was very glad that Joey had suggested it. As she had finished her shower she put on her favorite outfit, it was green carpi pants, white and yellow one shoulder tank top, and flip fops to accompany the outfit. As she had finished she came out of the bathroom and sat down on the bed that was to the left with Sue, who must have turned on the TV to watch, then Joey got up from the bed on the right side of the room, and headed into the bathroom.

He was getting undressed when he notice that he had an eight pack, his skin was darker, and his hair lightened up some. He looked at himself for a little bit, before getting into the shower. After looking at himself and realizing that with all the battles with the Dark Kingdom Zodiac that he had muscles everywhere. So he finished undressing and turned the shower on and made the water lurk warm. He got in and took a quick shower and got out after cleaning up, and washing everywhere; his hair and body. He got out dried off, put on his jean shorts, and sleeveless shirt before heading out of the bathroom. He put his tennis shoes back on with a clean pair of white ankle shocks. Then sat down on the bed to rest before they all went down to eat. As they all were watching TV, something had come to them; it was like a light was turned on in their heads. This realm is really different from all the ones they have been to.

On the TV was news cast about the weather, it looked like it my storm really bad. So they were glad that they had a place to stay the night. After the news was over they left the room went to the elevator, and went back down to the first floor to head to the restaurant in the inn, Breaking of Dawn, which turned out to be more a club than a restaurant, but they did have a menu of food. So they looked at the menu to see what they had, they had some money but not much. So they all order the cheapest food on the menu. Sue order a chef salad, Exie orders a Leaf Salad, and Joey order potato cheddar soup. They all gad sweet ice tea, which was light and very good; also the music wasn't bad either. So they stayed and listen to the music for a while, but then everything went silent. They stood up to see what was going on, then all the lights went off, as if the power was cut from the club. They knew what would come next, the Dark Kingdom Zodiac was about to attack them, somehow and some way.

"Welcome to my party of the year! I want to welcome some special guests that have been around. Welcome guardians' to the Unknown Realm, I'm your host, General Abria the General of Corruption. Please enjoy this party while you can, because this is also your last party." General Abria said with a very high laugh.

"So you finally show yourself." Sue said.

"It took you long enough." Joey said.

"I was waiting for the right time. Now it has come, can you overcome my darkness and push forward." General Abria said.

"Well you have us, show us your powers." Exie said.

Chapter 22

"**D**ARKNESS SPEAR FLASH!" General Abria called covering them all in pitch blackness. Then they were hit with spears that are so black they could not see the spears coming. So, Sue stepped up and used her own powers to give light to everyone.

"SUN BLAST!" Sue called. Making it so bright as if the sun was summoned. As the guardians' looked around they could tell that the people are all in a zombie light trance. The people kept dancing to the music when the guardians' realized that was the cause of their dancing, it was draining their energy. As they kept dancing making it hard for the guardians' to move, so they jumped on top of the both they had been sitting at when the Dark Kingdom Zodiac showed their ugly face here in this realm. So instead of trying to hurt the dances, they moved to another table, to avoid injury to the people. So Exie started to gather power to use against the General Abria, but before she could something hit her in the back. She went tumbling off the table before Joey could grab her, the dancers stopped dancing and grabbed her, and they held her so that her energy could be drained by the music. Then they all started to fall to the ground as the music kept playing.

"We need to do something about that damn music; it sounds like nails on a freaking chalk board." Sue said.

"How are we going to stop the music, if I summon a dragon in here, it might be more trouble than it is worth?" Joey said.

"Then let me use some more of my power to at least get to Exie, cause if not she could be dead before our own eyes." Sue called back.

"Give it a try." Joey suggested.

"SUN SHOWER!" Sue called as a lot of look like spears came raining down on the people hold onto Exie. As the attack hit them, they let her go, so Sue ran over to her to keep her from hitting her head on the floor.

"Well done Light and Travel guardian. Try this on for size. DARKNESS THRONES!" General Abria called. As a lot of thrones hit her in her back and side, she feels to the ground holding her side which got the worst of the attack. She was on her knees trying to hold her side, as well as trying to protect Exie.

"SUN SHIELD!" Sue called as another attack came this time; she was able to avoid injury. She was also able to protect Exie, who started to come too.

"What is going on?" Exie asked.

"You got hit really hard in the back which made you lose conclusions." Sue told her.

"Where is Joey?" Exie asked again, but more awake this time.

"I'm alright. Sue, I'm going to have to call one of my dragons, to at least slow her down." Joey said.

"Please be careful, the people are not at fault here. Okay?" Sue answered him.

"ROCK DRAGON, IRANETH. ROCK SLIDE!" Joey summoned his rock dragon. The attack hit the people only to knock them out. As the attack hit Abria, she moved by jumping out of the way and off stage.

"Well done guardian of summoning. You are better than I have heard. Please do keep entertaining me, I'm enjoying myself." Abria said laughing very loudly.

"SPRING SHOWER DANCE!" Exie called as rain started to pour down, but turning into swards of rain hitting Abria before she had a chance to react. The attack came a lot quicker than she had expected from the guardians.

"DANCING SUN!" Sue called as she was holding to daggers in her hand and she moved as fast as light. The attack was like she had been dancing with someone. She hit Abria right in the crest causing her to curse out loud and fall back only to get to her feet holding her arm, which was bleeding now by many cuts on her arm from Sue's attack.

"You stupid bitch, I'm not done with you guardian of Light and Travel. Just you wait; pay backs will be tens of thousands worse than they are now." Abria said.

"I look forward to it. So bring it on." Sue called at her.

"Then come to the castle in the middle of the lake, Ray of Sun, and see if you can beat me there. The task and travel will not be easy. I will make sure you will never make it there; all of you together, if even a live." Abria said as she disappeared.

"I look forward to it." Sue said with anger.

"Sue, are you alright?" Exie said.

"Yes, just a lot tired. Can we please go back to our room?" Sue asked them both.

"Sure, we can. Let us get our food, drink, and make sure that everyone is okay before we leave this club." Joey said.

"I agree; we need to heal them and then get out of here before anyone notices." Exie said.

"Joey, can you use your healing dragon this time?" Sue asked.

"Let me try, okay?" Joey answered back.

"I know you can do it, I have faith in you, both of you!" Exie said with a smile on her face.

"I SUMMON THE HEALING DRAGON, LYTH. HEALING WINGS!" Joey called; as a silver and pure white dragon appeared before them. She started to flap her wings and dust came down on them making their pain, and healing all their cuts up; caused from the battle that just took place. The healing also was giving the people back their energy that was taken from them by the Dark Kingdom Zodiac. As they people started to come too, the music started again, but this time there was someone D-Jing it.

They all looked around wonder why they were just on the floor, but their memories started to fade from when the club first opened up, and the music was playing. So the guardians' took that as a clue to leave, before anyone started to ask questions. As they were leaving the club to head back upstairs they rain into a woman who was wearing black leather vest that had a skull on it, plaid red, dark blue, gold, and black in the skirt, biker boots that went up to her knees with chains on them, she had a shirt on under the vest that had wholes all though it with a skull on the shirt. She looked as if she came out of a vampire book of some kind, but they notice that her skin was a peach color, eyes that shined like Twilight blues, pinks, purples, gold, and some green, red lip stick, hair color was blue with glitter highlights to the meddle of her back. She looked as if she was not met to be here.

"Excuse me." She said as she pushed past those three.

"Sorry about that." Sue called after as she entered the club.

"She was different." Exie said.

"Yeah, more gothic, than anything." Joey said.

"Well, let us be on our way please, before I pass out from that damn battle." Sue said getting annoyed.

"Okay, let us head back." Joey said.

"She was very tough to bet. It took a lot from all of us." Exie said feeling the drain her powers always caused.

"Yeah, she also made us advance some more in our own powers." Joey said.

"Yeah, we are differently going to have problems out of her." Sue also answered. As they all headed back the way they came from earlier in the day. They started to feel even more tired than they did when they came from the Nature Realm after that long battle.

"She has to be one of the tougher generals we have ever faced from the Dark Kingdom Zodiac." Sue said.

"Yeah, she might even be stronger than that damn prince of the Dark Kingdom Zodiac." Joey said.

"Yeah, well we have not come up against him since the Fire Realm Joey. So we are not sure if he has gotten stronger or if he has gotten weaker." Sue said.

"Who is this dark prince, you two are talking about?" Exie asked.

"He is the prince of the Dark Kingdom Zodiac. He also has taken one of our friends, and then he tried to take Sue. He was using his power to take hold of the Water and Ice Realm. So he tried to take the Fire Realm as well." Joey answered her.

"I see, so he is really strong if not very powerful. Do we have a chance against him?" Exie asked again.

"Yeah, as soon as we fine the last guardian, and find who our Star Princess is." Sue answered her this time.

"So what you are saying is that we have a very long hard battle against us." Exie answered. As they were still talking they had reached the elevator. It was still going up on one side, and slowly coming down on the other side. As they were waiting for the elevator to come down, they still talked about the Dark Kingdom Zodiac and the Dark Prince.

"So we will have to face them all in the end." Exie said.

"Yeah, there is a chance that the other generals that we have faced; will come back as well. The reason for this is because; as long as there is hate, anger, selfness, and pride in this universe there will always be a problem." Joey answered.

"How many have you two faced?" Exie asked.

"We have faced many generals over the past year. In the Crystal Star of Water and Ice, we went to school. So we should be almost over now. This means that Joey and I might have to repeat the grade. It is worth it all, if we can save our realms." Sue answered her back.

"I see, it seems that you two have been at this a while. How many realms have you seen?" Exie asked.

"We have been to nine realms. We started in the Water and Ice Realm, and ended up here in the Unknown Realm." Sue answered her.

"So you have been to that many realms then there are other realms that you have not been too yet?" Exie asked again.

"We have not been to our own realms. So we might someday go to our own realms. It just matters that we find the Star Princess first, so that we can stop the Dark Kingdom Zodiac for good." Sue said.

"It looks that we have a goal in mind, which we share." Exie said smiling at her new friends she has.

"Yeah, we all can look forward to that day." Sue said.

"What are the other guardians like?" Exie asked.

"They are really good friends. Andrew is the Prince of the Earth Realm, Faizah is the Princess of the Lightning Realm, Richard is the Prince of the Wind Realm, Lola is the Princess of the Fire Realm, Alena is the Princess of the Water and Ice Realm, Leroy is the Prince of the Elemental Realm, Autumn is the High Priestess (Princess) of the Healing and Spirit Realm, Alvaro Prince of the Darkness Realm, which you those two, Joey the Prince of the Summoning Realm, Me (Sue) Princess of the Light and Travel Realm, and then there is you (Exie) Princess of the Nature Realm. Each of us has special powers, but we all would get along because there are a lot of things that we have in common." Sue answered her back as the elevator had finally arrived. So they all three got onto the elevator to head back to their room for the night.

"What do you think the guardian of this realm is like?" Exie asked.

"I think that he or she might be a really great person, and that they have faced a difficult time due to the fact that the Dark Kingdom Zodiac has come here." Sue said.

"I think that they will be too." Exie said. As it reached the 16th floor the doors opened up and they all stepped out into the hallway and went to their room. They went to their room and went in. As they came in they put their stuff up and sat on the bed and turned the TV on. They turned it to a movie to watch while they relaxed for the rest of the night. They had requested an awake up call for the next day which would come early.

Chapter 23

Exie fell asleep first and started to dream, "She was near a water fall, with the stars shining down on her. She was waiting for someone, but didn't know who? She was wearing a dress so delicate that she was scared that she might rip it. The dress was in a hunter green color, with rainbow gems going down it, and strapless. When she moved it would shine, sparkle, and be very pretty. She had never worn anything like this before, so she could not stop looking at it. Then she started to look around, there was a Majestic Star Castle, a waterfall, she was standing behind the castle and there was also a stone path she had been standing on. The water fall would shine when the water fell down. It sparkled like the stars above her. She was happy and blushing because she was waiting on her true loves to meet her. She was still looking around when someone started walking up the path near her. She could not see who it was, but knew in her heart that he is who she had been waiting on. She went to say something to him, when she woke up by the phone ringing in the room.

"Hello." Exie said in a sleepy voice.

"Hello, this is the front desk calling you for your wake up call." Automotive service said.

"Oh, yes." Exie said. She looked over at the clock on the desk in the room, and it was 8:30 am. Which they had requested the night before. So she got up, and started to wake Sue, then they both got Joey up. After waking up, Exie got in the shower, and then Sue and Joey went last. After getting their things they went down to the lobby and checked out.

They left the inn, and went back out in the flow of people walking from one place to another. They looked around hoping to be able to ask someone how to get to the castle of this realm. So they went over to a bell hop, which was helping someone that was just checking in.

"Excuse me, but could you help us?" Sue asked the bell hop.

"Will you please give me a minute? While I help this person first, then I will answer your questions." Bell Hop answered.

"Okay we will wait." Sue answered back and the bell hop gave her thumbs up to show that he heard her. So they waited; sitting on the wall that was outside of the inn until the bell hop was done with his customer who wanted valet parking to the inn. So they had to wait for him to come back after parking the customer's mini-van for her. After waiting for a good half hour, here came the bell hop up the parking lot. He walked over to them to see what they wanted since it looked that the other bell hops was too busy to address them.

"How can I help you three?" Bell hop asked.

"We were wondering where the castle was located. That is surrounded by water." Exie asked.

"The castle is about a 2 hour drive from here. Do you have a car parked here?" Bell Hop asked.

"No we came here by bus. Can a taxi take us to the castle?" Exie answered and asked.

"Yes, a taxi can take you to the castle. It will cost you a bit of money. Would you like me to call a taxi for you?" Bell hop answered and asked.

"Yes, that would be great." Exie answered him back.

"Okay, give me a few minutes to call one." Bell Hop answered. So he walked away from them and went over to the phone. Picked it up, and dialed the number for a taxi. It was going to take about 20 minutes before the taxi will get there. So he walked back over to them and told them.

"It will take the taxi about 20 minutes to get here. Is this okay?" Bell Hop asked.

"Yes, that will be fine. We can go get some breakfast before the taxi gets here." Exie said grabbing her things, and looking at Sue and Joey to come with her. So all three walked away from the bell hop and went back inside the inn to get some breakfast before the taxi arrives. So they walked through the arch way and headed to a café that was nearby. It was called Java Chocolate, which had all kinds of cappuccinos', lattes, chai tea, gourmet coffees, fruit smoothies of your choice, flavored coffee, and food. So they waited in line to get their food and drinks.

"What can I get for you today?" Cashier asked.

"This order will be together? So, I guess; I will start. I would like a bagel with strawberry cream cheese spread and a large Chai Tea. Sue what would you like?" Exie asked.

"I would like a large banana-strawberry-mango smoothie and a blueberry muffin. Joey how about you?" Sue answered and asked.

"I would like a vanilla flavored large coffee with three pump of flavored, and I would also like a bowl of mini wheat, and that will be all." Joey answered.

"Okay, so we have a large Chai-Tea, large Banana-Strawberry-Mango smoothie, large vanilla flavored coffee with three pumps, a bagel with strawberry cream cheese spread, a large blueberry muffin, and a large bowl of mini-wheat, did I forget anything?" Cashier asked.

"No that is everything." Exie answered.

"Would you like to try a sugar cookie with sprinkles today?" Cashier asked.

"No thanks this will be all." Exie answered back.

"Okay, your total bill will be $45.63 today." Cashier said.

"Here is my Master Card." Joey said coming to the front once again to pay for their meal.

"Please sign on this line here for the credit card. Would you like a copy of your receipt?" Cashier asked.

"Yes, please." Joey answered back. As they went to a sat at a table near the window so they could watch for the taxi, and wait for their order to be ready. Sue was looking out and it had started to get cloudy outside. She was wondering if it might rain, when the cashier brought their order over to them.

"Here is your order. Also did you ask for a taxi?" Cashier asked.

"Yes we did." Sue answered her.

"Well, I just got word from the bell hop, and the taxi will be arriving in about 10 minutes. Would you like me to bring you a bag for your orders?" Cashier asked.

"That will be great. Thank you for the notice." Joey answered the cashier as the person walked away. After about five minutes the cashier came back with a couple of bags, containers for their food, and lids for their drinks, then handed it to them. Exie took the bag from the cashier and started to put their food in the containers when a black, white, red, and some yellow taxi pulled up to the valet parking. The bell hop went over to the taxi and said something to the taxi driving. Then the taxi driver pulled over to a parking spot to wait for them to come.

As they were finishing putting their things away when the cashier waved at them and they headed for the parking lot. They walked over to the taxi and he taxi driver got out of the taxi, and opened the truck of the taxi so that they could put their things in the trunk of the car. Sue and Exie put their things in first then went, and climbed in the back sit; while Joey had put his things in; then the taxi driver closed the trunk of the car, got back in the driver sit, as Joey was just getting in and putting on his sit belt. The taxi driver started the taxi up again, and waited for them to finish putting on sit belts before he spoke to them.

"So where are you heading?" Male Taxi Driver asked them.

"We are heading to the castle of your realm." Joey answered him.

"Okay, I charge a flat rate which is for longer driving, and I also charge an hourly rate as well. Since you are only going to the castle I will be charging you the hourly rate. Will this be a problem for any of you?" Male Taxi Driver asked.

"What is your hourly rate?" Sue asked from the back sit behind the taxi driver.

"I charge a $12.00 rate for hourly, and a flat rate of $150.00 if you are going more than a three hour drive. So for all of you it is a fee of $12.00 for all three. Will this do?" Male Taxi Driver asked again.

"No sir, it will be just fine. So do we pay you now or do we pay after you take us to the castle?" Exie asked this time.

"You will pay half now and when I get you to the castle you will be the rest. Will this be fine?" Male Taxi Driver asked yet again.

"That will be fine. Do you take credit cards?" Joey asked this time.

"Yes." Male Taxi Driver answered. So Joey handed him his Master Card so he could pay for the first $12.00 dollars. Then the rest when they get to the castle. After the taxi driver ran the Master Card and it was approved he backed out of his parking spot and went down to the end of the driveway, and waited to turn right out of the inn. After traffic cleared he then went, and headed straight for Rainbow Avenue which was about a 15 minute drive from the inn. Then he turned right and headed down Rainbow Avenue, to the I-33 (Interstate 33) to head to the castle. So Sue and Exie started to relax in the back sit, and started to drift off to sleep when they heard something. They sat up straight and started to look out the windows to see what made that offal sound. They couldn't see anything, but they started to get a bad feeling something was about to happen. So they knew that the Dark Kingdom Zodiac was up to something, they just didn't know how far they would go to take this realm from these people.

Then suddenly something hit the top of the roof of the taxi, and then claws started to slash at the top, until it got though. Then before they knew it, the beast or whatever it was, was on the hood of the taxi making the all the cars near the taxi sway, and causing crashes. Then the taxi driver slammed on his breaks to get the thing off his hood, but it had slammed its' claws into the hood of the taxi making the engine die. Everyone in the taxi went forward only to hit the back of the sits, and the dash. Then the thing swapped its' claws at Joey causing him to climb into the back sit with the girls. The taxi driver was so stun that he didn't know what to do. So Joey tried to open the doors but they were still locked because of being automatic. So he had to push the lock so that they could open the door. As he got the back driver side door a jar enough for someone to get through to at least get the thing's attention long enough for the others to get the taxi driver in the back sit to keep him from becoming a crew toy for the thing trying to kill them all. As joey tried to fit though the door he realized that he was too big that it would have to be one of the girls to do.

"Exie can you claim over both Sue and me to try and get through the door." Joey asked her.

"Yeah, let me try." Exie answered back. So she claimed over both Sue and Joey to try and fir though the door that was a jar. As she got closer the thing started to open its' month and a very hobble sound came out. Making them to cover their ears because it was that loud and bad. Then before they knew it, it started to suck in the air around them to spit something back at them. Exie had started to get through the door when the thing spit something at them all. As the green slim stuff hit the front window shield where it had not used its claws to put more holes in it. This stuff came all the way though heading for Joey's head, as he dunked to keep from getting hit, the back window of the taxi had a whole it the size of a softball. The slim melted it as if it was nothing. So Exie finally had gotten out of the taxi to run in front while Joey and Sue could get to the taxi driver before the thing choose to spit at them again.

As Exie ran in front of the taxi she now had a better view of the thing. It had bat wings the size of a semi-truck, a body the size of a mini-van in a melted color purple, claws that was the size of ice picks, a tail that had an arrow point on it, and teeth that was the size of knifes. This thing was ugly, what she could do to sum it up was that it looked like a bat that had been tampered with.

"Joey it looks like a bat from over here." Exie yelled to him.

"Okay, can you get its attention so we can get the taxi driver and ourselves out of this damn taxi?" Joey yelled back at her.

Chapter 24

✦✦✦✦✦

"**T**IGER CHARGE!" Exie called as she had called a tiger to her which looked like a bangle tiger from a whole different land. But before the others could react the tiger had charged the Bat creature and sank its' teeth into the flesh. As Sue was looking around for Exie she realized that she had shifted into the tiger to get the Bat creature's attention. It worked too, it had turned to were the tiger was and started after it. This was their chance to get out of the taxi and save the taxi driver.

"Let's move Joey." Sue called to him to take him out of his surprised looked.

"Sue, you go first, and see if you can pull the door open some more for me to get out." Joey said to her.

"Okay." Sue had replied. As she slid out the door with ease; she grabbed on to the door where it was opened; and pulled even more to see if she could open it up even a little bit more for Joey to get out. While Joey was pushing from the inside they both managed to get it to move a little bit more so that Joey could get out. He ran to the driver door and broke the window to get to the taxi driver who was still stunned by what he was seeing. As Joey used his fist to break the glass, the taxi driver chooses then to finally become un-stunned and turned his head away from the window while Joey was breaking the glass. While Joey's fist made contact the taxi driver undid his sit belt and used his sleeve of his jacket to get the rest of the glass out of the way so that he could climb out.

After Sue and Joey made sure that the taxi driver was unhurt they headed to where Exie was standing. She was no longer a tiger but herself again with a whip in her hand. They ran up beside her, and looked to that the whip had thrones all the way down it.

"So how is it going?" Joey asked her.

"This is not a time to be funny, you could help you know." Exie said feeling annoyed at Joey's approach.

"Okay, let us get rid of this thing before someone gets really hurt or killed." Joey said. So all three guardians was getting ready to use their powers when someone else came to their risqué.

"CIRCLE OF SWARDS. SHATTER!" Girl called as many swards in a circle shatter into an attack of many swards falling from the sky. It hit the bat creature causing it to shutter but not disappear. So the other guardians joined in the attack.

"WHIP OF NATURE. THRONE BRUSH ATTACK!" Exie called as her whip released many thrones at once looking like a bunch of needles coming from a brush which was her whip as the bat creature was hit knocking it back and coming up on its' legs.

"COME DRAGON OF NATURE, PHILIS. ROSE STRICK ATTACK!" Joey had summoned a new dragon from the Nature Realm releasing a powerful attack at the Huge Bat. Rose petals and thrones turned into what looked like a bunch of knives hitting the Huge Bat.

"SUN STROM!" Sue called as many sun rays came and hit the Huge Bat making it catch fire in orange, yellow, and red colors of the sun. Turning the bat to dust as someone else had arrived.

"Well done guardians. I see you got extra help this time. So guardian of the Unknown Realm it would seem that you came out of hiding." Abria said.

"What do you want with my realm you fowl general of the Dark Kingdom Zodiac?" Girl asked.

"We want to rule all the realms; we have been stopped by you worthless guardians for some time now. So we are going to get rid of you for good." Abria answered back.

"You can try, but you will not win. You have tried many times now to stop us but soon we will find the Star Princess and Prince and then there will be the end of you and your dark kingdom." Girl said.

"You maybe the guardian and princess of this realm but I still have control over your queen and king. How will you stop me?" Abria asked while laughing at her.

"We will stop you even if it means our own lives." Abria answered her.

"Then come to your home the castle of Rainbow." General Abria said while disappearing.

"We will be there. We will stop you and find our Star Princess and Prince." Girl said to General Abria as she was disappearing. Then she turned to the others and looked at them. She smiled and reached her hand out for them to shake it.

"I see that the guardians' are gathering finally. My name is Laverna-Grace Gale; I'm the crowned princess and guardian of this realm. It is nice to meet you." Laverna-Grace said to them.

"You are the girl we ran into last night leaving the club." Exie said.

"Yeah, I had to make sure that you were who you are before I could reveal myself to you all. I'm so sorry for not helping before, but I have been looking for the Star Princess and Prince and have had no luck yet." Laverna-Grace said.

"It is okay, we would have done the same thing if the Dark Kingdom had invaded our realms as well. By the way my name is Exie Green guardian and crown princess of the Crystal Star of the Nature Realm. It is nice to meet you as well." Exie said.

"My name is Sue Stang; I'm the guardian and crown princess of the Crystal Star of Light and Travel Realm. It is nice to finally meet you." Sue said.

"My name is Joseph Ryan; I'm the guardian and crown prince of the Crystal Star of the Summoning Realm. It is nice to meet you as well. We know who the prince is, but we have yet to find the Star Princess." Joey said.

"Really, so he has been found. So we just need to find the Star Princess and they can save all the realms from this darkness that is coming." Laverna-Grace said.

"Yeah, but first we need to save this realm and head back to the Crystal Star of Water and Ice where the other guardians' are. Do you have a way to get to the castle? We have about another 1hour and half before we get there." Joey asked her.

"Yes, I have a car that we can use. We need to hurry before they do more damage to my realm, then what they have already done." Laverna-Grace said.

"Okay we are with you." Exie answered.

"So let us get moving." Sue said this time as everyone followed Laverna-Grace to her 2013 Chevrolet Corvette Stingray that was pink with gold trim. As Joey came up the rare he looked at the car and his month dropped. He could not believe his eyes, this was one of the best sport cars ever made and he wanted one, but his father told him no because he felt he was too young for such a car. So the two girls got in the back, while Joey and Laverna-Grace took the front sits. Sue was not going to argue with her cousin to sit the front seat because she would lose that one. So she took the back while Laverna started up the car. It purred like a kitten when the engine started up. Joey was all smiles in this type of car.

After look to make sure that there was no more monsters to attack the interstate Laverna pushed the gas easily to go forward to get around the other cars that was on the interstate after the attack. She wanted to make sure that no one was hurt and that there would not be another attack if they left so she ease out slowly while clearing the cars all around. As she got further and further away from all the mess brought on by that bat monster she hit the gas; making everyone go back in their seats. This was like a car with super power speed. As she speed down the interstate heading to the Rainbow Castle to save her family and her realm with new companions which made her feel at ease because she was scared to return, not knowing what might happen if got there. Now she had friends to help her, which means that her guardian duty was taking over her princess duties which she was okay with. Her younger sister can take the throne and not her. She never wanted to be the crown princess of her realm, but her sister was all about it. Her sister was very pretty and she knew it. But she was never the one that got put in front a coward all the time dressed up in all kinds of gowns. Now she will get that chance because this was her chance to do what she was meet to do, and that was to be one of the guardians' that protected their future from darkness.

As the time went by she had turned the radio to station 103.5 FM on, so that the silence was not too hard to bear with the other guardians that are with her. As different songs came on the others started to relax again, but this time they were not on edge due to the fact that they had been attacked again which is never ending. Sometimes that is great other times when they are in a hurry; is bad. As they are all seating in the car while Laverna drove them to the Rainbow Castle, Joey reached over and turned the radio down so that they could talk to the new guardian who happened come help at the right time.

"Sorry for this but we need to talk before we arrive at the castle." Joey said as the other two girls sat straight up in the back to hear what he was saying and could not agree more.

"What do you want to talk about?" Laverna asked him.

"How did you know we needed help back there?" Joey asked her.

"I have been following you three for a little while now. Since you stepped out of the Light Portal in that alley back in the city." Laverna answered him.

"Why didn't you introduce yourself before now?" Joey asked again.

"I wanted to make sure that you were not with the Dark Kingdom Zodiac, and wanted to make sure that you are who you all are." Laverna answered again.

"So when we ran into you coming out of the club last night how come you didn't help then?" Exie asked this time.

"I wanted to see how strong you all are. To my surprise all of you are very strong indeed." Laverna answered her this time.

"Then how come you waited until we got on the interstate heading to the castle to finally help us?" Sue asked her this time.

"I waited for you three to leave the inn before I realized that something was not right. So I got my car from the valet parking which took longer than an expected. So I could not follow right away." Laverna answered Sue this time.

"So you just happened to be going this way when you see it attack us." Exie asked again.

"No, I got there as it was attacking you, but I was too far away to get near you three; to help right away. Also I was checking on the people that were driving the interstate when that thing came down on top of the taxi you were in. I also had faith in your abilities and power to be able to handle it while I was getting closer. I saw how powerful you three where back at the night club. So I knew you could at least hold it off until I reached you." Laverna answered.

"So, after getting there you didn't wait to see if we could finish it off or take it down." Sue asked.

"No, I knew you could. But the monster was very strong. So I needed to help in any way I could." Laverna answered. As the conversation kept going they had reached their destination the Rainbow Castle. It was very big; it had all different types of color on it. As the sun would hit it, the colors would change. They saw pink, green, red, purple, yellow, orange, blue, light blue, lavender, and all other colors. There was about six tear tops on the castle. It is just as pretty as the Majestic Star Kingdom Castle, but not as pretty, but still pretty in its' own right. As they pull up closer to the castle it looked to be empty, but they knew better, they had to get out of the car and reach the boat ramp so that they could reach the castle that was center in the middle of a lake called Rainbow Lake, they notice a speed boat that was yellow with flames. It was most likely that the castle was asleep or under some spell of some kind. So they approached with ease so that no one will detect that they are there. As they walk up to the front door Laverna went around to the back where there was a maze of brushes to get lost in.

"Where are you taking us?" Exie asked.

"I'm taking us to a secret entrance to the castle so that no one will see right away." Laverna answered.

"Does everyone know of this entrance?" Sue asked this time.

"No, the only ones who every use this entrance was myself, my younger sister, and the queen. She was the one who sowed it to us. Just in case we wanted to sink out if the castle or if the castle was every attacked by any enemies. This is how I got out when the Dark Kingdom Zodiac invaded our realm. My sister didn't make it out with me because she didn't want to leave our parents. Even though it was the queen who brought us to this entrance." Laverna answered.

"How does the queen know about this entrance?" Joey asked.

"Our father the king had it built for our mother before we were born. He knew that the queen love being outside. So as a wedding present he had it built, but did not want to know where the entrance was so he could not stop her from leaving the castle. After I was born, my mother would bring me out here as a child so I could run and play without getting yelled at for not acting like a child. When my sister was born my mother gave it to us so that we could have fun and be children. So we would use it to escape the castle for a while. If we were late coming back, my mother knew where to find us. Our father would be upset with us, but he never had it closed off. It is still open even to this day. I did come back one other time after the Dark Kingdom Zodiac had invaded us, but I didn't like what I was seeing. So I vowed never to come back until the time came for me to choose to be a crown princess or the guardian of this realm. I choose to be the guardian of this realm, and pass the crow to my younger sister who will take the throne when she is older." Laverna explain.

So the three guardians followed Laverna to the entrance of the maze and through the maze to a special spot that seem to be unnoticed by anyone. It looked as if it was a part of the brushes, but you had to get closer to know that it was just a dead end. Unless you knew of the secret entrance to the castle which she did. She reached her hand in the brush and pulled on what looked like a branch, but wasn't. It was a string that hung down so that the entrance could be opened. Then before they knew it the ground began to shake and then a door was reviled to them. They looked at it and was hoping that she was not lending them in a trap like once before. As she stepped forward she put her hand on a rail and started to walk down a set of stairs.

"These stairs go half way down, and there is a door to our right that we will enter to go inside of the castle." Laverna said to them so that they knew what to expect. So all of them stepped in the door way, and went down the stairs about half way down they went into the castle though the door. As they all stepped off the stairs they had enter a room that look to be a storage area for food or clothes.

"Listen up; we need to head to the throne room. So we will need to wear the maids and butler clothes that go to that area of the castle. The color for that area is Violet Vast, with white long sleeve shirt for the guys, Violet dresses for the woman, and both wear black dress shoes of some kind." Laverna told them. So they grabbed a set of maid clothes and changed into them; Joey had turned his back so that the girls could change first; and they did the same for him. So that they could walk around the castle unnoticed.

Chapter 25

After they all had changed they walked over to the door that most likely went into the kitchen or a hallway. Joey was wearing a Violet Vast, White long Sleeve Shirt, black dress pants, and black shoes. All three girls was wearing the same thing, Violet dress that went mid leg short sleeves, an apron, and black flat dress shoes. As they all were ready to face what came next they go ready for a battle that will take a long time. They make their way to the throne room where they are supposed to be.

As they walk the hall to the throne room, they start to notice that most of the staff looks like they haven't woken up yet, as if they are in a daze. Laverna is watching her people walk to and from the kitchen area and down the hall. One of the staff stops and looks at her as if they knew her, but thought otherwise. So they just kept walking down the hall till they finally came to the throne room. They all peak around the door frame so they could get a better look of the area. It is very big, pretty with wooden walls, high windows, wooden floor, four thrones at the front of the room each one different. Each throne bares a mark of the royal family that ruled this realm. But to their surprised three of the thrones had someone sitting in it. As they crept into the throne room not carry anything like a tray for food. So they knew that it was a matter of time that before someone might notice them. So they walked in with their hands behind their backs so that it looked as if they were coming in to get their orders from the royal family.

So all three of them made their way to the front of the room; with their hands behind them. As they approached, something seemed to be off, but it was just a feeling which none of them wanted to notice or think something could go really wrong. As they got closer they realized that there was some type of dark aura around them as if something or someone was controlling them like puppets.

When they approached the thrones both the queen and king looked at them as if they didn't see they or those they are dirt beneath their feet. The princess was no better she looked at them and she looked as if something flaw came in to the room.

"What do you want?" Queen asked them.

"My, lady we just want our orders for today?" Joey answered her.

"I would like that you three clean the floors, windows, and carpets in here and all over the castle." Queen said.

"As you wish my lady." Joey said bowing to her. As if he has had practice addressing a queen. So all three left the throne room with their orders from the queen.

"Joey, what was that all about? I thought we came here to free my family and the people of this realm?" Laverna asked him feeling very angry.

"It gives us a chance to look around for the enemy. It also gives us a chance to see what is really going on." Joey answered her.

"So, what are you planning? It would be nice to be included in it." Sue said to him.

"Sorry it was the spur of the moment. I just reacted to the queen and what they expect a servant to do." Joey told them.

"Next time will you please include us in your plan?" Exie said to him.

"You got it. So how about I include you now." Joey said with a smile.

"What are you thinking of." Sue asked him.

"I think; that we should split up and dig around for some information. Also we need to find out where the light portal is to the Crystal Star of Water and Ice Realm. So Laverna will take the East Wing of the castle, Sue will take the North Wing of the castle, Exie will take the West Wing of the castle, and I will take the South Wing of the castle. Also if any of you don't find anything; then we need to meet up with someone. Laverna will meet up with Sue in the North side castle is, unless Sue doesn't find anything then do the other, I will meet up with Exie in the West Wing of the castle, unless she fines nothing than meet up with me in the South Wing of the castle." Joey suggested.

"It sounds like a plan." Sue said.

"I agree." Exie said.

"I'm not sure, but it looks like we might have to do it this way. So we need to go different ways. Exie if you go out this way and head a few feet to an open space then take the left side, and keep heading in that direction Sue you just keep heading North, down this hall; and you will be in the North Wing, and for you Joey just head back the way we came from and it should take you straight to the South Wing. Everyone please be careful." Laverna said to them.

"Thanks you take care too." Sue said.

"I agree with Sue. All three of you take care." Exie said.

"Please check everyone room, door, and whatever else you come across. Please do be careful all of you." Joey said heading south. So everyone went their own way. It was hard for them to leave each other knowing that there could be an attack at any time.

Sue went the way she was told by Laverna and she started to wonder if there might be a trap anywhere in this castle. She was not hoping that something might attack her. As she kept walking she came to her first door, she checked to see if it was locked and to her special it was not. So she opened the door slowly so that if someone was inside they would not hear her. As she opened it up, her notice that it was nothing more than a sitting area for drinks, food, or maybe reading. She looked around checking for hidden doors, or a hidden drew. But there was nothing in this area, so she went back out into the hall, and continues down the hall until she came to another door. As she began to open this one something hit her hard in the back knocking her out. Before she knew it, she was in the enemies' hand which is not where she wants to be.

After making her way down the hall Laverna felt as if her heart had stopped. She knew something was up but was not sure what yet. She kept going checking as many rooms as she could before she had to stop and rest for a minute. She hoped that the other guardians' was doing okay, but she still had that feeling of dread in her heart. So instead of making her way down the East Wing of the castle, but stopped and went back the way she came. She knew that she needed to get to Sue, but could not figure out why.

Joey had gone to the way they had come from in the beginning. He was looking at each door he came too, but found nothing. He was starting to get worried about the others, when some movement caught his eyes from the corner. But before he could react to defend himself. He was knocked out and dragged to an area he routinized from earlier in the day. It was the throne room, he was starting to get a bad feeling that something has happened to the other guardians. He stated to look around when someone came in carry a person on their shoulders. He realized who it was from the golden sun color of the hair.

"SUE!" Joey yelled but got no response from her.

"Be quit guardian of Summoning. She is out for the count. We don't want to alert your other fellow guardians before my plan can work." Abria said to him.

"What have you done?" Joey said to her.

"Well it is a little game I plan on playing with you all." General said as the servant put Sue down next to him and tired her up just like him. Then there was something huge that moved in the background before he could react yet again; there were these huge tarantulas which were of different colors. There was the Rose Tarantula, Brazilian Tarantula, and Redknee Tarantula. There was venom coming out of their fangs' hitting the ground making it sizzle to almost nothing. There were huge holes in the floor all around them that they did not see before when they came into the throne earlier in the day when they had arrive. Also not only was there tarantulas there was also Spike Spiders. They are the Mangrove with Red Spikes, Black Spike with Red Spikes, and Flying Saucer Alien with Spikes which where even uglier than the tarantulas, just as dangerous because the venom comes out of their fangs and their legs. Joey couldn't move, and Sue was still knocked and just as Joey was starting to get loose from the ropes when Abria came over and knocked him out by punching him in the face.

Exie was in the West Wing of the castle when she felt something in her heart as if someone she cared about was being hurt. She knew that it could be anyone of the guardians', but she was hoping that it was just a feeling. She had just finished checking a room when she decided to go to the South Wing to find Joey. As she went to the South Wing she looked every, and could not find Joey. So she decided to head to the North Wing to find Laverna and Sue.

Laverna was looking around the North Wing for Sue and could not find her. As she was heading back to the main area of the North Wing she sees Exie standing in the main area looking around. She walks over to her to see what is up.

"Exie I thought you were supposed to meet up with Joey in the South Wing?" Laverna asked her.

"I was, but I can't find him. So I thought I would come looking for Sue and you. Where is Sue?" Exie answered and asked her.

"I don't know I can't find her anywhere? Let us go look for them together." Laverna said. So they both headed back to the throne room. They did not run into any of the servants which seemed very odd. So they rushed to the throne room, running down the halls to get there. As they approached the throne something seemed off. The queen, king, and princess was not anywhere to be found, but in the middle of a bunch of spiders with venom coming out of their fangs tired up is Sue and Joey. Both scrumming trying to get free from their bonds. But the spiders kept getting closer but are forced to back off. As they are watching they realized that Abria the General for the Dark Kingdom Zodiac; she was holding them against their will. SO they went back into the hall to come up with a plan to save their friends, then maybe they could also save this realm.

"What do you think we should do Exie?" Laverna said to her very worried.

"We need to save our friends, save this realm, the people, your family, and hopeful we would be able to stop the Dark Kingdom Zodiac." Exie answered her.

"You are right. We need to get our heads on straight." Laverna said.

"Okay, I will be the distraction, while you save Sue and Joey. So let us get to work." Exie said.

"Okay, let us do this." Laverna said also answering her unsaid question. So they both went back into the throne this time Exie went in first and then Laverna would follow only to get to the others.

"So what do you think of my babies?" Abria asked both Sue and Joey not expecting an answered.

"You just wait you witch once our friends know we are missing they will come looking for us. Then we will see how your little babies look like when we are done with you and your Dark Kingdom Zodiac." Sue said to her not holding anything back.

"We will see guardian of Light and Travel." Abria said to her with a sour look on her face.

"Don't worry I already know she has taken you two?" Exie said coming from behind a curtain.

"When did you get here?" Abria said to her with anger.

"I have been here for about a good 10 or 15 minutes." Exie said.

"Exie where is Laverna?" Sue asked her.

"She is around." Exie said.

"I will find her and I will destroy you all." Abria said.

"You can try, but it won't work." Exie said getting ready for her attack.

"This should be fun." Abria said with an evil smile on her face. So they faced each other waiting for the other to make a move. As Exie had done she distracted Abria from the others.

"Sue, Joey hold still." Laverna making Sue jump damn near out of her skin. Joey smiled at her. He was glad that they were both together and not in different areas of the castle.

"Thanks, we need to help Exie." Sue said.

"We will, but let me get you untied first." Laverna said. So she worked hard on the ropes that Sue and Joey was tied up with. She had pulled a knife out of her pocket of her maid dress to cut the ropes. As she went to work very fast the ropes became loose making it easier for them to move, and get freed.

Sue stood up and rubbed her wrist from the ropes bits. As she finally got the feeling back in her wrist she was getting very angry. Joey also had to rub his wrist so that he also could get the feeling back into his wrist as well. He was ready for a fight as well, and before they knew it the spiders where on them. While Exie was dealing with General Abria, which all they have done most of the time is look at each other.

"We need to get rid of these things, then help Exie, and take care of General Abria." Joey said.

"Let us deal with these first, then take her out." Laverna said.

"You got it." Sue said in agreement with them both.

"MOONLIGHT SHOWER!" Laverna yelled making the attack hit the spiders on one side leaving the others to deal with the rest. The attack was beams of moonlight which looked like swards of some kind.

"SUN DANCE!" Sue yelled taking out a lot of spiders with her dangers of dancing light. She looked as if she was dancing to a song only she can hear.

"RAIN DRAGON, SHANGDI! RAIN ATTACK!" Joey called. The attack was like spears of rain hitting the last of the spiders that was blocking their way. After they had disappeared, Abria had turned around to show the horror shock on her face.

"YOU DAMN GUARDIANS' WILL PAY FOR THIS. MY BABIES!" Abria said with tears in her eyes as the last of her spiders disappeared.

"Now, there is only you!" Exie said to her with a smug look on her face. As Exie ran over to her friends' sides', relived that they are okay.

"This is enough. It is the end of you and your Dark Kingdom Zodiac in my realm." Laverna said.

"We will see about that." Abria said too her.

"BRING IT ON!" Exie and Sue said together.

""VEMON STRIKE!" Abria yelled when a whip of her own came out dripping with poison, making more small holes in the floor of the throne room. As she lifted it above her head it was aim at them all.

"MOON REFLECTION!" Laverna yelled. As a barrier that looked just like the moon and the attack did not hit Sue, Joey, Exie, and herself.

"ROSE PETAL SHOWER!" Exie said as a bunch of rose petals turn into some deadly attack.

"RAIN DRAGON, SHANGDI. RAIN DANCE!" Joey yelled as the rain dance attack with such force, which is the same power as a storm. Turning Abria in a whorl pool of power.

"SUN DANCE!" Sue yelled which looked as if she was dancing. After she had hit Abria, she yelled with such pain and was turned to dust.

After what seemed to be a very long day and week. The Unknown Realm was finally freed from the holds of the Dark Kingdom Zodiac.

"Thank you everyone for your help." Laverna said to them all.

"You are welcome. We are glad we could help." Sue said breathing hard after her attack, but she was shining. They all were. Everyone was coming around as if waking up from a very long sleep. After what seemed to be years people started to talk in the halls wondering how they got there. So they started running to the throne room. After everyone was finally out of danger the Queen, King, and Princess came walking into the throne room holding hands and looking scared. They looked into the middle of the throne room was where the guardians' was standing laughing glad that the battle is finally over; this one at least.

"My darling daughter you are safe." The Queen said to Laverna as she turned around she was in her mother's arms before she knew.

"Mother, I'm safe, I'm glad that you are too. Thanks to my new friends." Laverna said trying to keep from crying.

"It would seem you have done well my child." The King said to Laverna. He also walked over to her putting his arms around his daughter and wife.

"Oh, Laverna. I'm so sorry I didn't come with you. I'm relieved that you are safe and okay." Sherry said to her older sister.

"It is okay. I have missed all of you too. The threat is over now. We can be in peace for once." Laverna said as her family let her go.

"It will only be over when the true ruler is found. The one that can save us all from this darkness." The Queen said.

"Well, I could not do it without my friends, whom are also guardians' of their own realms." Laverna said to her family.

"It is nice to meet you. Thank you for helping Laverna and our realm." The King said.

"You don't have to thank us. It is what we are born to do. But I'm sorry; we need Laverna to come with us. So that we can find the Star Princess who will bring us back to peace." Joey said to him.

"I understand, but it is up to her. She had grown into a very wonderful and powerful young woman. Laverna what will you do?" The King asked her.

"Father, I'm glad that you and everyone are safe. But I would like to be the guardian for this realm, and help to find the Star Princess." Laverna said.

"But Laverna? What about me?" Shelly asked.

"I think you will be just fine. I pass my crown to you. Please watch over this realm as our parents have." Laverna said to her little sister.

"Then it is settled. Please be careful my dare. I do believe that you are going down the right path, my dearest daughter." The Queen said.

She looked at her sister once more and saw that she was wiping tears from her face, but she is as beautiful as ever. The Queen hugged her daughter very tight to let her love sink in. She hugged her mother back to let her know that she can feel the love from them all.

"If you would please follow me out of the throne room. We need to head to the North Wing where the portal is located. So they all headed that way. Into the room that Sue had looked into and could not find anything in there. Here there was a secret door in the far back of the closet. As it opened there was a long stairway heading down. So they all headed down to the bottom of the stairs and there was a huge crystal that shined many colors as does the realm.

"This is the portal of our realm which can take you anywhere you need to go in all the realms. Please use guardian of Light and Travel for it is you who is the only one that can control it." The King said to Sue. She nodded to let him know that she understood what he was saying. So, Sue walked over to the crystal and touched it. As she did the portal lite up. She knew where they needed to go.

"Everyone we need to head back to the Crystal Star of the Water and Ice Realm." Sue said.

"Okay, what do we need to do," Exie asked.

"All you need to do is walk through the portal and we will all be on the other side." Sue said. So Laverna gave her family one last hug, Exie stepped into the portal felt as if she would turn into water, Joey went behind them bowing to the King, Queen, and Shelly, and last Sue had stepped though.

Return to the Land of the Crystal Star: Water and Ice Realm

Chapter 26

As they stepped out of the light portal they all covered their eyes to cover them from the sun, which was shining very bright. As Sue and Joey looked around they are the Warehouse and Business Area of the City.

"Welcome to the city of Lima. We have arrived back to the Crystal Star of Water and Ice Realm." Joey said looking around. The city of Lima looked as if it is bad up of ice. All the buildings had a lot of glass in them, and there heard the water around them. Before they knew it, it started to rain to make the city look even more beautiful they all thought.

"We need to get a hold of the others." Sue said.

"Then let us get to a payphone so we could call them. Maybe they can meet us somewhere nearby." Joey said heading to a nearby office building and they all went inside. As Joey stepped in from the rain; which now they all where wet from head to toes. The office building they had walked into is the federal building where Joey's father worked. He knew that his father would most likely want to see him. He turned to his friends to let them know that they need to go to the 64th floor.

"Well guys this is where my father works. If we could, I would like to go up and see him on the 64th floor. Sue, I know he would want to see you as well." Joey asked his friends.

"Sure we can go see your father Joey." Laverna said. So they all headed to the 64th floor of the federal building. It was a long ride because there was almost one stop on each floor between the 1st floor and the 64th floor. The interior of the building is white walls, very expensive paintings, some crystal bowls, and there was many different types of furniture in the building each floor seemed to have its own theme. One floor was all gray with black furniture; another floor was yellow and orange, and so on all the way up to the 64th floor of the building. As they stepped out of the elevator the theme for this floor is light sky blue walls, midnight blue lamps, and blue furniture. It seemed to be comfortable. Joey walked down the hall until he came all the way to the end of the hall and to their left was a huge door that read Thomas J. Ryan on it. Joey knocked on the door waiting for an answer.

"Come IN." Joey's father said. So they walked into the office. Joey's father is on the phone with another business partner. So they waited for him to notice them. So there was some couch, couple of chairs, and a coffee pot that had fresh coffee. So Exie and Laverna went over to the coffee pot, so they got a cup just to make time go bye as they are waiting for the man behind the desk dressed in a carol black high end suit. Now Exie can see where Joey got his looks from. His father has light brown hair, hazel eyes, and his skin tone is a tan color. He most differently has control over a lot of things. After what seemed to be an hour, Joey's father finally hangs up the phone and then turns to be surprised that his son and friends are in his office.

"So, Joey what do I owe this visit? On another note, where the hell have you been?" Mr. Ryan asked his only son. Joey shuffled in his' father's gaze and was trying to find his voice.

"Well dad, I have been a round you could say. Also I was wondering if I could use the phone. So I used the phone in the lobby, and felt I needed to pay you a visit." Joey told his father.

"Well, I think I have time for you to start explaining something. Also what the hell is going on around here? Who are these people?" Mr. Ryan said scanning the room and his eyes land on Sue. He smiled and walked from behind his desk. Walked over to his niece and held her very tightly. She could not believe he is doing this. It has been a very long time since she has seen her uncle; she smiles into his suit jacket.

"Father, this is Laverna and Exie. They are my friends, and they are from far away." Joey said.

"Well, it is nice to meet you all. Where are you both from?" Mr. Ryan asked the girls.

"We are differently not from around here. You would not believe where we are from." Exie answered him.

"Please explain further. I would like to know where my only son and niece have been. By the way, Sue your parents have been calling for a long time now asking if I have seen you. So please call them." Mr. Ryan said to them all.

"Mr. Ryan, to fake and honest I don't think you would believe us if we told where we have been." Laverna answered him.

"Try me." Mr. Ryan said with a firm stair.

"What do you want to know?" Joey asked his father.

"Everything." He answered.

"Fine we have been in different realms of the universe. Also I'm a guardian from the Crystal Star of the Summoning Realm." Joey told his father.

"I see. It would seem that it is time that we had a long talk. I think you should head to our house." Mr. Ryan.

"Okay father. We will head to our house. Can you at least call the car for us please?" Joey asked his father.

"Yes, I'll can the car for you and your friends. By the way your friends can stay at our house. Sue call your parents, they have been very worried about you." Mr. Ryan said.

"Yes, Sir I will call them as soon as I get to your house. Will that be fine?" Sue asked.

"Yes, that will be fine." Mr. Ryan answered her.

"You are not going anywhere." Someone said.

"Who the hell are you?" Mr. Ryan asked.

"It would seem that the guardians are stronger than we had thought. But you will not make it to your friends. I'm General Phoenix. THIS IS THE END!" General Phoenix.

"What the hell do you want with these kids?" Mr. Ryan said.

"To stop them from finding the Star Princess and meeting up with their other guardian friends." General Phoenix answered him with a smile.

"Bring it on. DAD; GET. OUT. OF. HERE. NOW!" Joey yelled at them.

"I'M NOT LEAVING YOU OR YOU'RE FRDINEDS!" Mr. Ryan said to his son.

"IF THAT IS THE CASE THEN HOW ABOUT I PUT YOU ALL OUT OF YOUR MISABLE LIVES!" General Phoenix said.

"BRING IT ON!" Exie said to the general. This will be the last stop for you and this damn Dark Kingdom Zodiac.

"PHOENIX FIRE BOMB ATTACK!" General Phoenix yelled when a bunch of fire balls came down on them all.

"LEAF SPEAR ATTACK!" Exie called when a whirl wind of leaves came from around her turning into spears attacking the general.

"MOON STRIK ATTACK!" Laverna called when a huge beam of moon light which was cutting into the general.

"SUN RINGS ENCIRCLE THE PHOENIX!" Sue called as many rings caught General Phoenix and holding him still for Joey to finish him off.

"WATER DRAGON, WINA. WATER CYCLONE!" Joey summoned. When a huge water whirl sucked up General Phoenix causing him to disappear back to where ever he came from.

After the battle they all fell to their knees catching there, breathe. Since they arrived back in this realm after their fight in the Unknown Realm they have spent most of their energy to keep the dark forces at bay. As it is this is only the beginning, they needed to find their other friends and get together.

Mr. Ryan looked at his son and could not be more proud of him than in this moment.

"Joey, you look tired. I will call down and have the car brought around front so that you could head home. I will join you." Mr. Ryan said.

"Thanks dad." Is all, Joey could say after the battle the just had. The girls all looked up at them, and smiled. Mr. Ryan had picked the phone up and called his secretary, Jessica to call for his car.

"Jessica, please call my car around front. Also cancel all my meetings for the rest of the day. I'm going home with my son. He is finally home again." Mr. Ryan said to his secretary. The phone rang in the office and Mr. Ryan picked it.

"Yes." Mr. Ryan said.

"Your call is ready sir." Jessica said.

"Thank you. Take the rest of the day off as well, Jessica." Mr. Ryan said.

"Thank you sir." Jessica answered back.

So they all got off the floor and headed to the door. Went back down the hall and got back on the elevator, went back down to the 1st floor of the federal building. As they stepped out of the elevator and headed to the doors. Mr. Ryan was stopped by another co-worker and they started to talk. He waved them all, letting them know he will be there shortly that he had to deal with this person first.

So they all went out to the valet parking and waiting for them was a Black Limo. They walked over to the limo and the valet opened the door for them. They looked in and the limo had leather black seats, mini bar, and a stereo system that had Bluetooth so that you could listen to your phone or mp3 player. They all claimed in and got comfortable, when the door opened again and Mr. Ryan claimed in after them.

"Is everything okay dad?" Joey asked his father.

"Yes, it is fine." Mr. Ryan answered his son.

"Where too sir?" Limo driver asked.

"Home, please." Mr. Ryan told the driver.

"Okay, sir." Limo driver answered back. So Mr. Ryan rolled the window back up so that they all could have some peace from the driver. So the driver pulled out of the federal building and turned right, then had to take another right to head to Joey's home. Exie,

Sue, Joey, and Laverna were looking out the windows at all the blue skies. It had stopped raining for now, but looked like there might be another storm coming in. There were all kinds of trees, buildings, cars, and other things. They could hear birds, dogs, cats, and even bugs. It felt good to be back. As they kept driving for what seemed forever they had arrived at a long drive with an iron fence that had some kind of design on it. But it had opened up before the girls could see what kind of design it had. They were pulling up to a White Mason that had an old Greek look to it. As they pulled up to the steps of the mason the driver opened the door and they all got out. Claimed the stairs and a butler opened the door for them.

"Welcome back young master, and master." Butler Johnny said.

"Thank you, Johnny. It nice to see you." Joey said to his butler. Mr. Ryan just tilted his head to let the butler know he heard him. The house was huge; it had all kinds of things. Joey looked around and it looked as if his father had something changed. On the stand near the door in the lobby was a cordless phone Sue walked over to it and dialed her parents' number.

"Hello?" Mrs. Sting answered.

"Hello, mother. It is Sue." Sue said back. Her mother shirked in the phone dropping it. She heard her mother yelling for her younger brother and father. Sue could not keep the tears out of her eyes. How she had longed to be home, now she is it seems different somehow. She smiled into the phone.

After her mother picked up the phone again she was glad that she had called her. After what seemed like hours she talked to her family she didn't realized that she had walked into the living room and sat down. She looked at her friends who had made themselves at home. They were waiting on dinner, when Joey and his father came out of the office to the right smiling.

"Now you know what had truly happened to your mother and brother. She was like you. She also noticed the signs with your brother when he started to get older. It would seem that you are the stronger of the two. I would not change it for nothing so you know. I loved your mother with all my heart, and no one can take her place. When I first heard you came up missing my heart sank to the bottom of the ocean. So, I asked to be stationed here for good so we would never need to move again and you would not be alone. So you know I love you son with all my heart, because you are our son. You are what I have left of your mother. So next time try and get a hold of me before taking a long trip like that. Okay." Mr. Ryan said to his son.

"I will father. I love you too. I do miss them very much, but it is getting easier to deal with." Joey said.

"We will together. You have guest and your cousin here for the first time in a long time. Enjoy it why you can." Mr. Ryan said.

"You got it father." Joey said with a smile. Then looked at his friends sitting in the living room. Sue was still holding the phone, but seemed to be off of it now.

"Hey, Sue. Call Alena and let them know we are back, please. Everyone else if you will follow me into the dining room, diner is done then maybe we can get some great sleep." Joey said to his friends.

"Okay, Joey I will get a hold of her." Sue said as she started to dial Alena's number. It rang for about a minute when someone answered.

Chapter 27

"**H**ello, this is the Patches house, Faizah here." Faizah said into the phone.

"Oh, Faizah it is Sue we are all back we also have the last of the guardians'" Sue said as Faizah was yelling in the background for Alena. Handing Alena the phone.

"Hey, Sue it has been a while. Glad that you guys are okay. So what is up?" Alena asked.

"We need to get together all of us so that we can make a plan. You guys game? Also did Alvaro and Autumn make it?" Sue asked her.

"Yeah, Sue they made it. It would seem that we finally have found all the guardians'. Now maybe we can find the Star Princess." Alena said.

"Yeah, glad that they made it. They are really great people and very strong. Let us hope so." Sue said to her.

"Yeah, we get a long really well. The girls have been staying with me, and the guys have been staying with Leroy. Where do you want to meet at Sue?" Alena asked her.

"Let us meet at Red Dawn Beach sometime tomorrow, okay?" Sue asked.

"Sounds great to me, I will let everyone else know. Then maybe we all can be in one place at one time." Alena said.

"Yeah maybe, I look forward to seeing you all really soon. I got to go we are getting ready to eat, bye Alena it was nice talking to you." Sue said.

"It was nice talking to you as well Sue, bye." Alena said as Sue was hanging up the phone and heading into the dining room which was just as big as the rest of the house, it had a huge table that could sit at least 16 people very comfortably. So, Sue walked over to the table and too a set next to Laverna and she was served a clam coward soup to start off with, and then the entrée was of black sea bass, carrots, salad, mashed potatoes, and corn bread, to top it off with a diet-dr. pepper chilled. She was starving which she could believe. It had been a long while since any of them had a really great home cooked meal. So they all ate in silence and in record time. After their meal was done they brought out dessert which was a variety of different things, like ice cream sundaes, pies of all kinds, Jell-O, and fruit parfaits. Sue wanted an apple pie slice with vanilla ice cream on top, Joey had a sundae topped with a cherry, Laverna had a mint chocolate ice cream in a bowl, and Exie went for the fruit parfait, which was very good. After they all had finished completely they started to feel tired.

"Everyone there is rooms ready for you when you are ready to go to bed." Mr. Ryan said.

"Thank you Mr. Ryan." All the girls said together.

"Thanks Dad." Joey said.

"You are all most welcome. Now sleep well." Mr. Ryan said taking his leave from the dining room. So everyone headed up the stairs to the rooms. Each one took a room and went right to sleep.

Laverna had drifted off to sleep almost immediately and started to dream of a castle that was made up of crystal. It was so beautiful that she held her breathe just to take it all in. She could not believe the view it had as well. It was very mysterious and she wanted to explore more than anything. But knew that she could not, for she was waiting on someone. But who? Well as she dreamed so did the others of a place so beautiful, peaceful, warm, loving, and kind that it was hard to walk away. Before they all knew it morning had come and the servants came into all their rooms to wake them, as well as give breakfast in bed. Exie had two eggs over easy, toast, coffee with cream and sugar, fruit, and bacon. Laverna had an omelet that had almost everything in it, roll, coffee that was black with sugar, bacon, and fruit. Joey had scramble eggs with salsa, coffee with cream only, bagel with cream cheese, bacon, and an orange. Sue had pancakes topped with blueberries, whip cream, orange juice, toast, bacon, and an apple. After everyone had eaten their food, they all got showers because each room had their own bathroom; they changed cloths that were brought for them. Joey was wearing jeans, t-shirt, white shocks with tennis shoes, and a black leather jacket, which made him look even hotter than with his normal cloths on. Sue was wearing pink leggings, long cream color see though top with a pink tank top under it, and cream colored ballet flats, Laverna is wearing black leather skinny pants, a vest with black and purple strips, a black top, and black Mary Jane platform shoes. Exie is wearing a golden color top with sparkles on it, white skinny Capri pants, golden saddles, and sunglasses. Each of their clothes is name brand clothes, and made them look even cuter and hotter than their normal clothes did. After they all had gotten dressed and headed down stairs to meet up in the living room. The first one in the room was Exie, Laverna, Sue, and Joey they all sat down for a few minutes waiting on the car to be brought around. After about 20 minutes the butler Johnny came into the living room handing Joey some car keys.

"Here you go sir. Your father said to give these to you." Butler Johnny said to Joey.

"Thanks Johnny. I guess that we all should be going." Joey said to them all. So they all got up from the couch and headed for the door. It was opened for them by the butler Johnny.

Chapter 28

As they all stepped out onto the pouch there in the driveway was a SUV Ford Escape 4x4, four doors, 2014. It was black, with tan seats. They all went down the steppes to get a better look at the SUV. So they all got in, and Joey got in the front on the driver's side so that he would be the one driving. He knew that there was a chance that there might be a fight they have to avoid or somehow keep from getting out of hand with their powers so that no one can see them use their powers. As he got in along with the others the seats are heated for each person, there is a stereo system with Bluetooth, also in the rear seats there are DVD players so that a person could watch a video if they so choose to do, and the SUV also can sit up to three rows of seats at once, which is good considering that they will be meeting up with their friends in a few hours.

"Joey is we ready to go?" Sue asked.

"Yeah, it will take us a couple of hours to get to the Red Dawn Beach from here. So please get comfortable everyone." Joey told them.

"You got it." Exie said claiming into the front seat with Joey, while Sue and Laverna got into the back. They knew that it would be while before they would be able to get out and stretch. So they all took off their shoes expect Joey because he is the one driving for now. Joey had turned the radio station to 93.9FM so that they could listen to the music for a while. Sue curled up in her seat to listen to the music as Joey starts driving down the long drive and out of the gate. He turned right and head straight for the state route they will be taking. It is going to be a long drive.

"Everyone we will stop at some restaurant to eat lunch, but beforehand we are going to stop at a grocery store to get some things to drink. Okay?" Joey asked them all.

"Sounds great to us." Exie answered for them all which they all agree anyway. So they stopped at a corner store a few blocks from Joey's house. He went in and got them all a couple drinks for the road until they stop for lunch. There are many stores in this area that would want the money. He also got them some snacks for the road trip. He brought a case of A&W Root Beer, Pepsi, Dr. Pepper, and Orange Soda. He got chips, corn nuts, fruit snacks, and Debbie cakes for them all since they had a really big breakfast the snacks would hold them over until they stop for lunch near the beach for which they are heading. Now that they all have what they need they headed for the state route 45. The road went on for a while only seeing farms and hills, they came to a sign that had pictures showing them that there are restaurants on the next exit. The sign read "Sleep, Food, and Gas next right exit 31 ramps" which they are going to take because it was about 1pm. So Joey took the next exit so that they could stop and eat before they get to the beach. He pulled off onto the ramp, and had to stop at that red light at the end of the road.

"Where do you guys want to eat?" Joey asked them.

"It doesn't matter to me." Sue answered him.

"I down with anything." Laverna said.

"You choose Joey." Exie said.

"Okay then let us go eat at Texas Road House. I will pay. Is this okay with everyone?" Joey asked.

"Yeah, sure considering some us are out of money right now." Sue said rolling her eyes. Joey started to laugh because he knew she had. So he turned right and went about half mile before they came to Texas Road House. He pulled in and notices that he still had about ¾ tank gas in his SUV which he loved. This must be for his 17th birthday which had already passed. He was glad that his father got him a car. Which he needed considering his mustang was still good, but this is better considering they are in the Crystal Star of Water and Ice Realm. It does get really cold here sometimes. So they all got out and headed inside to be seated. They are waiting in line for a table for four people.

"Sue will you please call Alena and Leroy and let them know that we night be a little because we stopped for food." Joey asked her to do.

"Sure Joey I will call her. Hand me your cell phone since mine is dead and I have not had a chance to charge it." Sue told him with a smile.

"Here, dad also got me a new smart phone so it has really good reception anywhere." Joey said handing Sue his HTC One Smart Phone. She took it and started to dial Alena's number. After a few minutes she answered.

"Hello." Alena asked.

"Hey, Alena it is Sue, I was just calling to let you all know that we are going to be a little late. We stopped to get something to eat. Okay?" Sue answered.

"That is fine we will see you guys there." Alena said. After a few minutes conversation with Alena, Sue called Leroy and he answered on the second ring. She told him the same thing she had told Alena and he is okay with it. Sue came back in from making her calls and handed Joey back his phone.

"So did you tell them?" Joey asked.

"Yeah, they are both okay with us all being a little late." Sue said.

"So where are they going to meet us at?" Joey asked.

"They are going to meet us at the café on the beach." Sue answered.

"Okay, we will sitting here in about 10 minutes they said. Our number is 154." Joey told her.

"Okay, so that gives us time to use the restroom, and wash up." Sue said.

"Yeah." Joey said heading to the men's restroom, while the girls all headed to the women's restroom. As they all was finishing up their number was called. So they all headed out of the restroom and were shown to their sit. It was a booth that looked out on to the parking lot, when they started to get that feeling that something is about to happen. As they started to look around the waitress came over to their table to get their drink orders. As they gave their drink orders they picked up their menus and were still looking around. They looked over the menu and choose what they wanted. The waitress came back with all their drinks and took down their order and put it in. As they are all sitting, something started to feel off. As if they have been submerged into water, they looked around and before them was the enemy. They got up and got ready for a fight.

"Well it took me a while to find you guardians." General Waywear said.

"So what do you want with us?" Laverna asked.

"To stop you from ever finding the Star Princess and meeting up with your other guardian friends." Waywear said.

"Try and stop us, cow!" Exie said.

"So be it!" Waywear said.

"Bring it on!" Joey said.

"WATER SPITE BOMBS!" General Waywear called as a water spite came out up out of the floor now covered in water. Everyone in the restaurant seemed to be out cold. Then the bombs hit them all knocking them all back about a few feet. As they started to get up another bomb hit them hard. Making them all jump out of the way, as they landed on their feet this time, Sue went down springing her ankle from dodging the attack.

"Enough of this!" Exie said. When another attack hit this time missing them all together. Because Laverna used her powers to protect them.

"TIME BARRIER SHIELD!" Laverna yelled. So the attack missed hitting a window near them instead of them. It helped, making it easy for them all to get out of the restaurant by claiming though the shatter window.

"Well it looks like you all have fight in you. But trying to escape won't help you at all." General Waywear said laughing when another attack hit them but the time barrier shield held only to knock Laverna on her ass because of the force of the attack.

"SPRING DANCE!" Exie yelled as an attack hit the general straight on and making him fall back. The attack was of rain drop spears and dangers.

"SNOW DRAGON, KELLI! STAR DANCE ATTACK!" Joey called as the dragon appeared and sent sharp star shape snowflakes at Waywear hitting him again this time making him fall to his knees holding himself. As Sue got up, even though her ankle hurts like hell, she still managed to use her powers.

"SUN DANGER SHINE!" Sue yelled as many dangers hit Waywear head on and making him disappears back to the Dark Kingdom Zodiac. It looked as the dangers became a sun ray which is a new attack for Sue.

After the battle was over they all got up and went back into the restaurant. Everyone was back to normal, but didn't seem as if anything was out of place. The waitress came back to their table as they all were sitting back down. As the waitress finished sitting down their meal, she asked if they needed anything else and Joey spoke up.

"Yes, can we please bring us some carry out containers we changed our mind we want the meal to go." Joey told the waitress.

"Sure." The Waitress answered. So she went and got them carry out trays so that they all could put their food in the carry out container. As well as cups to go for their drinks. After a few minutes Sue was limping out the door of the restaurant. They were leaving the restaurant and getting back in the car.

"Sue, are you going to be okay?" Exie asked from the front seat.

"Yes, I just need to prop my ankle up and rest. Thanks." Sue told Exie who seemed to be okay with that answered. So they all are back in the car eating their food, except Joey who was driving. After about another half hour they came to the rest stopped and everyone got out except Sue who just stayed in the car to rest her ankle and finish her food. Everyone else went to the rest room, and sat at a picnic table so that Joey could eat. As they all sit Sue started to drift off to sleep. After about another half hour they were on the road again. After another hour they made it to the beach around 3:30pm.

Chapter 29

They had pulled over so they could get a better look at the beach and see if they could spot their friends. The beach had red sand, with crystal clear blue water, palm trees, umbrellas, yachts, a floating bar, bar, rocks, and all kind of sea animals. As they are looking down they could spot different things like colorful umbrellas which had a lot of people on the beach. It would seem that everyone still was enjoying what they had of summer left. For the rest it is the first time that they could even get to a beach due to the fact that they have had battle after battle. They knew today would not be any different from the other days. Just as it is they got back into the car a headed to the beach for more fun in the sun, if they could enjoy it for a little while.

As Joey started up the car, they all got back in; Sue still popped her ankle up just to keep it from hurting. She must have sprung it worst then she thought. So she just leaned back in her seat to relax and hoping that just by putting her ankles in the cool water it will help with the thumbing. She knew that she would not be much good if they were attack now. So she took a deep breathe to claim herself so that she would not think about what she can't do but what she can do. She is a guardian just like everyone else, she is strong and she knows it. She will fight if she has too. Maybe Autumn can heal her ankle for her so that she could help if an attacked happened.

As they got closer to the beach they all could see that there are more people there than they thought from looking down from on a top the hill. As they pulled into a parking spot Joey got out and opened the door for Sue and helped her out. She took his hand and limped around the car to the other two. As they look around for Alena or even Leroy for a clue that they are here waiting for them and was not attacked by some enemy from the Dark Kingdom Zodiac.

They spotted the bar for which Alena said to meet them all at. So they all walked over to the bar, Tiki Bar. They all took a seat at the bar while waiting to spot their friends. The bar tender came over to them and asked them what they wanted. Joey order drinks for everyone which was cool and refreshing. He also paid for them so that the others did not have to worry. Then before they knew it someone was walking up to them and waving like a crazy person. Then they realized that it was Faizah running to them.

"Hey guys it has been awhile? So who are these two?" Faizah asked while pointing at Exie and Laverna.

"Faizah these two are the last of the guardians' we had to find. Laverna-Grace Gale guardian of the Crystal Star of the Unknown Realm and Exie Green of the Crystal Star of The Nature Realm. So where are the others'?" Sue asked told her. She started to shack their hands holding onto Laverna-Grace hand a little longer than intended. Laverna bushed pink than red. There was something about her that Faizah just could not shake.

"Alena, Lola, and Autumn are in the water swimming still. Leroy and the others are running late just like you four." Faizah said.

"Oh, Okay. So as soon as the others get here we can talk about finding the Star Princess." Joey said.

"Yeah, we can. Sue what happened to your ankle?" Faizah asked her.

"I hurt it fighting another general from the Dark Kingdom Zodiac at the restaurant we stopped at on the way here. So how long have you guys been here?" Sue answered and asked her.

"Well, Alena's mother is on vacation and rented a cabin here for a couple of weeks. So when you called her we, were just at the house getting extra supplies for the rest of the week." Faizah answered.

"Well that is good, maybe we could stay here too. Joey how does that sound?" Sue said and asked Joey.

"Sounds great to me. Let me call my dad and ask if our cabin is free for the rest of the week." Joey answered back. As he took out his phone and dialed his father's number. He answered on the second ring.

"Hello, Ryan here." Mr. Ryan answered.

"Hey, dad it is Joey. I was wondering if our cabin is free for the rest of the week." Joey asked his father.

"Yes, you can use it. Just make sure it is stocked full for your friends and you. I will see you at the end of the week." Mr. Ryan answered him.

"Thank you dad. See you then." Joey answered back. After he got off the phone to his father Joey went back to the bar and sat back down with everyone else.

"So is it okay that we use the cabin then?" Laverna asked.

"Yes, he said it is fine that we use the cabin." Joey answered her. So they finally got some more to drink when Autumn came looking for Faizah. As she came closer to the car she could see that Faizah was talking to someone. As she got even closer she seen Exie, Sue, and Joey sitting at the bar talking with Faizah, she ran the rest of the way to them. As she finally got to them at the bar, Sue had her ankle popped up on another stood. She looked at Sue and then the others; there was one she didn't know.

"Sue what happened to you? Also who is this?" Autumn asked Sue and pointed at Laverna.

"Hey Autumn, this is Laverna and I hurt myself in a fight with another general at the restaurant we stopped at to eat. Can you heal my ankle for me please?" Sue asked her.

"Sure, just give me a minute okay. I need to get catch my breath after that swim and running up here to see you all." Autumn answered.

"That is okay with me." Sue answered her back.

"HEALING RAYS!" Autumn called. After a few minutes Sue started to move her ankle and it did not hurt anymore. So she got up from the bar and started to walk around when she saw some guys pull up in a Red, black, and orange flames on the Jeep 4x4 Wrangler. Before she knew it there before her was Andrew looking straight at her. She ran to him, Joey and the others got up to see where she was going. Before they knew it, they all started to run for the Jeep. Joey gave Rich, Leroy, Alvaro, and Andy all hand shacks.

Lola was coming u the beach when Joey turned around and before anyone knew it he was holding Lola in his arms, giving her a big kiss of longing, and want. She smelled of burnt oak wood which he is oaky with. Andy was still holding Sue and gave her a kiss that took her breath away. His touch sent shivers down her spine and back up her spine. It fleet good to be back in his arms. Alvaro gave Autumn a hug and kiss on the check. When they all was done shacking hands, and hugging each other. The others notice both Exie and Laverna. Rich looked at Exie and he walked over to her.

"Hi, My name is Richard Springer, you can call me Rich. What is yours?" Rich asked Exie.

"Hi, my name is Exie Green; I'm the guardian from the Crystal Star of the Nature Realm." Exie told him.

"It is nice to meet you." Rich said back at her.

"It is nice to meet you too." Exie said.

Chapter 30

Alena came running to the parking lot to where the others where to see what was going on. As she approached them she could see why everyone had disappeared from the water. The twelve guardians' have gathered together finally. It is going to be one hell of a party. Each person has someone that is right for their powers, healing and spirit to darkness, sun light to earth, lightning to unknown, and wind to nature, fire to summoning, and maybe water and ice to elemental. Each one can balance out the other.

"Hello everyone. Welcome to my realm of Water and Ice, I'm Alena Patches. Let us introduce ourselves, please?" Alena said to everyone.

"Hello everyone, my name is Laverna-Grace Gale from the Unknown Realm. It is nice to meet you all." Laverna said.

"Hello everyone, my name is Faizah Carter. I'm from the Lightning Realm. It is nice to meet you all." Faizah said.

"Hello, my name is Richard Springer, please call me Rich. I'm from the Wind Realm. It is an honor to meet you all." Rich said.

"Hello, my name is Exie Green; I'm from the Nature Realm. I'm glad I will get to know each of you." Exie said.

"Hello, my name is Sue Stang. I'm from the Light and Travel Realm. I look forward to working with you all." Sue said.

"Hi, my name is Leroy Addams; I'm from the Elemental Realm. I am the Crown Prince and promised to the Star Princess. I hope we all can become really great friends." Leroy said.

"Hello, my name is Andrew Brown, you all can call me Andy; I'm from the Earth Realm. I look forward to helping you all." Andy said.

"Hello, It is nice to meet you all. My name is Alvaro Sky; I'm from the Darkness Realm. I hope that we can spend a lot of time getting to know each other well." Alvaro said.

"Hi, my name is Lola Scarlet; I'm from the Fire Realm. I am glad that I got to become friends with you all." Lola said.

"Hey, I'm Joseph Ryan, please call me Joey; I'm from the Summoning Realm. I hope that we can kick butt together." Joey said.

"Hello to you all, my name is Autumn Williams; I'm from the Healing and Spirit Realm. I look forward to working with each and every one of you." Autumn said. After everyone had introduced them they all headed back to the Tiki Bar, sat down and had a cold drink. As it would seem time seemed to be going by fast. I guess that is what happens when you are having fun.

"So everyone, there are fireworks tonight here at the beach, let us enjoy them together as a group of friends enjoying themselves." Alena asked them all.

"Sure, let us enjoy some peace while we have it." Sue said.

"We all agree." Laverna answered.

"Glad to here. There is also an solar eclipse happening after the fireworks. We can watch it. It is the first time in over a thousand years since all realms lined up." Alena suggested.

"YEAH!" Everyone cheered. As they all had another drink it started to get late. As 10pm came the guardians' all made their way down the beach to watch the fireworks which lasted for a good hour. After the fire works the guardians' stayed to watch the solar eclipse. As the solar eclipse started the guardians' got up and before they knew it; they started to get a feeling of unease.

"Well I can see that all the guardians' have gathered together." Prince Jordan said.

"What the hell do you want?" Alena said to him.

"I've come for what is mine!" Prince Jordan said.

"There is nothing here that belongs to you." Sue said.

"But you are wrong. I have come for your heads." Prince Jordan said.

"Bring it on." Leroy said.

"DARK FIRE STRIKE!" Prince Jordan yelled. As his attack had missed.

"WIND SHIELD!" Rich said to block the attack from the Dark Prince Jordan.

"DARKNESS STAR DANCE!" Alvaro yelled as his attack hit the dark prince only to knock him back.

"WIND SANDS ATTACK!" Leroy yelled as his attacked hit the prince only to hit back with the attack.

"TIME SHIELD!" Laverna called countering Leroy attack that was sent back to them.

"ANGELS' WINGS'!" Autumn yelled as angel wings turned to spears hit the dark prince only to send him back some more.

"SUN DANCE!" Sue yelled as she looked like she was dancing, only to be matched hit for hit by the prince.

"SNOW STAR!" Alena yelled as she looked to being throwing stars at the dark prince only for him to reject them.

"ROSE PETAL SHOWER!" Exie yelled as a shower of rose petals turned into thrones of spears only to be bounced off the prince shield.

"COME IFIRT. FIRE STORM!" Joey summoned as a fire dragon appeared to hit the prince only for it to be blocked once again.

"LIGHTNING STRIKE!" Faizah said as a huge lightning bolt came down only to be reflected by the shield the Dark Prince was being protected.

"EARTH QUAKE!" Andy said as the earth spilt into two. Only to not touch the Dark Prince at all.

"FIRE BOMB!" Lola said only for her attack to reject as well. Prince Jordan was laughing because he was being protected by the eclipse. Before they knew it the eclipse had finished and all the realms was lined up. Then the Dark Prince Jordan was thrown back by the light beams of all the realms shining down on each of the guardians. As they looked around they notice that they could not move.

"What does this mean?" Exie asked.

"Maybe it means that the Star Princess will be reviled to us and her location." Joey said.

"Let us hope." Autumn said. Then something started too happened. Both peace's of the crown that the Star Princess is to wear came into view. The peace from the Wind Realm and the pieces from the Fire Realm came together. Before their eyes the crown became whole and in the middle of them all was Alena. Both pieces had a star and a moon on it. Only to come together and look like the star and moon are one. It was the crown tiara that was given to the Star Princess as a baby when she was first born, for it to be lost and broken in two so that it is protecting the Star Princess and that when all guardians were together whether on the same side or not would become one and be placed on the head of the true heir to the Majestic Star Kingdom. The crown tiara is gold with laurel leaf patterns on it, which would wrap around her head to sit just right on her forehead.

The crown floated above her head before being placed on her head. She started to feel more power. The love of all her friends, the love of each realm, and the love she felt for Leroy in her heart.

All the guardians' could not believe their eyes.

"WOW!" Sue said.

"MY LOVE, I HAVE FINALLY FOUND YOU!" Leroy said.

"OUR STAR PRINCESS HAS BEEN FOUND!" Faizah said with tears in her eyes.

"YEAH!" Everyone else screamed.

"NOW SHE IS MINE!" Dark Prince said.

"SHE WILL NEVER BE YOUR'S!" Alvaro yelled back.

"YOU ARE A GUARDIAN OF THE CRYSTAL STAR OF WATER AND ICE. I KNEW YOU WERE SPECIAL. NOW YOU ARE ALSO THE STAR PRINCESS; THAT I HAVE BEEN WAITING FOR." Dark Prince Jordan said.

"YOU LIE!" Exie said. Before their own eyes, the dark prince came down, and stood behind Alena; and then knocked her out. Picking her up, by putting his right hand under her head, and his left hand under her knees. He started to step back into the black whole behind him. Leroy started to come forward only to still be frozen in the same spot. Prince Jordan knew that once the other guardians' are freed they would come fore him just to get back the Star Princess who is supposed to bring all the kingdoms together and heal the Dark Zodiac Kingdom if there was any hope for that now. For he is the last and finally guardian of the Star Princess.

"NO!" Leroy yelled as they disappeared into the void of darkness together.

THAT IS ALL FOR NOW

Printed in the United States
By Bookmasters